>>> This title is part of The ˙   Room, our series dedicated
to making available   ard-to-find titles by classic
crime writers

C ˙   ̂irror to society. The
ᴠ   ᴜnal murder and the
en   ̶ow we are obsessed with
the   ̶ death. And no other genre has so
captiᴠ   ̶ᴜled readers.

Vast troᴠ̶s of classic crime writing have for a long time been
unavailable to all but the most dedicated frequenters of second-
hand bookshops. The advent of digital publishing means that
we are now able to bring you the backlists of a huge range
of titles by classic and contemporary crime writers, some of
which have been out of print for decades.

From the genteel amateur private eyes of the Golden Age and
the femmes fatales of pulp fiction, to the morally ambiguous
hard-boiled detectives of mid twentieth-century America and
their descendants who walk our twenty-first century streets, The
Murder Room has it all. >>>

The Murder Room
Where Criminal Minds Meet

themurderroom.com

Helen Worrell Clarkson McCloy (1904–1994)

Born in New York City, Helen McCloy was educated in Brooklyn, at the Quaker Friends' school, and later studied at the Sorbonne in Paris. From 1927–1932 she worked for Hearst's Universal News Service after which she freelanced as an art critic and contributor to various publications, including the *London Morning Post*. Shortly after her return to the US she published her first novel, *Dance of Death*, in 1933, featuring her popular series detective-psychologist Basil Willing. The novel *Through a Glass, Darkly*, a puzzle in the supernatural tradition of John Dickson Carr, is the eighth in the Basil Willing series and is generally acknowledged to be her masterpiece. In 1946 McCloy married fellow author Davis Dresser, famed for his Mike Shayne novels. Together they founded Halliday & McCloy literary agency as well as the Torquil Publishing Company. The couple had one daughter, Chloe, and their marriage ended in 1961. In 1950 Helen McCloy became the first woman president of the Mystery Writers of America and in 1953 she was awarded an Edgar by the same organisation for her criticism. In 1987, critic and mystery writer H.R.F. Keating included her Basil Willing title *Mr Splitfoot* in a list of the 100 best crime and mystery books ever published.

By Helen McCloy

Dr Basil Willing

Dance of Death (1938)
The Man in the Moonlight (1940)
The Deadly Truth (1941)
Who's Calling? (1942)
Cue for Murder (1942)
The Goblin Market (1943)
The One That Got Away (1945)
Through a Glass, Darkly (1950)
Alias Basil Willing (1951)
The Long Body (1955)
Two-Thirds of a Ghost (1956)
Mr Splitfoot (1968)
Burn This (1980)
The Pleasant Assassin and Other Cases of Dr Basil Willing (short stories) (2003)

Standalone novels

Do Not Disturb (1943)
Panic (1944)
She Walks Alone (1948)
Better Off Dead (1951)
Unfinished Crime (1954)
The Slayer and the Slain (1957)
Before I Die (1963)
The Singing Diamonds and Other Stories (short stories) (1965)
The Further Side of Fear (1967)
A Question of Time (1971)
A Change of Heart (1973)
The Sleepwalker (1974)
Minotaur Country (1975)
The Changeling Conspiracy (1976)
The Impostor (1977)
The Smoking Mirror (1979)

Cue for Murder

Helen McCloy

An Orion book

Copyright © Pollinger Ltd as Literary Executor of the Estate of Helen McCloy 1942

The right of Helen McCloy to be identified as the author of this work has been
asserted in accordance with the Copyright, Designs and Patents Act 1988.

This edition published by
The Orion Publishing Group Ltd
Orion House
5 Upper St Martin's Lane
London WC2H 9EA

An Hachette UK company
A CIP catalogue record for this book is available from the British Library

ISBN 978 1 4719 1242 9

www.orionbooks.co.uk

Printed and bound by CPI Group (UK) Ltd, Croydon, CR0 4YY

To A. D.

Contents

CHAPTER ONE

Prologue

THE MURDER MYSTERY at the Royalty Theatre was solved through the agency of a house fly and a canary.

The fly discovered the chemical evidence that so impressed the jury at the trial, but the canary provided a psychological clue to the murderer's identity before the murder was committed. Basil Willing is still troubled by the thought that it might have been prevented if he had read the riddle of the canary sooner.

It began with the canary. Though birds are unblessed with public relations counsels this one made the first page of the *Times* one spring morning when a weary make-up man snatched a filler at random from the galley file to plug a hole at the bottom of column three.

BURGLAR FREES BIRD

New York, April 28—Police are puzzled by the odd behavior of a burglar who broke into Marcus Lazarus' knife-grinding shop near West 44th Street shortly before dawn yesterday. Nothing was stolen but the intruder opened the cage of Lazarus' pet canary and set the bird free. The shop is hardly more than a shack in an alley leading to the stage door of the Royalty Theatre.

1

On April 28 at eleven o'clock in the morning, Dr. Basil Willing unfurled a copy of the *Times* at breakfast on a plane from Washington to New York. He read the war headlines with the sensation of individual littleness that an ant must have during an earthquake. It was a relief to come across such a human item as BURGLAR FREES BIRD. That was criminal behavior on a conceivable scale; pleasantly trivial after the murder of peoples, the robbery of continents, and the perversion of cultures. The little puzzle teased his imagination as prettily as a problem in chess or mathematics.

Why risk incurring the severe penalties for burglary by breaking into a shop without stealing anything? Why prolong the risk by lingering on the premises to free a canary from its cage? Was this erratic burglar a man of sentiment who broke into the shop solely in order to free a bird from a cage that was cramped or dark or dirty? A telephone call to the A.S.P.C.A. would have been far less risky and more permanent in its effect. But if freeing the bird were an afterthought, what sort of burglar would be distracted from the serious business of burgling by such a frivolous impulse?

At the moment Basil believed his knowledge of this "crime" would always be limited to the few facts contained in the news item. The construction of a plausible hypothesis within such narrow limits was a mental exercise as strict, and therefore as stimulating, as the composition of a sonnet. But the longer he played with those few facts, the more clearly he realized that no hypothesis he could construct embraced all the facts adequately. If this were an anagram, some of the letters were missing. The letters he had spelled only nonsense words and stray syllables, unintelligible and tantalizing as a message in an unknown code.

That afternoon Basil stopped at Police Headquarters to discuss a sabotage case with Assistant Chief Inspector Foyle of the Police Department.

"Well, well!" For once the Inspector's shrewd, skeptical face was off guard, relaxed and friendly. "I thought you were marooned in Washington for the duration!"

"At the moment I'm working with the New York office of the F.B.I."

"As a psychiatrist or an investigator?"

"A little of both. Very much the sort of work I used to do for the D.A. If it weren't for you I'd be in uniform by this time."

"What have I to do with it?"

"You gave me my first chance to apply psychology to the detection of criminals. Now I'm supposed to be applying it to the detection of spies and saboteurs. But I ought to be with some medical unit. I'm under forty-four, I have no wife or children, and I've been in the Medical Reserve Corps ever since the last war. I went straight from Johns Hopkins to a casualty clearing station, and it was through shell-shock cases that I first became interested in psychiatry."

"Don't worry, doc," said Foyle dryly. "They'll call you up quick enough if they need you. They probably think that anybody who speaks German like a native and reads a crooked mind like a book is more useful doing what you're doing now. . . . Funny thing happened to me the other day. I was walking down Whitehall Street sort of fast, the way I always walk when I'm thinking, and a recruiting sergeant sees me and comes rushing up to me with a big smile. Then suddenly he stops and his smile goes out like a light and he shakes his head and turns away. When he *first* saw me he thought I might do because I'm still thin and wiry and can move fast; but when he got close enough to see my gray hair and the lines in my face he wasn't interested any more. I suppose I should've been glad in a way, but I wasn't. I felt the way I did the first time a truck driver called me 'pop' instead of 'buddy.'"

War talk brought the morning paper to Basil's mind, and that in turn reminded him of the canary.

"Yeah, it was sort of funny," admitted Foyle. "I got a report on it from the precinct this morning. I thought it might be a publicity stunt."

"For whom?"

"Wanda Morley. Her new show opens at the Royalty in a day or so, and the knife-grinder's shop is right next door. But her press agent swears he doesn't know a thing about it, and her name hasn't been mentioned in connection with it. If there were any tie-up it would've come out by this time."

"Is there anything of value in the shop?"

Foyle laughed. "You should see it! Nothing but a grindstone and a lot of rusty old knives and scissors."

"Has Lazarus any enemies who might do a thing like that just to annoy him?"

"He says not. If people wanted to annoy him wouldn't they have stolen something? Or injured the bird? It was perfectly all right—just out of its cage flying around the room when Lazarus came to his shop to work yesterday morning. Then he noticed the door of the cage standing open and the broken latch at the window. Those were the only signs that anyone had been there."

4

"But *why?*" persisted Basil.

"That's your headache, doc. My job is to catch the guys who do wrong—not to worry about *why* they do it! Maybe you can tell me *why* they always push forward at a fire when we tell them to stand back?" The Inspector weighed his next words. "I wish it hadn't been a knife-grinding shop."

Basil's interest quickened as if someone had supplied one of the missing vowels to his anagram. "So that's it?"

"Looks that way. We made quite sure nothing had been stolen. That can mean only one thing: "Somebody wanted to sharpen a knife—without witnesses."

"Murder?"

"Sure. With malice prepense. But there's nothing we can do about it. No fingerprints. No clues. . . ."

Outside in Centre Street, the east wind struck through Basil's spring overcoat with a sudden, keen thrust. *Somebody wanted to sharpen a knife. . . .* In his mind's eye, he saw the dark, faceless figure in the gray, dreamy light just before dawn sliding a moistened thumb along a blade secretly sharpened to a slicing edge. There would be the low humming of a grindstone and a spray of cold blue sparks; but no one would be likely to see or hear anything at that hour in a little shack in an obscure alley running through the theatrical district. Why such stealth unless the purpose were murder in its most inhumane form—with the premeditation of a surgeon and the callous blood-letting of a butcher? That was sound enough as police logic, but . . .

With an almost audible click, new facts and old fell into juxtaposition. His anagram had become less intelligible than ever. If this were murder in its most inhumane form, why free the canary?

Like most modern psychiatrists, Basil Willing believed that no human being can ever perform any act without a motive, conscious or unconscious. The unmotivated act was a myth like the unicorn or the sea serpent. Even slips and blunders had their roots in the needs of the emotional nature. He had used his knowledge of that fact to solve his first murder case. But what was the motive here? What feeling had informed the hand that unlatched the door of the canary's cage yesterday morning?

However pitiful a winged creature in a cage may be, a murderer planning to use a knife against a fellow human being is hardly in the mood for pity. . . .

CHAPTER TWO

Persons in the Play

THE MODERN ART GALLERY was inclosed in a penthouse on Central Park South. The architect prided himself on being "functional," but he had forgotten that the principal function of a modern building is resistance to air raids. He had made the north wall of the gallery one great sheet of sheer plate glass. After Pearl Harbor, the management had supplemented the glass with two-inch bands of adhesive tape, criss-crossed in a series of tall X's and sealed flat and taut with an electric iron.

Outside, winter lingered in the Park like an insensitive guest who has long outstayed his welcome. The turf was bald and dry and brown. The skeleton trees made a black mesh against a sultry streak of saffron at the western edge of the white sky. Nurses and children, hurrying east to home and supper, bent their heads forward, unconsciously streamlining themselves in order to cleave the April wind. There was not a hint of green in the landscape, but there was a new freshness in the air that hinted of all the green things to come in a few weeks.

Inside, a crowd of invited guests—largely feminine, furred, perfumed, and voluble—pretended there were no such things as wars and east winds. Soundproof walls shut out traffic noises. A thermostat maintained a temperature as mild and even as that of an embryo. Brilliant, artificial light from concealed sources was refracted in every direction by three blond walls of wax-rubbed pine. There were no shadows. The gallery was a solid cube of light, a medium where people moved and had their being like fish in a tank of illuminated water.

Now and then one of the guests remembered to glance at the paintings on the walls and tell the exiled artist in schoolgirl French that his *oeuvre* was *épatante* and *vraie Parisienne*. For the most part, they sipped cocktails, nibbled macaroons, admired fragments of T'ang pottery on the twin mantelpieces, or sat down to gossip on settees covered with tight, slippery leather in jade green.

A young man and a girl were sitting on one of these settees—the one with its back to the glass wall. The girl was pretty, but there was nothing remarkable in her prettiness. Hundreds of girls have chestnut-brown curls that gleam red when light touches them and gray eyes that seem blue under a blue hat. The freckles across her short nose were faded as if she had changed an outdoor life for an indoor light in the last few years. The women in red fox and rayon velvet and flowered hats looked at the beautiful severity of her tweed suit and decided that she was underdressed. The women in silver fox and bagheera and clever black hats looked at the same suit and wondered if they could be overdressed. Something in the short curl of her upper lip and the tilt of her small, stubborn chin suggested that she cared little for their opinions. Her manner was composed and detached, rather businesslike. On her knee was a sketch pad; in her right hand, a soft, black pencil. From time to time, she sketched something in the crowd that pleased or amused her—a piquant profile, an impossible hat, or an ungainly silhouette.

The young man had slumped down on the seat beside her with his hands in his trouser pockets. He was a shade fairer than the girl and about her own age—in the late twenties. His eyes were too round, his mouth too wide, his legs too long; yet the general effect of his appearance was pleasing, for he had the look of youth, health, high spirits, and an affable disposition. At the moment he was not being affable. Neither was the girl.

"I don't see why we should wait any longer."

"Don't you?" The man's eye followed her pencil.

"Maybe we'd better call the whole thing off."

"Now, Pauline—" he began.

She cut him short. "I don't like secrets—particularly secret engagements. And I don't see any reason for it. Both our parents were delighted. Though you don't seem to realize it, there are other men in the world. Some of them ask me out to dinner and—so forth. If they knew I were engaged to you they—well, it would make things easier all around. As it is, I'm neither engaged nor disengaged. I'm suspended in a vacuum. It's hard to act as if you were an engaged girl when nobody knows you are. It wouldn't matter for a short time, but it's been going on for several months now. Honestly, Rod, I'm tired of keeping my ring in a bureau drawer and looking self-conscious whenever your name is mentioned. I can understand waiting until after the run of the play to get married, but why can't we tell people we're engaged?"

"Because we just can't."

"Why?"

"It's—well, you wouldn't understand. You'll just have to take it on trust that we can't."

"How are we ever going to get along after we're married if you don't trust my understanding enough to tell me things that matter so much to both of us?"

"And how are we ever going to get along if you don't trust me at all?"

Pauline closed the sketch pad and slipped the pencil into a slot in the cover. "Rod, we can't go on like this. We will have to call it off."

"All right, then do!" Rod assumed an elaborate nonchalance. "May I get you a cocktail?"

"If you will be so kind." What a dreadful thing politeness was: always the mask of hostility between sexes or classes; never the medium of true friendship or true love. Pauline watched Rod as he rose and disappeared into the crowd. Her lips parted as if she were going to call him back, then closed again without making a sound. To think that so much could be ended by so little! A few sharp words spoken under cover of a chattering crowd and the whole thing was all over.

Mechanically, she pulled out the pencil again and reopened the sketch book. But the line faltered. Her hand was trembling. Her throat felt swollen and raw. *I mustn't cry. There are hundreds of people looking at me.* Her eye caught the outline of a short, fat woman in a short, fat, fur coat pushing through the crowd like a tug through heavy seas. Her quick, nervous pencil pinned the fugitive absurdity to paper with three strokes. She felt the bench yield to a weight at the other end. Someone had sat down beside her. Her eyes were on the sketch pad as a man's voice spoke.

"You couldn't be more detached if you were sketching monkeys at the zoo."

She started and turned an arrogantly blank face in the direction of the voice. Then a light came into her eyes. "Basil! What are you doing here?"

"*Sur-réaliste* painting is just another form of psycho-analysis to me. What are *you* doing here?"

"I thought I might get some ideas." The pencil noted a young girl's frivolous, feather hat perched above a solemn, old face.

"For a portrait of mutton dressed as lamb?"

"No, costumes. I design them, you know. For the stage. Or perhaps you didn't know."

"No, I didn't. The last time I saw you, your chief interest in life was—let me see. . . . Was it the rhumba? Or beagling?"

"Beagling. But that was ages ago."

"About fifteen years ago. You were thirteen or fourteen."

"And you were an old man—thirty-two or three. But now you're just about my own age. I believe Einstein was right!"

He laughed. "When I first saw you, you were fifteen inches long and weighed eight pounds. That was during the last war."

She nodded. "I was three when the Armistice came. The family never let me forget that I remarked: *Won't it be funny not to have a war any more?*" Her gaze explored his lean, ageless, brown face; his dark, penetrating eyes. In the bright light she saw two single gray threads in the thick, brown hair. She would have said he was thirty-five—thirty-eight at the most. But he must be a year or so over forty now; for she knew he had been in her father's class at Johns Hopkins in 1916 and had left it for the Medical Corps in 1917.

"Basil, you're old enough to be honest with me. Will you answer a personal question frankly?"

"Depends on the question."

"Thank heaven you're not polite!" She sighed. "How do I look to you? Pretty or ugly?"

"I thought women's handbags were provided with mirrors."

"I thought psychologists taught that people never see the same face in the mirror that they show to other people."

"My dear Pauline, you are a Baltimore girl and all Baltimore girls are pretty." He looked at the ringless left hand holding the sketch pad. "Any particular reason for doubting it?"

Pauline's eyes were on the crowd around the buffet. "I just wondered if maybe I was—well, plainer than I realized. You get so used to your own face you can't see it objectively; and it always looks young to you because you get it mixed up with your memories of youth. That's why old women wear such youthful hats."

Basil smiled. "You can still wear youthful hats, Pauline. But you do look a little pale—possibly anemic." His clinical glance considered her. "Been dieting?"

"No, only working. I've just finished Wanda Morley's new show. It opens tonight at the Royalty."

"The Royalty?" There was a new note in Basil's voice. "You mean the Royalty Theatre on West 44th Street?"

"Of course. Sam Milhau puts on all Wanda's shows at the Royalty. It was a tough job. Adaptations of Victorian styles. She's reviving *Fedora*."

"Sardou's *Fedora?* Isn't that a pretty musty old piece of fustian?"

Pauline smiled. "Modern playwrights don't go in for sugared ham. That's Wanda's meat, so she has to play revivals. It was *Candida* and *Mrs. Tanqueray* last season. It'll be *Lady Windermere* or *Madame X* next. Wanda wants to do everything that Bernhardt and Ellen Terry and Fanny Davenport did. She even imitates their foibles. And yet, goodness knows, she *looks* modern off-stage!"

Basil's glance followed Pauline's through a sudden rift in the crowd to a woman who had just entered the gallery. She would have drawn glances anywhere. She was thin and supple as a whip, with a flashing, feline grace that made every gesture a work of art. Her black hair was parted in the middle, sleekly waved and brushed up in two little wings above either ear. Her face was a creamy oval, slashed with a long, thin mouth, stained scarlet. Her eyes were tilted and tawny, their golden spark heightened by gold and topaz earrings. She wore black with a leopard-skin cap far back on her dark head and a leopard-skin muff on one arm.

"Wanda Morley?" asked Basil.

"Yes. Fascinating, isn't she?" There was a tart flavor to the speech. "And yet you can't say just why," went on Pauline. "It's a sort of miracle. Hollywood has just established a formula for female allure—bleached hair, blubbery lips, tapering hips, and great udders that make you wonder about the butter-fat content per quart of human milk. Then along comes Wanda and breaks all the rules—dark hair, thin lips, no hips, and no bosom —and yet she makes all the finished products of the

Hollywood beauty factories look as *ersatz* as they are. You can't reduce her to a formula. Her eyes are too slanting, her mouth too wide, and all of her is too thin. She ought to be downright ugly, and she would be if she just weren't so extraordinarily beautiful. Basil, do you suppose beauty is purely psychological after all? Put Wanda on paper and she's hideous. She's easier to caricature than any other actress on the stage. But there's something in her nature that pulls all her features together and suggests the idea of beauty almost hypnotically. Why don't you psychologists find out what makes women like that tick?"

"It's probably a kind of suggestion," agreed Basil, "based on self-suggestion. Some of the French psychologists have a theory that luck is a product of self-suggestion. Perhaps a woman is only beautiful when she believes in her own beauty sincerely without any conscious effort."

"Then beauty is really vanity!"

Basil caught an undertone. "You don't love Wanda, do you?"

"I hate her." Pauline spoke as tonelessly as if she were saying: *It's going to rain.*

"Any particular reason?"

"She's an intellectual fraud, and she can't act."

"That might account for dislike but—hatred?"

"I was just being colloquial. But I don't like her. She says things."

"What sort of things?"

"Well, what I suppose you'd call catty things. At home I used to read novels where women talked like that; and I always thought the author was just using them as mouthpieces for his own spite, because I never knew any woman in real life who talked that way. But the minute I met Wanda I thought: *There really are women like that, and this is one of them!*"

Basil's thoughts reverted to Pauline's home environment—secure, kindly, generous. He had never heard Pauline's mother or sisters say anything spiteful or envious, or even gossipy. To a girl coming from that environment, it would be a shock to meet one of those simple-minded climbers who know no other form of social intercourse but war.

"I'm just as bad as she is now," Pauline was saying. "You have to hit back."

Wanda Morley had reached the buffet. People turned to look at her. Some smiled and spoke, but her responses were brief. She paused to speak to a man. Rod joined them. Wanda refused a cocktail with a gesture, took a cigarette from her bag and put it between her lips. Both men produced matches. She smiled impartially at either, hesitated a moment, then leaned toward Rod.

Pauline's pencil traced a side view of Wanda, exaggerating her fluent suppleness so that it looked boneless and snaky. The line wavered. Pauline's hand was shaking. She crossed out the imperfect sketch with slashing strokes.

"Black hair and golden eyes," remarked Basil. "Rather like a puma. Those three would make a neat composition. You could call it *Puma with Stag and Sheep.*"

Rod was the stag—long-legged and fleet-looking, with a round, intense eye and a flaring nostril. The other man was the sheep—narrow forehead, pendulous nose, dull eyes set close together.

Pauline's answering smile was cheerless. "Pumas prey on deer and sheep, don't they?"

"That's the point. Do you happen to know these victims?"

"The sheep is Leonard Martin. The stag is Rodney Tait. They're both in Wanda's company. Rod brought her here this afternoon. He's supposed to be getting a cocktail for me now, but he seems to have forgotten all about it."

"Can I—?"

"No, I don't believe I want one after all." There was a snap as the point of Pauline's pencil broke. "She only does it to annoy because she knows it teases!"

"Does what?"

"What's she's doing now. Preying."

There was something a little avid in the red-lipped smile and the bright, yellow eyes set off by the pale face and black clothing. The color scheme was carefully planned, vivid as a playing card, and the features looked just a little larger than life. The face would have been eye-catching on a hoarding or a stage, but it was a little overwhelming at close range. Wanda was a poster, Basil decided, and Pauline a miniature. Wanda's beauty would bloom under a spotlight that would wash out Pauline's softer coloring and more delicate features.

Wanda was talking to the two men with animation. Her thin mouth writhed against her face like a small, red snake. It was extraordinarily mobile—proud, wistful, ironic, beguiling in bewildered succession. Smoke trailing from the cigarette in her hand traced the suave line of each gesture as visibly as sky-writing. To Basil, it seemed that Wanda was performing the part of the charming and successful actress; conscious of many eyes upon her, yet less sensitive to their impact than a person unused to living in public. Just as an object that is constantly handled acquires a patina—worn, hard, smooth, glossy and a little soiled—so the surface of Wanda's personality seemed to have been glazed and tarnished by the curious glances that were always sliding over her face and figure wherever she went.

"Oh, Lord, here she comes!" murmured Pauline.

Wanda had dropped her cigarette in an ash tray. Her flat, limp muff was tucked under one elbow as she drew on long, beige gloves. She moved forward slowly, still talking to Rod and Leonard, her small, dark head tilted on the long, flexible white column of neck. She drew them in her wake as a magnet draws steel filings.

"Why, Pauline, darling! What a surprise to see you *here!* Somehow one just never thinks of a costume designer as being interested in *real* art."

Pauline smiled. "If ever you meet any of your friends in heaven, Wanda, I'm sure you'll say: Darling, what a surprise to see you *here!*"

Wanda wasn't listening. Her eyes had shifted to Basil. Their glance was as intimate as a caress. "Aren't you going to introduce us?"

"Dr. Willing, Miss Morley. Mr. Tait, Mr. Martin." Pauline was curt.

"Not Basil Willing—the famous psychiatrist!"

Even as Basil told himself this was boloney his ego began to purr.

"To think of actually meeting you! Pauline, dear, you must bring him to my opening tonight. You have an extra ticket, haven't you? Dr. Willing, it would mean so much to me to know *you* were in the audience! We're all going to have supper at the Capri afterward and wait up for the reviews in the morning papers. You will join us, won't you?"

The very suddenness of the invitation made Basil hesitate. "Well—"

"Of course you will!" Wanda swept on imperiously, and he saw she didn't really care whether he came or not. In the language of the stage, she was simply using him to feed her lines in her chosen role of Fascinating Femininity. At the same time, he realized that some men would fall for this sort of thing. Certainly Rod and Leonard seemed to be falling for it.

"I wish I could stop to talk now," pursued Wanda, "but I'm giving an interview to a reporter from the *Sun* at six-thirty, a photographer from *Vogue* is coming at seven, and I must have at least one hour's rest before I go to the theater. You have no idea how I *hate* all this fuss and bother and publicity! It's so *false*. If only I could live a *real* life in some quiet little suburb doing all my own housework and caring for a husband and children!"

"Why don't you?" Pauline's voice was small and dry. "It's a free country."

"My dear girl!" A hint of shrillness broke through the smooth surface of Wanda's trained voice. A hint of color darkened her cheeks. Basil had seen similar symptoms in neurotic patients brought face to face with the cause of a neurosis they would not admit. He decided that Wanda was one of those chronic self-deceivers who becomes allergic to truth. At least truth had much the same effect as a chemical allergy on her vaso-motor system. But she rallied quickly with practiced ingenuity. "Special talents impose special responsibilities. I can't just think of myself as if I were a nobody. I have a duty to my public and my art. Think of all the people who would be thrown out of work if I disbanded my company. Not only actors, but stage-hands and ushers and—people like that!"

Pauline laughed.

"Now Dives daily feasted and was gorgeously ar-
rayed
Not at all because he liked it, but because 'twas
good for trade."

"Really, Pauline, that sounds almost communistic to me." Wanda looked at a slender gold band on her wrist. The little watch was covered with a cabochon topaz in place of the usual crystal. "Heavens, it's nearly five-thirty now! I must dash! Good-by, darling! Dr. Willing, I'm counting on you tonight. Good-by, Leonard . . .

Rod started to go with her, but she stopped him with a hand on his arm. "Don't bother to come with me, Rod. Sam Milhau is driving me home. We have a few things to talk over before tonight. The boy who was to play *Desiré* has fallen ill, and we'll have to cut out his lines. Fortunately there are only a few!"

Rod seemed a little piqued at this dismissal. Pauline was amused. Leonard's thoughtful eyes followed Wanda as she passed through the crowd like a breeze through a field of poppies, leaving a trail of turning heads behind her.

A waiter presented a tray of French pastry. Pauline took a strawberry tart. Basil and Rod followed suit. Leonard eyed the remaining tarts and *savarins* with distaste and shook his head.

"Poor Wanda!" cried Pauline. "She's beginning to ham off-stage as well as on!"

Leonard's long face broke into a wry grin of apprecia-tion, but Rod was dismayed.

"That's not like you, Pauline. Great artists have to be conceited. Don't you remember what Huneker said about Rodin? His vast store of conceit kept him going all the years the public neglected him."

"The public isn't neglecting Wanda," returned Pauline. "Not with two press agents working night and day to keep her on every theatrical page in town. And it's not her conceit I mind; it's her hypocrisy. She leads the sort of life most suburban housewives would give their eye-teeth to lead; but she flatters them by pretending that they're the lucky ones and that she's the martyr to circumstance who deserves everyone's sympathy. She never sends her picture to the papers without a covering letter to explain that she just *hates* publicity. She never wears an orchid without telling everyone present that what she *really* wanted was a simple bunch of violets. You're never quite sure whether she's apologizing for being a success or rubbing it in. I suppose it's her idea of being 'democratic.' I prefer honest snobbery."

"Pauline!" protested Rod. "That isn't fair."

"Isn't it?" Pauline lifted her chin and looked at him. "I believe you're half in love with her!"

It was the true word spoken in jest. Rod chose to take it lightly. "Don't be silly!" he cried. "We're just good friends."

"You sound like an old, divorced couple!" Pauline shut her notebook with a snap and rose. "Can I give anyone a lift uptown?"

"Yes," said Rod. "If you're including me."

"Of course." Pauline took a narrow envelope out of her purse and turned to Basil. "Here's your ticket for tonight. She thrust the envelope into his hand. "Do

20

come if you can! Better dress. Wanda likes her first nights plushy. Good-by!" Pauline slipped away in the crowd. Rodney Tait followed her.

There was a flicker of mild amusement in Leonard Martin's eyes. In a close-up he looked sickly and underweight; he was gaunt to the point of emaciation. Loose skin sagged in folds and creases on his long face as if he had lost flesh recently. It had a dark tinge, nearer bronze than tan, that contrasted vividly with his pale blue eyes and the fringe of sandy hair above his ears. His high, bald forehead shone waxily in the brightly lighted room. His manner was gentle, almost apologetic. Basil wondered what part such a tired, discouraged, quiet, little man could play in a dashing melodrama like *Fedora*.

He was speaking now in a voice as mild as his eyes. "I suppose we've confirmed your belief that all theater people are crazy?"

"Stimulating is the word I should have used."

"Wanda is certainly stimulating." Leonard exhaled a deep sigh. His breath was heavy as if he had been eating overripe fruit. "She's rather like an X-ray," he mused. "When you're first exposed to her, you think there's no harm done! Her technique is so obvious! Then weeks, or even months later, you may discover you've been badly burned."

"Is that what happened to young Tait?"

"I don't know. But Wanda ought to leave Rod alone. He's only a boy and she—well, she wouldn't like me to say how long she's been on the stage. . . . I must be off now. Shall I see you this evening?"

"I expect so." Basil looked down at the ticket envelope in his hand. It was covered with fine print, but two words stood out in larger type: *Royalty Theatre*. "Have you seen the pictures?" he asked suddenly. "There's a rather curious animal study over here."

They squeezed through the crowd to the first row of a group standing in a semi-circle before a small painting in oils. At a little distance it looked like a turquoise matrix. There was a brown plain wide open to a turquoise blue sky mottled with tan clouds. Cunning perspective gave the spectator a feeling of infinite distance, airy and sunlit. In the foreground, drawn on a small scale, there was a row of crumbling Doric columns. A tiny brown ape sat on one of them, cross-legged, holding a yellow bird. He had just pulled off its wing. Three pear-shaped drops of dark red blood were falling toward the ground, high-lighted like rubies.

Leonard looked at the painting, and Basil looked at Leonard. His only response seemed to be the same mild, quizzical amusement he had shown as they discussed Wanda.

"The draughtsmanship is sound, but I'm afraid the subject is a little over my head. Is it supposed to inspire pity or cruelty? My chief feeling is disgust. I suppose that's because I don't like monkeys. And I do like canaries!"

CHAPTER THREE

Enter First Murderer

WHEN BASIL set out for the theater the evening was young, and he decided to walk. He turned into 44th Street from Fifth Avenue, the east wind at his back, pushing him along with surprising force. With the reluctance of a busy man, he had obeyed Pauline's injunction to "dress." Now the pavement felt hard under the thin soles of patent leather shoes, and white doeskin gloves impeded his efforts to dig loose change from a hip pocket when he stopped at a newsstand for an evening paper. He amused himself with the thought that this unaccustomed splendor was almost as good as a disguise. No one was likely to recognize Dr. Willing, the active member of the District Attorney's staff, or Dr. Willing, the studious psychiatrist, in this drone's livery.

As he came to the Royalty Theatre, he stepped back to the curb and looked up with a certain curiosity. It was one of New York's older theaters. A gloomy façade of plum-colored stone with white trim suggested a wedge of fruit cake with vanilla icing. The marquee blazed with electric bulbs:

Sam Milhau presents WANDA MORLEY

in FEDORA

with RODNEY TAIT *and* LEONARD MARTIN

Light flooded two great posters at either side of the box-office door—fleeting impressions of Wanda caught on paper with a few slashing brush strokes in sepia and red. Her head was a small, dark ovoid poised on a long, sinuous, white column of neck. Her tilted eyes were half shut in a provocative side glance over a shrugging shoulder. The wide mouth with its thin, scarlet lips curled in a sardonic smile. It might not be art, but it was Wanda. One sketch showed her against a Muscovite skyline of onion-shaped domes; the other, against a summery background of oleander and mimosa. Nothing in either suggested that anyone else appeared in the play. But apparently Wanda was what the public wanted. Already a long queue besieged the box office and an extra traffic policeman was telling a pair of autograph seekers to move on.

Basil glanced at his watch. It was only eight, and the curtain would not rise until eight-forty. He looked about for a place where he could read his evening paper.

To the left of the theater stood a gaudy, Broadway hotel; to the right, one of the low buildings called "taxpayers" because their rentals just cover the landlord's tax bill. This one housed a row of small shops and restaurants, and the first of these was a cocktail bar.

The moment Basil entered the place he knew it was expensive. There seems to be an unwritten law in New York that the more expensive a drinking place, the dimmer the light; and this place was so dim that he could hardly see across the room. Night gathering in the street outside turned the plate glass window into a huge mirror. Behind the bar, another mirror doubled the reflection of amber bottles with golden highlights. Wherever there wasn't a window or a mirror, there was a highly polished surface of wood or metal, so the whole place shimmered like a faceted jewel in the half-light. The air was close and spicy with an aroma of mixed drinks. Soft music came from a radio turned low. A solitary bartender mixed his highball and inquired if there were any news about the opening next door in the evening paper?

Basil turned to the theatrical page.

Openings Tonight

At the Royalty Theatre this evening, Sam Milhau is reviving Sardou's *Fedora* starring Wanda Morley. According to Mr. Milhau's office, *Fedora,* usually considered a romantic melodrama, will be staged tonight with the strictest realism. Action and dialogue have been brought up to date. The Russian Revolution of 1917 replaces a Nihilist plot in the original version, and the players will appear in modern dress. Miss Morley is, of course, playing the title role created by Bernhardt. Rodney Tait, her leading man, is making his first appearance on Broadway after winning laurels on the West coast; and a distinguished supporting cast includes Leonard Martin who is returning to the New York stage after a year's illness.

"That all?" The bartender was disappointed.
"There's something under *Stage Notes.*"
They read it together.

There may be jealousy and bickering in some the-atrical companies, but according to Sam Milhau, the company that is opening tonight at the Royalty in his revival of *Fedora* is just one big, happy family; and no member of that family is more beloved than the star, Wanda Morley. Even the stagehands have fallen under Miss Morley's spell. They have all clubbed together in order to send her a floral tribute on the opening night. "Just because she's regular guy," explained one of the electricians. "And we want her to know we're all root-ing for her!"

The bartender grinned. "The things them press agents think of!"

The street door flew open as if a gust of wind had blown it in. A young man swaggered up to the bar. He was about Basil's own height, just under six feet, and he was dressed as Basil was dressed—patent leather shoes, dark overcoat, white gloves and muffler, and what Parisians used to call a "hat with eight reflections." But there was a difference. Perhaps nothing tells more about a man's temperament than the angle at which he wears a top hat. Timidity carries it as straight as a book balanced on top of the head to improve posture. Tough-ness pushes it far back to expose a tousled forelock. Gaiety tips it to one side. But arrogance tilts it as far forward as possible, carrying the head high and the chin thrust out to keep the brim from sliding down over the eyes. This young man was arrogant. Hat balanced pre-cariously just above the bridge of his nose, he peered through the shadow the brim cast across his eyes like a half-mask and gave his order curtly: "Rum, gum and lime."

The bartender was polishing a tumbler. He paused

to rest two hands on the counter and responded deliberately: "That's a new one on me."

"Two jiggers of rum, one of lime juice, and one of sugar-cane syrup," retorted the young man impatiently. "If you haven't any syrup, grenadine will have to do. And fill it up with ice and soda."

The bartender measured the ingredients gravely. The young man took a sip from his tall, pinkish drink and made a face. "Sugar-cane syrup is better!"

The bartender cast an eloquent glance at Basil. Sugar-cane syrup indeed! What next?

Basil remembered that Adler, the psychologist, claimed he could always tell whether a man had been the eldest, youngest or middle child of his family the moment he entered a room. Surely Adler would have classified this young man as a youngest child or an only son. Once he must have been the "baby" of a doting family, and he had never got over it. There was perennial immaturity in every word and gesture, though physically he looked about thirty. His face was fair and smooth. He might have been handsome in a sulky way if his lower lip had not been so full and protruding it was almost pendulous.

He had finished his drink. He took out a billfold of black pinseal. It contained a thick wad of greenbacks and some sort of official card in a cellophane pocket. He peeled off a five-dollar bill and slapped it down on the mahogany counter. "Where's the stage door of the Royalty Theatre? I've been walking all around the square looking for it!"

The bartender returned the four dollars' change. "It's right next door. You have to go down the alley to get to it."

The young man took a cigarette from a crumpled packet and stuck it in his mouth so it dangled damply from his lower lip. Somehow that was as insolent as the exaggerated angle of his hat. A match flared in the dusk and spotlighted his face. As the mirror behind the bar caught the image in the window, there seemed to be dozens of fair young men in shiny black hats lighting cigarettes in a long vista of reflections like a visual echo. He tossed his burnt match on the floor and the picture vanished. He strode through the doorway, his unbuttoned overcoat swinging from his shoulders as loosely as a cloak.

"Some young fool with too much money for his own good!" surmised the bartender. Basil paid for his own drink and went outside.

Night had fallen. In the pallid glare of the street-lamps the pavement was a dusty gray blushing here and there under neon signs. Down a narrow alley that ran between theater and taxpayer a dingy light shone on a sign painted *Stage Door*. The warm evening had brought out several flies that banked and plunged like miniature dive bombers around the kitchen door of the cocktail bar. Half-way down the alley a frame shack huddled against the side wall of the taxpayer. There was a crude sign outlined in white paint:

MARCUS LAZARUS
Knives and Scissors Ground
Saws Filed and Set
If it has an edge, we sharpen it!

Curiosity drew Basil toward the scene of the "burglary." As he turned the corner into the alley, the wind passed him with a thin tuneless whistle. Light shone from one small, unshaded window in the wall of the shack. Through a broken pane he saw an old man in shirt sleeves sharpening a pair of shears. A shower of blue sparks sprayed from a humming grindstone worked with a foot treadle like a sewing machine. The light from an oil lamp picked out each finest wrinkle in the cobweb of lines that seamed the old face and left the rest of the workshop in shadow. It was like a little *genre* painting of the Dutch or Flemish School. Fancy supplied catalogue notations: MAN WITH SHEARS; *attributed to Rembrandt or his School. Note mellow, golden flesh tones and fine detail in treatment of face and hands . . .*

Basil's glance searched the shadows beyond the lamplight. Something dangled from a wire hooked to the ceiling. It was covered with a piece of burlap. It looked like a birdcage . . .

A sudden swishing sound startled him. As he turned his head, something darted past his eyes and fell at his feet with a crisp rustle. It seemed to be a booklet bound in paper, about the format of a theater program but more bulky.

As a psychiatrist he had often observed that most people never look above their own eye-level without provocation. He himself was no exception to the rule. Though he had been looking all around him since entering the alley he had not looked up once. Now he raised his eyes. Beyond the low roof of the taxpayer, skyscrapers were piled as carelessly as a child's blocks against an inky, blue sky. The side wall of the theater towered on his right, sheer and blind as a cliff. A red glow pulsated against the drab stone like the flicker of firelight. Apparently it came from the winking neon signs on Broadway beyond the taxpayer. A fire escape zigzagged down the wall. On the top landing, Basil could just make out a dark, faceless figure—a still shade among shadows that quivered as the light came and went. It was so shrouded in some sort of long cloak or overcoat, he could not see if it were man or woman. It was motionless as an animal when it "plays dead" in order to escape notice.

"Hi! You dropped something!"

No answer. Had the wind carried his voice away?

He picked up the booklet. It was a typewritten manuscript bound in paper with brass staples. When he lifted his eyes again, the figure was moving.

Like most theater fire escapes this one was substantial —an outside stairway built of flat iron bars with its first flight anchored securely to the ground. On impulse Basil stuffed the manuscript in his overcoat pocket and started up the stairs. The wind met him half-way, howling and dancing like a dervish over the roofs of the city. The higher he went, the more urgent the blast. He clutched his hat with one hand and clung to the iron railing with the other, while his overcoat flapped about his knees. Through the bars overhead he saw the dark figure move again. It seemed to melt into the wall of the theater. When Basil reached the top landing there was no one there.

At this height, the red glow he had seen from below was flickering all around him, and he could see over the roofs of lower buildings to its source—letters of fire, flashing and fading their message with the regular beat of a pendulum:

Time For Tilbury's Tea!

Other tubes of neon gas shone uninterruptedly, outlining the hands and numerals of a great clock. At first glance it seemed suspended between heaven and earth without means of support. Then as his eyes grew used to the uncertain light, he saw that the figures of the clock were merely unframed and uncovered, set flush with a block of stone in the darkened tower of a skyscraper that blended with the night sky. It was just eight twenty-five. He glanced at his own watch and found it ten minutes slow. Automatically, he set it right.

Beside him in the theater wall, a fire door stood open. Someone passing through the doorway in a hurry had not given the door a hard enough tug from within to counteract the pull of the wind and catch the snap lock. Basil stepped inside and drew the door after him. He had a brief tug of war with the wind before he got it closed.

He was standing on the top landing of another iron stairway—the sort you see in factory lofts, composing rooms, and other places where durability comes before comfort or beauty. Below, four stories deep, lay the fascinating confusion of a theater backstage on the eve of an important opening. There was no one else on the stairs now, but there were a hundred places in that huge windowless barn where a dark figure might have hidden: the dressing rooms opening onto the staircase; the maze of flies and catwalks overhead; and the wings far below where a mixed crowd of actors, stagehands, firemen, dressers, press agents and men from the producer's office pullulated like ants around an ant heap. None of them noticed Basil as he stood looking down at them. Like him, none thought to look above eye-level without provocation. Any one of them might have been the dark figure he had seen. Or had the whole thing been an illusion born of the shifting shadows? His hand went to his pocket. The manuscript was still there. That much at least was solid and real.

He took it out and leaned forward to catch the light from below. The cover was made of coarse blue paper. It was labeled:

FEDORA, *A Drama in three acts*
By Victorien Sardou

He turned the pages. It was an English translation of the old French play, revised and modernized. All *Desiré's* lines were crossed out, and all Fedora's lines were checked with blue pencil. This must be Wanda's script —the one she had used in learning the part of *Fedora*. At first he thought there were no other marks. Then he saw that one line spoken by another character had been heavily underscored in lead pencil:

SIREX: *He cannot escape now, every hand is against him!*

II

Basil went down the stairs. On each landing he passed a door. On the floor level he saw one embellished with a silver star. He rapped lightly.

The door flew open. "Oh, you're late. I—Oh . . ."

It was Wanda herself. Dark hair streamed loosely across her shoulders. There was something snakelike about the small, flat head, the long neck, the lithe body and tilted jewel-bright eyes. Sulphurous yellow satin billowed around her—the color of a canary's plumage. From throat to hem it was fastened with tiny buttons and loops of the same material. There must be at least twenty or thirty of them. Could she have fastened so many tricky little loops in the two or three minutes since he had seen a dark figure on the fire escape?

As she recognized Basil, her smile went out as if someone had snapped off a switch. For a moment her face was a cold, clay mask, painted rather garishly. Then she assumed artificial animation. "Dr. Willing!" This time her smile was a muscular effort. "Will you excuse me? I'm on in the first act, and I must dress now. I do hope you'll enjoy the play!"

"I'm beginning to enjoy it already."

Her eyes opened wide. "What do you mean?"

"Hasn't the play begun already? Or, at least, a play?" He held out the manuscript. "I believe this is yours." He showed her the first page with all *Fedora's* lines checked.

"Why, yes." But she wasn't looking at the manuscript. She was looking at the hand that held it. "What have you been doing to your gloves?"

He looked down. The palm of his white glove was streaked with black dust. He laughed. "Your fire escape needs a spring cleaning. I was in the alley just now when you dropped this, and I followed you up the fire escape."

"Are you crazy? I was never on the fire escape! What would I be doing there?"

"I don't know, but I couldn't help wondering. And I couldn't help thinking it odd that you marked one line spoken by one of the other characters. A rather sinister line." Basil read it aloud: *"He cannot escape now, every hand is against him!"*

Wanda's pupils dilated until her eyes looked almost black. "I never marked that line!"

"Then who did?"

"I don't know. Why should anyone else mark a line in my script?" Her gaze went beyond him.

He turned. There was no one there, but he had an impression she was waiting for someone.

"You really must excuse me," she said hurriedly. "I'll see you after the play, I hope." She stepped backward, closing the door. She had forgotten all about her script.

With something like a shrug, Basil put it back in his overcoat pocket and wandered off in search of a door to the front of the theater.

The stage was already set for the first act. Every way he turned, he was blocked by a frail wall of muslin canvas stretched on frames of lathe, held upright by wooden braces nailed to the floor, and ropes running through pulleys anchored to the roof. It seemed to be the wrong side of a box set enclosing the stage completely on three sides. In the rear wall there was a small three-sided projection—apparently the obverse side of an alcove opening into the set. Beyond this alcove in the right wall of the set there was an open window. Outside the window, a backdrop was painted to represent snow-covered roofs against a starry sky—the view from the window. An electrician was just placing a blue-shaded lamp so that it would shine on the snow to simulate moonlight. A formidable tangle of wires filled the small space beyond, so Basil turned and went around to the opposite side of the set. There he found a door in the canvas wall. Facing it was another backdrop painted to represent a marble wall. In front of the wall stood a small table supporting a bowl of beaten brass. Apparently this was the segment of hallway beyond the door that would be visible to the audience when the door was opened during the action of the play. To an audience under the spell of a dramatic scene, that door would seem to lead to a whole houseful of rooms and beyond to a street and a city full of people. Actually it led to a few inches of backdrop with nothing beyond but the brick wall of the theater.

The door opened. For one dreadful moment, Basil feared the play had begun and he was going to be caught on stage. But it was Pauline who came off the set, shutting the door behind her. It closed with the dry snap of real wood and he saw that it was made of plywood set in a lath frame.

There was a thread of frown between Pauline's brows. Her mouth drooped disconsolately. She stopped when she saw him. "What are you doing here?"

"Looking for a way out."

"Are you good at finding things?"

"What's lost?"

"Nothing very important. And it isn't exactly *lost*. It's only . . . Rod and Leon can't find it, and neither can I."

"Then it's probably lost. What is it?"

"A knife."

Basil's composure hid a sense of shock. "What sort of knife?"

"Well, it's like this," Pauline went on wearily. "Sam Milhau is awfully keen on what he calls 'realism.' That doesn't mean that he likes human characters or possible situations in the plays he produces. It just means that he likes the details of a production as literal as possible. Only he doesn't call it 'literal.' He calls it 'authentic.' Real food if there's a meal, real flowers if there's a garden. He'd have real fires in stage fireplaces if the fire department would let him. Tonight Rod plays the part of a surgeon who has to probe a wound for a bullet, and Milhau wants Rod to carry a real surgical bag with real scalpels and what not. Of course Milhau didn't want to pay a lot for his realism, so the prop man tried to get a surgical bag second hand. He couldn't get one because surgeons are donating all their old instruments to the Red Cross these days. Then Rod remembered that one of his uncles was a retired surgeon, and he got hold of this uncle's old kit. The knife blades were awfully blunt and rusty, but he polished them up a little so they'd look clean and bright—more 'realism.' He's been carrying the bag at pre-views and try-outs, and tonight—about ten minutes ago—he opened the bag and saw that one of the knives was missing. He says it's the same knife he used at the pre-views, so I went on stage just now to see if he'd left it on the set, but it isn't there. Suppose you come and take a look around his dressing room."

Pauline led the way to another door on the floor level and tapped lightly. A voice shouted: "Come in!"

They entered a room about sixteen feet square. Rodney Tait stood in front of a dressing table examining the contents of its drawer. A dressing gown of light blue flannel was belted tightly around his waist. Leonard Martin was pacing the floor—five steps in one direction, stop and turn, five steps in the other direction, and *da capo*. He, too, wore a dressing gown, but his was silk of a vivid, cardinal red.

Rod grinned at sight of Basil. "Got a criminologist on the job?"

"Well, the knife is missing." Pauline perched on the arm of a chair. "It could have been stolen."

Leonard laughed. "Who would steal an old surgical knife? Some ardent Red Cross worker?"

"Are you sure the kit was complete in the first place?" asked Basil.

"No, I'm not." Rod shut the drawer with a slam. "I never examined it very thoroughly until tonight, but I have an impression that all the pockets were filled when I first used it." He turned to Leonard. "Haven't you?"

"Yes, but it's just an impression," responded Leonard. "I could be mistaken."

"Well, you didn't leave it on the set," announced Pauline. "I looked all over the alcove, and it just wasn't there."

The bag stood on the dressing table—a very ordinary bag of black calfskin scuffed and cracked with age. Basil looked inside. Sewn to the lining were loops and pockets something like the interior of a woman's sewing bag. All but one were filled with surgical instruments. There was nothing to indicate whether that one had contained a knife recently or not. Basil took out a probe and examined it in the intense glare that came from the high-powered bulbs framing the mirror. The blade bore the name of a Boston manufacturer. It was good steel, freshly cleaned, though the edge was dull. The handle was engraved rather elaborately with a spiral pattern of grooves and "lands" like the interior rifling of a gun barrel in reverse, though the grooves were much deeper and the lands correspondingly higher.

"This is the instrument you'd probably need if you were probing for a bullet," said Basil, picking up a probe.

"Is it?" Rod was interested. "Then I shan't worry about the missing scalpel. What do I take the bullet out with?"

"Rod, don't be an idiot!" cried Pauline. "As if anyone in the audience could see what you're using when you're way back in the alcove. All they get is a flash of light along the blade. You might just as well use a bread-knife."

"I don't care whether they can see me or not," retorted Rod. "I'm like Milhau—I want realism. Everything must be authentic."

Pauline and Leonard laughed. Evidently Milhau's "realism" was a running gag.

But Rod was serious. "Even if the audience can't see the knife, I can."

"For the gods see everywhere?" suggested Basil.

"Exactly," agreed Rod. "It has a psychological effect on me to know I'm doing the right thing in the right way whether the audience knows it or not. I never could see anything funny about the fellow who blacked all over for *Othello*. I'd do the same thing myself!"

"Are you sure it was a scalpel you used during re-hearsal?" asked Basil.

"Well, it was a knife like this." Rod held up a scalpel. "That's another reason I'm pretty sure a knife is missing. I have a distinct impression that there was a pair of these, and now there's only one."

Basil turned to Pauline. "Did you search the set thoroughly?"

"Indeed I did. I spent about five minutes poking into everything there."

"And you're sure the knife isn't in here?" Basil turned back to Rod. "You might easily have laid it down some-where in this room instead of returning it to the bag after the pre-view."

"That's what I thought. But I've looked and so has Leonard, and it just isn't here."

Basil's glance swept the small room. It was furnished sparingly—rug, couch, dressing table, bench, wardrobe, and washstand. All the movable furniture was pushed back against the walls leaving a space about fourteen feet square in the middle of the room.

"No windows?" remarked Basil.

"There are no windows backstage even in dressing rooms," explained Leonard. "If there were, daylight might filter onto the set in the wrong place. Or a draught might blow against a sturdy brick wall until it flapped like a flag, and the audience would see it was only painted canvas."

Basil sat on the upholstered couch and slipped his hand down between seat and back. He fished out a cigarette stub, two hairpins, a broken pencil, a ten-cent piece, and a small nail file, but nothing that remotely resembled a surgical knife.

Pauline was watching him curiously. "You really think it matters?"

"Well . . . a sharp knife isn't a good thing to leave lying around." He made his voice casual.

"But it wasn't sharp!" protested Rod. "Those knives haven't been used for years."

"Then your realism didn't extend to sharpening the knife?" murmured Basil.

"No. Too much like work when they're as blunt as that. Besides, I've cut myself with a razor too often to hanker after handling a really sharp knife on stage."

"They're quite sharp enough as they are." Leonard displayed a small, dark cut on his right forefinger. "I did that just now when Rod asked me to go through the bag for him."

"Better put iodine on it," said Basil. "Tetanus germs thrive in dusty places."

Leonard laughed, but Pauline found a bottle of

iodine on the dressing table and insisted on applying it.

Basil pulled out the dressing-table drawer. Nothing there but the expected array of cosmetics, combs, and brushes.

"When did you first realize the knife was missing?"

"Just about ten minutes ago. I opened the bag to put in some gauze dressings I had bought for tonight—more realism—and I noticed that empty pocket. I wasn't sure whether it had been empty before so I went to Leonard's room and asked him if he could remember. He said he thought the kit was complete the last time I had it on stage. That was yesterday. He came back here to help me look for it. We met Pauline outside, and it was she who suggested I might have left it on the set. She went off to look for it there."

Basil nodded. Apparently each one of the three had been alone ten minutes ago. Any one of them could have been the dark figure on the fire escape. . . .

"Could the knife be on one of the other sets?"

Rod shook his head. *"Dr. Lorek* and his surgical bag only appear in the first act. I play another part in the second half of the play. Sardou wrote before the days of Equity salaries, and he didn't care how many characters he had. Milhau has cut out all the walk-on parts he could and doubled up on those that appear only in the first act."

"I hate to break up this party," drawled Leonard, "but do you realize the curtain will rise in three minutes, and I have to go on in seven minutes?"

Basil rose. "If I were you, I'd be careful of that knife on stage tonight. Perhaps it would be wiser to forget realism for once and carry an empty bag. You could make the motions of probing for a bullet without any probe."

"But that would spoil everything!" exclaimed Rod. "The flash of light along the blade of the knife is what makes that scene!"

Leonard was gazing at Basil in astonishment. "You don't think this knife business is serious, do you?"

"It's probably just mislaid—a case of first-night jitters. But—" Basil hesitated.

What did it all amount to? A surgical knife lost . . . a burglar who broke into a knife-grinding shop without stealing anything . . . a canary let out of its cage . . . a script of Sardou's *Fedora* with one rather ominous line underscored. . . . The rest was "atmosphere," not evidence. The District Attorney's office was not interested in atmosphere. Neither was the Police Department. . . .

III

Pauline led Basil briskly through the semi-darkness, swerving now and then to avoid a tangle of rope or a dangling wire. The canvas wall was on their left, the brick wall of the theater on their right; and the roof so high above their heads that the ceiling was lost in shadow. They passed the plywood door and came to the end of the canvas wall. There was a narrow gap between it and the proscenium arch. Through this gap Basil had a glimpse of men gathering around a table set for a game of dominoes—actors assembling on stage to be discovered by the audience when the curtain rose.

Beyond them at the rear of the stage there was a double doorway. As Basil watched, it opened, and a woman came out drawing the doors together behind her.

She crossed the stage with a firm, slow step. The glare of the footlights fell on a hard, sun-browned face—eyes narrow; nose sharp; lips thin and resolute. Light brown hair, straight as pine needles, coiled in a neat roll on the nape of her neck. Her sun-baked skin was almost the same shade of tan as her hair, but her eyes were light. She wore no make-up save a slight reddening of the lips. Her dress was a stiff silk, striped diagonally in black and white. It was crisp, severe and dashing—a style that suited her. Cloak and gloves were black. As the cloak flowed behind her Basil remembered that the figure on the fire escape had been a dark one.

She reached the gap in the wings. Her pale eyes dwelt on Basil briefly—a cool, inimical stare. Then she passed him, disappearing among the shadowy shapes beyond the stage.

Pauline touched his arm. "What are you waiting for? We must hurry!"

Directly in front of them was a heavy door covered with green baize. A faint buzzing came through it, as if bees were swarming beyond. When Basil opened the door for Pauline, the buzzing became a shrill clatter of many tongues. They were on the frontier between reality and illusion. In one step they passed from the actor's raw world of seam and packthread to the cushioned, gilded world of the spectator where canvas is stone; spotlight, moonlight; and rouge, the first bloom of youth.

On this side of the curtain all the hangings were ripe red plush; all the fringe a glittering gilt; all the paneling figured walnut; all the pillars veined marble, and all the chandeliers dripping with crystal prisms. The domed ceiling was painted with a billowy Aphrodite supported by bulbous cherubs on pink cotton clouds against a turquoise blue sky.

"A perfect setting for *Fedora*," whispered Basil.

"Isn't it?" responded Pauline. "Sam Milhau was pretty clever not to streamline this place. If only the footlights were gas jets Belasco's ghost could feel at home."

As if their entrance had been a signal every light in the house went out except the dim red exit lights that pricked the darkness far back under the first balcony. They were at one end of a corridor that embraced the orchestra seats in a half-circle. They hurried around to the head of the center aisle. As they reached it, the footlights flashed on—a crescent of yellow glare that sculptured the lower folds of the curtain while everything above swam in a watery twilight without color or contour. The clatter of tongues died away in a silence taut with expectation.

They were stopped half-way up the aisle by an usher with a flashlight. "Your tickets?"

Basil fumbled in his breast pocket, found the envelope Pauline had given him. "We've just been backstage. Can you take the stubs and check my hat and coat for me?"

"I shouldn't, but I will. This way, please."

He led them down the center aisle to seats in the fourth row and thrust souvenir programs into their hands—sumptuous affairs of cream-colored parchment bound with crimson cord and a sketch of Wanda on the cover. The star did not believe in hiding her light under a bushel. . . .

Basil glanced toward the critics' row. "Wonder what they'll say?"

"Formula X31B2," answered Pauline. *"Last night the brilliant artistry of the American theater's first lady, Miss Wanda Morley, infused life and passion into the sawdust and tinsel of a creaky old melodrama by Victorien Sardou. When will our theater provide the gifted Miss Morley with a vehicle worthy of her great talent and beauty?* It never occurs to them that Wanda chooses bad plays on purpose so she'll always seem better than the play."

"And the audience?"

"They'll eat it up. Look at them now—watering at the mouth."

Every seat in the house was filled, and filled magnificently. A Wanda Morley opening was one of the few events that could make a New York theater look as festive as the opera. Every silver fox farm in the West must have contributed its quota of pelts to the scene, while Siberia must have been entirely denuded of mink and ermine. There was a vast display of bald heads and boiled shirts among the men; of shaved armpits and shoulders coated with liquid powder among the women. In spite of the elaborate artifice of jewels, silks, and coiffures, the feminine faces looked strained and haggard in the cold twilight as their eyes settled hungrily on the curtain.

Basil's glance came back to Pauline and dwelt approvingly on her simple, long-sleeved, long-skirted dress of clear azure. "You're the only one who doesn't look like a *singe endimanché.*"

"Well, a costume designer ought to know something about clothes!" She lifted one hand in a self-deprecating gesture. The palm of her white glove was streaked with black dust.

"How did that happen?"

Silk rustled, and a woman behind them leaned forward to hiss: "S-s-sh! Will you please be quiet?"

The curtain was rising.

IV

Act I, *St. Petersburg. Winter. The house of Count Vladimir Andrejevich. A parlor in the antique Muscovite style with Parisian decorations* . . .

Sam Milhau's stage designer had interpreted Sardou's directions luxuriantly. There was a low, domed ceiling formed by interlacing ogive arches. Synthetic firelight drew monstrous shadows on walls enameled in barbaric blues and reds, yellows and greens. The painted figures seemed to dance a stealthy measure whenever you didn't watch them closely. Candle-flames made white highlights in a silver samovar. A tea service of blue and gold Sèvres and a few brittle Louis XVI chairs gave the Parisian touch Sardou had insisted upon.

In the left wall Basil recognized the single door he had seen from the other side. From here, the plywood looked like stout oak carved intricately. In the right wall, he looked through the window to snow-covered roofs. Could that chill moonshine really be coming from the blue lamp he had seen backstage? At first he was puzzled by the double doors that stood closed in the rear wall of the set. Why hadn't he noticed them on the other side? Then he remembered the three-sided projection of lathe and canvas he had passed at the rear of the set. As he had surmised, it was an alcove. It must be reached from the stage by these double doors, now closed; and apparently they were its only opening.

The rising curtain disclosed the domino players Basil

had seen on stage from the wings. They were supposed to be servants gossiping informatively as stage servants did in Sardou' day. There was a general coughing and shuffling and rustling of programs as the modern audience grew restive. First-night nerves seemed to have congealed the actors playing these minor parts. They spoke and moved as stickily as flies on fly-paper.

Then everything changed.

A bell rang.

The Princess!

Stage servants scattered in guilty haste, hiding dominoes and tea cups. One ran to open the single door at left. An outburst of hand clapping rippled through the audience.

Fedora, in full evening dress, closely wrapped in furs, enters hurriedly ...

Bernhardt herself could not have looked the part more superbly. Wanda was cloaked from head to heels in dark, supple, plumy sables. A few flakes of stage snow clung artfully to hood and shoulders as if they had just fallen while she stepped from *troika* to *porte-cochère.* As she reached the stage fireplace, she tossed her small round muff on a chair and stretched out ungloved hands to a red cellophane fire, chafing them with a realistic shiver. Her hood fell back, and she allowed her open cloak to slide down to her elbows without dropping it altogether. Her shoulders were bare and dazzlingly white above the dark fur. For this scene Pauline had designed a dress of golden gauze, sleek at the waist, and foaming about the feet in a frothy glitter. Diamonds blazed at her throat and crowned her dark head, heightening the golden flash of her eyes. Obviously they were the real thing, cold and heavy. Her small head bore the weight proudly as she turned from the fire and spoke her first line. *Is the master away?*

No more shuffling of feet or rustling of programs. There was something in Wanda that bewitched an audience—a vitality, only partly sexual, that could be felt across the footlights like the warmth of a fire. She had the politician's knack of infecting a crowd with uncritical enthusiasm for everything she did. Even the other actors on the stage responded to her vivacity. It was not a mere quickening of tempo, but a surge of power from a personality geared to a higher voltage than theirs. In a few moments the fate of Wanda as *Fedora* had become a matter of personal moment to every member of the audience. Would she discover that *Vladimir* had gone out to carouse with other women on the eve of his marriage to her?

Wanda dropped into an armchair before the fire. Its light turned her gauzy skirts to rose-gold. As a servant parried her questions, her glance strayed toward the closed double doors. *What's that?*

The bedroom.

Wanda ignored the sly undertone in the servant's voice. A charming tenderness infused her smile as she turned back to the fire.

Again the doorbell rang. Again a servant hurried to open the door at left. Wanda, lost in her own thoughts, did not turn her head as a man in the uniform of a Tsarist police officer entered brusquely. *The count's room—quick!*

This was an actor Basil did not recognize, but he was reminded a little of his friend, Inspector Foyle. This was the universal policeman—robust, hard-headed, unimaginative, doing his duty as his superiors saw it and asking no inconvenient questions of God or man. It was a caricature, shrewdly observed, subtly suggestive, and the actor contrived all this without any help from Sardou who had roughed in *Grech,* the police officer, as carelessly as he sketched all his minor characters. Wanda had brought the warmth and color of a brilliant personality into the play and captured the sympathy of the audience. But for all her charm the play itself had remained an emotional illusion. Only when *Grech* entered the scene did the illusion suddenly become reality itself. Now the blue spotlight really was moonlight, and the painted roofs beyond the window really were the roofs of Moscow while Broadway and New York and even America were thousands of miles away.

Grech snatched off heavy, leather gauntlets and thrust them in his belt. The servant pointed to the double doors mutely. *Grech* strode upstage from left to center and threw the double doors open with a wide gesture.

Something between a gasp and a sob was wrenched from the audience. The alcove was a shallow oblong, and, as Basil had seen from the other side of the set, there were no doors or windows in the side and back walls. Within the alcove the only light came from a red-shaded candle that burned before a black and gold icon on the rear wall. It was furnished with a rug, a small table, and a narrow bed. On the bed a man lay on his back—a long figure stretched at full length under a crimson quilt. Only his head and one arm were uncovered. The arm dangled limply, lax fingers trailing to the floor. The head was turned toward the audience. Dim as the light was, Basil would have known that handsome, sulky face anywhere. It was the man he had seen in the cocktail bar.

But for him the alcove was empty.

His face was made up with considerable skill, Basil thought. It was exactly the shade of dirty white he had so often seen on faces of the dying and the dead in his medical experience. The make-up man had even contrived to suggest the sharpened nose and the pinched, blue look around the lips. Or perhaps that was another of the electrician's blue lamps focused on the mouth . . .

The audience sat in almost cataleptic stillness as it realized that *Vladimir* had been lying wounded—perhaps dying—in this inner room all the time that Wanda and the servants, unaware of his presence, waited in the alcove for him to come home. Fur cap, military tunic, and high boots lay in a heap on the floor as if he had dropped them there before he crawled blindly into bed exhausted, scarcely conscious . . .

Even now *Vladimir* did not move or speak.

Grech was the first to enter the alcove. He leaned over the bed with his back to the audience, hiding *Vladimir* from view. After a moment he turned. How like Inspector Foyle and all the other policemen Basil had ever known was the curt, businesslike tone of *Grech's* voice as he rapped out one word: *Wounded.*

Wanda had turned her head from the fire at the sound of the doors opening. As *Grech* approached the bed she had risen. Now with a cry that seemed torn from her heart, she ran into the alcove and dropped on her knees beside the bed. Her arms cradled *Vladimir's* head. She sobbed aloud, her face against his shoulder.

Grech came downstage center and spoke to the nearest servant: *Who is that woman?*

Only then, when *Grech* stood for the first time in the full glare of the footlights, did Basil recognize him as

Leonard Martin. Basil was so fascinated by this discovery that he could not take his eyes off Leonard for some time after. The colorless brows and lashes had been darkened. A wig hid the bald head and thin fringe of sandy hair. A full-skirted overcoat with broad shoulders made him look larger and more formidable. But it was not make-up alone that gave Leonard all the rugged virility he had seemed to lack off-stage. Everything about him was different—voice, gait, gesture, and bearing were those of another man. Wanda had won the sympathy of the audience by the intensity of her own personality. For that very reason she had not acted at all. It was *Fedora* as Wanda Morley, not Wanda Morley as *Fedora*. She could control the expression of her emotions at will, but they were always her emotions. She could not simulate another character alien to her own temperament. With Leonard it was different. He was more than an actor—he was an artist. He didn't use *Grech* as a vehicle for exploiting his own personality. He didn't even act *Grech*—he *was Grech*. He destroyed his own personality temporarily in order to make *Grech*, the policeman, a living, breathing individual with a robust personality all his own that had nothing to do with a quiet, sickly little actor named Leonard Martin. Wanda was merely an alluring woman. Leonard was a creative artist. Basil wondered if the audience appreciated the difference between sex appeal and art.

Perhaps Wanda was afraid of comparisons, for now she went out of her way to draw the attention of the audience to herself. How could anyone watch *Grech* question the household servants near the footlights, while Wanda, in the alcove, kept her hands in constant motion by straightening *Vladimir's* pillow, stroking his cheek, lifting his arm back onto the bed?

The door at left opened to admit *Dr. Lorek*. His entrance completely destroyed the illusion of reality on stage which Leonard Martin had created. Once again the moonlight was just blue lamplight; the roofs of Moscow, painted canvas.

Even if Basil had not known who was playing *Lorek* he would have recognized Rodney Tait at once. He was supposed to be a distinguished surgeon called in to save a valuable patient lying at the point of death; but he only succeeded in being exactly what he had seemed off stage—a personable, debonair young man without a care in the world. His success in the theater was obviously owing to a pleasing voice and easy manner, rather than any talent as an actor. His good-humored presence served him well enough when he played young men like himself. But, like Wanda, he was incapable of portraying any character alien to his own nature. Tonight he was miscast in just such a role. He was trying—too hard. With artless solemnity he divested himself of padded overcoat, fur cap, and fur-lined gloves, piling them neatly on a chair. You could almost hear the beat of the dramatic school metronome between each carefully spaced syllable when he exclaimed woodenly: *An accident?*

The fluid perfection of Leonard's delivery was a painful contrast as he answered: *Attempted murder.*

Rod picked up his black bag and moved toward the alcove. He had an unfortunate trick of relaxing between his lines and forgetting all about his part while he allowed his eyes to roam the stage, examining the set, the other actors, and even the audience with the detached interest of a spectator. Then, when he heard a cue for his next line, he would come to with a start and begin to "act" again. In the alcove he went through the motions of examining *Vladimir* with mechanical precision—lifting an eyelid, groping for a pulse, frowning portentously. He scribbled a prescription and sent one of the servants to get it filled. He called for hot water. Wanda hurried downstage to relay the order to the household. Rod was left alone with *Vladimir* in the alcove. Rod set his little black bag on the bedside table and opened it. He leaned over the bed. Candlelight struck a glancing beam from a steel blade in his hand. The flash dazzled Basil so he couldn't see whether it was a probe or a scalpel. But he thought he understood why Rod had decided to bring the knife on stage after all. He probably believed that realistic bits of stage "business" would help out his deficiencies as an actor.

Only a second or so had passed when Rod laid down the knife and came out of the alcove to discuss the case with Leonard.

"Quickest extraction of a bullet on record!" whispered Basil to Pauline. "What price realism now?"

She smiled—and just then Basil was startled by a familiar line: *He cannot escape now, every hand is against him!*

Basil's glance returned to the stage. The line had been uttered by an actor Basil had not noticed particularly until this moment—an elderly man who had entered just after Leonard. He had announced himself in the play as "Jean de Siriex of the French Embassy." Basil riffled through pages of luxury advertisements and intimate chats on *What The Man Will Wear* until he came eventually to the business end of the playbill:

Jean de Siriex...............Seymour Hutchins

Pauline saw what he was doing and whispered: "Who's playing *Vladimir?*"

"Don't you know?"

"I've no idea. They used a dummy at the pre-view." Basil's eyes ran down the entire cast.

Fedora Romazov ....Wanda Morley
Grech, a police officer........Leonard Martin
Lorek, a surgeon.............Rodney Tait

"*Vladimir* isn't listed."

"What a pity! He's good. That's what I call realism."

Basil lifted his eyes to the stage once more. "Too realistic to be real."

In the cocktail bar the fellow had not looked like an actor. Now, in Basil's opinion, he was overacting with such extreme exaggeration that he made the whole play seem false and forced—the usual fault of the amateur in any art. Basil had heard that a death scene never fails on the stage. No matter how poor the play or the players, the drama of death must always transcend their limitations. But this time the old saying did not hold good. This death scene was failing drearily. *Vladimir* lay utterly still with limp, curled fingers, half-closed eyes, sunken cheeks, and colorless lips parted in a soundless moan as if each breath were drawn in agony. Yet somehow it was such a blatant bid for pity and terror that the natural reaction of the spectator was: *You're not fooling me! The minute the curtain's down you'll be up and off to a champagne supper!* Even malnutrition cases in the public ward of a free hospital didn't look quite so

drained of vitality when they checked out. Or if they did
—well, that was one of the things Basil came to the
theater to forget. . . . He felt a certain relief when Rodney returned to the alcove and stood with his back to
the audience hiding *Vladimir* from view.

Swiftly the scene was building to a climax. *Vladimir's*
assailant had escaped. That gave Leonard a chance to
draw a malicious thumbnail sketch of a policeman so
absorbed in the strategy of a man-hunt that he was happily oblivious to all the human feelings of his quarry.
Rod came out of the alcove and crossed the stage to
Wanda and Leonard.

Madame, it is the end.

She clasped her hands, staring into his face. *Dead?*
The word was a sigh. Rod bowed his head.

Wanda squeezed all the melodrama there was out of
those last few moments. *Vladimir!* She ran into the alcove. *Don't you know me?* She threw her arms around
the motionless figure on the bed, kissing the still lips.
Vladimir, speak to me! She fell across the body, sobbing
loudly.

Basil felt a light touch on his arm. It was Pauline.

"Let's slip out quickly before the rush."

The curtain was falling as she led the way up the
center aisle and down the side aisle to the door that
gave back stage. They paused at the narrow gap in the
wings. Wanda was taking curtain calls with Leonard and
Rodney on either side of her. A messenger boy brought a
big gilt basket of roses down the center aisle and hoisted
it over the footlights to her. As the curtain fell again
Rodney and Leonard retired to the wings opposite.
Wanda took the last bow alone on an empty stage with
her blood-red roses. No, not quite alone. *Vladimir* was

still lying on the bed in the alcove. Basil felt grateful for that. He hated to see a stage corpse coming to life to take a curtain call.

At last the curtain was down for good, muting the thunder of applause. Wanda turned toward the wings. She seemed to be looking for someone. Then she glanced back at the alcove and smiled.

"You can get up now, darling!" She called gaily. "First act's over, and your job is done. Was it very hard?"

No answer. Wanda laughed and picked up her sable cloak. "Get up! Is this your idea of a gag? The stage-hands have to shift the scene. Next act in Paris."

Dark fur cloak trailing from one arm, gauzy, golden skirts fluttering around her, she seemed to drift rather than walk to the alcove. Still laughing, she leaned over and touched *Vladimir* on the shoulder. Her smile died. She lifted her knuckles to her lips as if stifling a cry.

Basil crossed the stage to the alcove. Pauline, Rodney, and Leonard were close behind him. Wanda's tawny eyes were wide open, staring straight into Basil's.

"He's—dead." Her breath separated the words. Her eyes closed. She swayed and toppled. She lay on the bare boards of the stage as still as *Vladimir* himself. Pauline knelt beside Wanda, drawing the fur cloak over her, taking a crystal phial of smelling salts from Wanda's purse. A stagehand came up to the edge of the group. "Listen, we gotta shift this scene now."

No one paid any attention to him. Everyone was looking at the man on the bed. His half-shut eyes were filmed, his open lips were pale and dry. There was a little saliva at one corner of his mouth and one tiny drop of blood. It might have been caused by a pinprick.

Basil touched the neck. It was still warm. He pulled

down the crimson quilt that had covered *Vladimir* all during the first act. The grooved handle of a surgical knife protruded from the chest just above the heart. There was no breath, no pulse. The dangling arm was rigid.

"Who is this man?" Basil lifted his eyes to Rodney and Leonard.

"I don't know," said Rodney.

Leonard nodded in sober agreement. "Never saw the fellow before in my life."

The stagehand moved forward. "I don't know the guy. Is he—?"

"Dead." Basil supplied the word quietly. "And apparently murdered. Will you notify the Police Department at once?"

"But—the show—?"

A hint of grim amusement flickered at the corners of Basil's mouth. "This is one time when the show will *not* go on." He glanced at his watch. "It's nine-forty, and—"

"One moment," interrupted Rodney. "I make it nine-thirty."

"You're slow." Leonard was looking at his own watch. "It's exactly twenty minutes of ten."

"Well, split the difference," said Basil to the stagehand. "Tell them we discovered the death at about nine-thirty-five."

"For the love of Pete, what's going on here?" A plump, swarthy little man in a dinner jacket who looked as if he had been stuffed and varnished pranced across the stage in great excitement. "What are you doing here?" He stared at Basil. "I'm Milhau, the producer, and I must ask you to get off the stage at once. The man can't shift the scene unless you—" His voice trailed away. Some of the stuffing seemed to ooze out of him and his patina lost a little of its gloss. His eyes were on the knife handle protruding from *Vladimir's* chest. "W-why —w-what—Is this a gag?"

"No. It's the real thing."

"My God!" Milhau wailed and wrung puffy hands.

"Who is this actor?" inquired Basil.

"That's no actor! Oh, my God!"

"Then who is he? And what is he doing here?"

"I don't know."

Basil began to lose patience. "You say you're the producer of the play in which this man played the part of *Vladimir;* and yet you tell me he is not an actor, and you don't even know who he is?"

"That's right," answered Milhau. "I know it sounds cockeyed. But I can explain. *Vladimir* has no lines to speak. He has hardly any acting to do. He just lies still.at the back of the stage in a dim light and plays dead. He doesn't have to be an actor any more than the dead men in *Arsenic and Old Lace* or the convicts in *The Man Who Came to Dinner.* He isn't listed on the program. When Bernhardt did *Fedora* in Paris, *Vladimir* was always played by one of her boy friends who was not an actor. Edward VII was one of them, and nobody in the audience recognized him. The gilded youth of Paris got a kick out of being kissed by Bernhardt in public—all the thrills of going on the stage and none of the hard work. As soon as Wanda heard about that she wanted to invite one of her pals to play *Vladimir* here on the opening night. I said 'Okay' and never thought anything more about it. We used a dummy during rehearsals. I suppose this must be some guy she invited, but—. Good Lord, I have no idea who he is!"

CHAPTER FOUR

Ad Lib

THE HANDS of the Tilbury clock were pointing to ten-fifty-eight when a long, black limousine turned into West 44th Street from Broadway. The crowd was so dense that the car had to crawl an inch at a time. A mounted policeman leaned down from his horse and yelled at the chauffeur: "Wha'd'ye think yer—Oh." His voice died away and his hand touched his cap as the pale beam of a street lamp crossed the tight, unsmiling profile of a man who sat alone in the darkness of the tonneau. "This way, Inspector!" The horse plunged ahead forcing the crowd back from the path of the car. It halted at the mouth of an alley. The door opened, and a compact, wiry figure just tall enough to meet the physical requirements of the New York Police Department stepped out. Eyes that darted here and there took in the scene swiftly. Then with the straightened back of a man resisting the drag of a heavy burden newly placed upon his shoulders, Inspector Foyle walked down the alley to the Stage Door of the Royalty Theatre.

A lieutenant from the Homicide Squad met him at the door and conducted him to the stage itself. The curtain was raised, the auditorium empty. Under the glare of footlights and a double bank of auxiliary lights overhead, the scene looked rather absurdly like the second act of a routine mystery play. An assistant medical examiner was working over a still figure in an alcove at the rear of the set. A police stenographer was writing in a notebook at a table in the foreground. A fingerprint man was busy with lens and insufflator over a silver samovar and a set of Sèvres tea cups. A police photographer was focusing a camera on the stage from the wings. Other detectives were comparing a designer's drawing of the set with an architect's plan of the theater building and scrutinizing every square inch of the actual boards and scenery.

Close at hand there was no illusion of a princely "parlor in the antique Muscovite style." Here it was painfully obvious that the carved oak doors were plywood encrusted with plaster and paint, the Byzantine frescos crude oils on canvas, and the burning embers in the fireplace an artful contrivance of red cellophane and winking electric light bulbs.

A fat fly from the alley had drifted through the stage door with the Inspector. Now it cruised lazily around the set on transparent wings exploring the scene with detached, almost scientific interest in the odd behavior of the human species.

Without removing hat or coat, Foyle dropped into the armchair before the "fire" where *Fedora* had waited for *Vladimir* during the first act. Shoulders hunched, chin sunk on his chest, he listened impassively to the lieutenant's verbal report.

"And no one in the theater could identify *Vladimir?*"

"No one."

"Where is Miss Morley now?"

"Her maid took her to her dressing room before we got here. There's a doctor with her now. The others are in Milhau's office."

"Is that all?"

"Yes, sir. Except one witness who says he knows you. Some name like Billings." The lieutenant consulted his notes. "No, Willing. A Dr. Basil Willing. I didn't pay much attention to him. Put him with the others in Milhau's office. There's always one fellow in these mix-ups who claims to be an intimate friend of yours or the Commissioner's. It usually turns out he sat next to you at a ball game once twenty years ago."

A smile softened the Inspector's close mouth. "New to Homicide, aren't you?"

"Transferred from Narcotics when Lieutenant Samson was detailed to Enemy Aliens, sir."

"Well, if you stick around long enough, you'll find out that Dr. Willing is a mighty handy man to have around when you're trying to break a tough case. Incidentally, he's one of the D.A.'s medical advisers. I'll see him at once."

The lieutenant colored richly and withdrew. When he came back Basil was with him. "If you'd only said you were in the D.A.'s office . . ."

"I was going to. Then I realized that the moment I did every witness would shut up like a clam in my presence. I thought it would be more interesting to wear an invisible cap for a while."

Foyle asked the lieutenant to collect *Vladimir's* belongings and then greeted Basil with a tired grin. "Hello, doc. Who did it?"

"Isn't that a little premature?" Basil had retrieved his

hat and overcoat from the usher. He piled them on the sofa and sat down. "I'm not that good!"

"But you have the knack of seeing things other people miss. Where did you sit during the first act?"

"Fourth row, center."

"Good Lord, you were practically on the stage!" Foyle sat up and stared. "Your eyes are good. You're a doctor of medicine. How could you be so close to *Vladimir* and not see that he was dying?"

"You underestimate the murderer." Basil took out his cigarette case. "As I'm on stage now I suppose I can smoke?"

Foyle shrugged. "That's the Fire Department's headache not mine. I believe the stage is the one place where you can smoke in a theater."

Basil lit his cigarette and inhaled a deep draught of smoke. "I needed that. How do actors endure the No Smoking regulations back stage night after night?" He annexed one of the Sèvres saucers as an ash tray and settled himself more comfortably against the back of the sofa. "This crime was hatched in an ingenious brain."

"What do you mean?"

"The character of *Vladimir* is supposed to be dying all during the first act. He has no lines to speak—no gestures to make. He just lies still on the bed in that alcove at the rear of the stage. The only light in the alcove comes from one votive candle burning under a red glass shade in front of the icon on the wall. Candlelight flickers deceptively and a red-shaded light is always dim. Not only that, but *Vladimir* is made up to look like a dying man—white face, blue shadows around eyes and mouth, gray lips. He is even supposed to assume the look of a man exhausted by pain, scarcely conscious. Now do you see what an unique opportunity for murder that provided? No one on stage or in the fourth row or anywhere else in the audience can tell at what moment the look of pain and exhaustion on *Vladimir's* face ceased to be artifice and became reality. No one knows when he first turned white from a mortal wound under his white mask of grease paint."

Foyle's glance went swiftly to the alcove and then to the fourth row of seats in the orchestra. "I can see how you and the rest of the audience might mistake the real thing for acting and lighting and make-up at that distance, but what about the other actors on the stage? Are you asking me to believe they didn't see that *Vladimir* was really suffering?"

"If they say so, how are we going to prove they are lying?"

"Conspiracy?"

"It might be. Or it might be the truth. Either way it protects the murderer. According to Milhau, the producer, who also directed the play, the first act is supposed to run forty-eight minutes—from eight-forty to nine twenty-eight. It's impossible for us to fix the moment within those forty-eight minutes when the murder was committed. That makes it practically impossible to discover who committed the murder."

"Why should that depend on timing?"

"When the curtain rises, four actors are discovered on stage playing dominoes. All four were on stage tonight when *Vladimir* crossed the stage alive and well and entered the alcove before the curtain rose. One of them spoke to him. He is said to have answered with a grin as he shut the double doors of the alcove behind him. The alcove has no other door and no windows or openings of any kind backstage. It even has a ceiling so no one could have climbed over the walls. After *Vladimir* entered that alcove, he could only be reached by someone crossing the stage to the double doors in full view of the actors on the stage and the people in the audience.

"During the first act, there were only three people who entered the alcove, actors who approached *Vladimir* separately on three different occasions as part of the action of the play.

"Therefore the murder must have been committed in full view of the audience by one of those three actors. But as we cannot fix the actual moment of the murder within the forty-eight minutes the first act lasted, we have no way of proving which of the three people who could have murdered *Vladimir* actually did so.

"As a rule a murderer tries to escape detection by dissociating himself from his murder with a false alibi, and that is often the very thing that leads to his detection. This murderer realized there is safety in numbers. Instead of giving himself an alibi, he has merely obliterated the alibi of two other people. Instead of dissociating himself from the murder, he has contrived to associate other people with it on the same terms as himself. He has dissipated suspicion by diffusing it equally among three people. He's perfectly willing for us to know that he was at the scene of the crime when it was committed, because at least two other people were in exactly the same place at the same time. In ordinary circumstances no murderer could take the risk of having two witnesses to his crime. But the peculiar circumstances of *Vladimir's* role in this play made it possible to commit a murder before several hundred witnesses on the stage, in the wings, and in the audience before their very eyes.

"It looks very much like the perfect crime. We're up against the laws of physics. I saw murder committed with my own eyes and yet—thanks to the limitations of space-time—I don't know when the murder was committed or who did it or even who was murdered."

Foyle got up and walked over to the alcove. Basil remained on the sofa placidly smoking his cigarette. Foyle nodded to the medical examiner and walked around the alcove, tapping the canvas walls, examining floor and ceiling. He came back frowning and stood with his back to the stage fire facing Basil. "It's funny to think of those flimsy canvas walls being just as effective as bricks and mortar three feet thick!"

"For this purpose they are," returned Basil. "There's no way of getting around or under or over them. The canvas is stretched taut and the lath frame nailed to the floor. You couldn't lift it and crawl under as if it were a tent. It's a real box set—there are no gaps, except a very narrow one between the canvas wall and the proscenium arch. To reach the alcove doors that way you have to cross the stage just as you do if you come in by the single door at left, and there are no other doors to the set. When they shift the scene, they hoist the ceiling to the flies, push back the furniture, and drop the second act set inside the first act set. The ceilings of alcove and parlor are all in one piece. You couldn't budge one without attracting attention of actors and audience."

The fly from the alley buzzed inquisitively around the Inspector's head. He brushed it away. "Who were these three people who came near enough to *Vladimir* to stab him during the first act?"

Basil had been waiting for that inevitable question.

He answered with a sigh: "Wanda Morley, Rodney Tait, and Leonard Martin." He liked the two men, and he was beginning to be a little sorry for Wanda.

"Are you sure all three were close enough to *Vladimir* to stab him on stage in full view of the audience?" pursued Foyle.

"Perfectly sure. Wanda, playing *Fedora,* was alone with *Vladimir* in the alcove on two occasions when all the other actors were downstage near the footlights. Both times she threw her arms around *Vladimir* and clung to him, groaning and weeping in a theatrical frenzy of grief. She could have stabbed him easily without anyone realizing what she was doing.

"It was Leonard, playing the policeman, *Grech,* who opened the alcove doors on stage the first time after the curtain rose. He went straight up to *Vladimir's* bed and stood there for a full minute. His back was turned to the audience, and he was bending over *Vladimir.* In the play he was supposed to be ascertaining whether or not *Vladimir* was alive. He did the same thing again just before his exit to search for *Vladimir's* murderer.

"Rodney, playing the surgeon, *Lorek,* was supposed to make a medical examination of *Vladimir's* gunshot wound and extract the bullet. Rodney actually brought a surgeon's bag on stage, took out a surgical knife, and pretended to work over *Vladimir* with it for several minutes. No one in the audience or on the stage could see what he was really doing."

The Inspector made a sour grimace. "Then any one of three different people could have committed the murder on five different occasions, and one of them was actually seen with a knife in his hand bending over the murdered man?"

"Exactly. This whole thing was planned by a remarkably bold, clear, and original mind. The bold are so often reckless and stupid; the calculating, timid and meticulous. But this time, we have a justly balanced combination of boldness, calculation, and utter ruthlessness; for two innocent people are going to suffer just as much as the guilty third."

The medical examiner came down to the footlights and laid a knife on the table. "Hiya, Willing!" He was a stolid young man to whom murder was just a "case" and nothing more. "Stabbed right through the heart so far as I can see without an autopsy. Awkward angle— couldn't have been self-inflicted. Hardly any external bleeding. What there was was under the bedclothes."

"Somebody with medical training?" suggested Foyle, hopefully.

"Not necessarily—in wartime, when every man, woman and child has taken a first-aid course in anatomy. The knife is a surgeon's scalpel. Judging by the tarnished handle it's an old one, but the blade has been sharpened recently, and rather amateurishly. There's a lot of deep spiral grooving on the handle. You won't get any fingerprints. Ideal weapon for murder."

So far as Basil could see it was exactly like the scalpel Rodney had displayed in his dressing room before the curtain rose—except for the dark stains on the blade.

"Can you fix the time of death within forty-eight minutes?" demanded Foyle.

"I could. But I'd just be guessing," returned the examiner. "Onset of *rigor* varies too much with constitution and circumstance, and you can't go by temperature. Indoors in a warm room a dead body only loses heat at the rate of two degrees an hour."

"Anything particular about the body?"

"Youngish—thirty to thirty-five. Healthy and clean, athletic, well-fed, rather sunburned. So far as I can see without stripping him no scars or deformities or chronic diseases. Might've been a horseman. Slightly bow-legged but so tall you wouldn't notice it if you saw him walking around. Will you need me for anything else?"

"No, you can go."

The inquisitive fly made a perfect six-point landing on the handle of the knife, folded his wings, and palpated the grooved metal with proboscis and forelegs.

"Damn that fly!" The Inspector made a mighty swoop at the knife. Quicker than human hand or eye, the fly spread his wings and rocketed into the air with a derisive buzz. But he didn't go far. He hovered just above the knife handle.

The Homicide lieutenant came through the door at left carrying an overcoat, a dinner jacket, a white waistcoat, a top hat, and a bundle of small things wrapped in a handkerchief. He put them all down on the table. "*Vladimir's* belongings—they were in Miss Morley's dressing room." Foyle's hands moved briskly over the clothes. "Good quality. No labels. I suppose he was wearing costume on stage?"

"Not exactly, chief. *Vladimir* is supposed to wear just a shirt and trousers and socks. This man wore his own."

As Foyle picked up the top hat, Basil recalled all the vitality in the cocky angle at which the dead man had worn it when he sauntered into the cocktail bar. Now it was just a shiny black silk beaver like any other.

"Pockets?"

The lieutenant opened the handkerchief bundle. Gold watch—silver cigarette case—linen handkerchief

—five quarters—three dimes—one nickel—leather wallet. And a small sheet of lined paper torn from a notebook with some letters and numbers scrawled across it: RT, F:30.

"That's your department—conundrums and riddles." Foyle pushed the slip of paper over to Basil and picked up the wallet. "Money—no draft card—no driver's license—"

"There was an official looking card of some sort in that cellophane pocket," said Basil. "I saw it when he paid for a drink in the bar next door."

"No sign of a card now," insisted the lieutenant.

"Could it have been taken from him on stage?" demanded Foyle.

"He carried the wallet in the breast pocket of his waistcoat," answered Basil. "And he didn't wear the waistcoat on stage."

"Detail two men to search the theater for an official-looking card," Foyle instructed the lieutenant. "Any fingerprints on this cigarette case? Or lighter?"

"Yes. We've photographed them already. All his own."

Foyle wiped both objects clean with his own handkerchief. "See if Miss Morley is ready to be questioned."

The Homicide lieutenant returned in a few moments. "Miss Morley's physician says she's in no condition for questioning, but I told him she'd have to identify the body."

There was a sound of footfalls beyond the canvas wall. The single door at left was thrown open. Foyle and Basil rose as Wanda Morley made the most dramatic entrance of her long stage career. She was still wearing *Fedora's* dress of golden gauze, but it was crumpled since she had lain down in it, and the gilt glitter looked tawdry under a harsh, direct light. She had removed her diamonds. Dark hair hung in stringy locks about her ravaged face. At close range her coarse stage make-up buried her beauty like a barbaric mask of tragedy. Blackened brows, bronzed eyelids, and reddened lips were as grotesque as a clown's paint beside cheeks that must have been gray under the ivory powder. She was supported by her personal physician and her lawyer on either side. They were followed by her press agent and Milhau. Next came her dresser carrying the sable cloak, a jewel case, and a phial of smelling salts.

"Sorry to trouble you, Miss Morley," said Foyle gravely. "I am an Assistant Chief Inspector of Police. My name is Foyle."

Wanda looked at him with dull eyes. This scene was unrehearsed, its lines unwritten, its cues untimed, its peripeties unplanned. She was on her own, improvising everything she said or did as she went along without the guidance of script or director. There was no prompter to come to her aid if she faltered, no understudy to fill her place if she collapsed. She seemed to be stumbling and groping through an unfamiliar world. "Oh . . . yes . . ." Her voice was hesitant, uncomprehending.

"This way, please." Foyle led the whole group toward the alcove.

Wanda followed slowly. She made an apparent effort to look down at the dead man's face. It was still coated thickly with the corpse make-up—marble white and ash gray with a blue tinge around lips and eyes. Yet it was a comely face now, with the sullen temper that had distorted the mouth gone forever. She bit her lower lip as it started to quiver.

"I—" She turned back to the Inspector hastily. Tears stood in her golden eyes. "I'm sorry." Her voice was a mere breath. "I don't know this man. I never saw him before tonight!"

Was it Basil's imagination? Or was there something terrible about this denial. Somehow it seemed like a betrayal. . . . He tried to recall her smile as she turned toward this man in the alcove when the curtain fell. *You can get up now, darling! First act's over and your job is done.* . . . Was it the smile she would give a stranger?

Basil's quiet voice ended the silence. "You called him 'darling.'"

Wanda closed her eyes. "I call everybody 'darling.' It means nothing in the theater."

"But Miss Morley!" protested the Inspector. "I understood that it was you who secured this man to play the part of *Vladimir* tonight?"

"I—there is some mistake . . ." Wanda opened her eyes and looked at Milhau. "I had thought of getting some friend of mine to play the part, but you said you'd rather have a professional, Sam, don't you remember? And I let the whole thing drop. So naturally tonight I assumed that . . . this man came from you."

There was more realism in the theater than Milhau had bargained for. Real candles and real food were one thing, but a real murder was another. His round face was sallow and oily with sweat. He wrung his hands again. "But Wanda—you were so stubborn about it! Don't you remember? I finally said 'Okay, have it your own way!' So I didn't get anybody, and tonight when this fellow walked in I assumed that he came from you! My God, who did send him? And why? I've got eighty

thousand of my own money in this show and now—
it's ruined! I'm ruined! You're ruined!"

Wanda closed her eyes again.

Foyle could be ruthless on occasion. "Miss Morley!
On the stage you actually kissed the dead man on the lips
just before the curtain fell. Are you asking us to believe
that you didn't know then whether he was alive or dead?
Or did you stab him yourself at that moment?"

"I—Oh—" Wanda slumped and the arms of her doctor caught her. Apparently she was unconscious.

The doctor addressed Foyle sternly. "Miss Morley is in
no condition for questioning. She is a great artist, and
her nervous system is too sensitive to bear shocks of this
sort. I must get her home at once."

Lawyer and press agent bristled, obviously determined to back up the doctor if necessary. Foyle wasn't
afraid of law or medicine, but he had a healthy respect
for the press.

"All right," he sighed. "Take her home."

The dresser wrapped Wanda in her sable cloak. The
lawyer helped the doctor carry her out to her car. The
press agent followed to fend off reporters. As the stage
door opened, Basil heard the "Ah's" and "Oh's" of the
crowd. Flashlight bulbs flared briefly in the alley. The
door closed.

Foyle turned to the lieutenant. "Mr. Tait next."

II

Like a master of ceremonies the lieutenant brought
his next number through the wings onto the stage. The
immaculate morning dress of *Dr. Lorek* had wilted con-
siderably. The Ascot tie was loosened, the stiff white
collar unbuttoned, and sweat mingled with pink powder

and grease paint to make Rod's face a shiny red. His round eyes, lengthened by a few strokes of eyebrow pencil at the outer corners, rolled in their sockets displaying white rims like a startled horse. As he sat down he ran his fingers through his hair in a nervous gesture that disarranged all the neatly brushed waves. He looked very young and very distressed but not in the least guilty.

"Mr. Tait, do you recognize any of these things?" Foyle pointed to *Vladimir's* belongings on the table.

"No."

"Have you ever seen this before?" Foyle handed Rod the cigarette case. Rod turned it over, unconsciously leaving beautiful impressions of his fingertips on the freshly wiped surface. He returned it to Foyle with a shake of the head. "No."

Foyle remained standing, hands behind his back, looking down on his victim. "Mr. Tait, on stage during the first act you approached the actor playing the part of *Vladimir*. Was he alive or dead at that moment?"

"Good Lord, I—I don't know."

"Do you really ask me to believe you could stand so close to a man and not know whether he was breathing or not?"

"But the light was so dim!" cried Rod. "He was made up to look like a corpse. He was supposed to act like a dying man—eyes half closed, lips parted, body still. When people are lying down they breathe quietly. Ordinarily you don't notice whether people are breathing or not unless they're panting or snoring. How can I tell now whether he was acting the part of a dying man or really dying? I wasn't thinking about him then. I had my own part to think about."

"Try thinking about him now," suggested Foyle.

Basil intervened. "Take it step by step. When you first came on stage you took off your wraps—hat, coat, and gloves. As I remember you took them off slowly and piled them on a chair. Was that your own idea or part of the play?"

"It was Milhau's idea. He directed. Leonard as *Grech* was supposed to rush in excitedly, tearing off his gauntlets and thrusting them in his belt in order to keep his hands free for his revolver." Rod smiled slightly. "Milhau's idea of a police officer at the scene of a murder—a sort of disciplined hustle. Then I was supposed to come in slowly and take my things off methodically and leave them neatly on a chair—the professional man who makes haste slowly and refuses to be rushed or rattled. Contrast. Get it?"

"Then it was part of Milhau's direction that you should both remove your gloves?" continued Basil.

"Why, yes." The question seemed to puzzle Rod.

"And then you entered the alcove and—take it on from there."

"I went up to the bed and that was the first time I looked at *Vladimir*. I—I thought he was doing a pretty good job. He really looked like a dying man. He didn't move or speak. His face was sort of relaxed. Usually when you play a dead man on the stage you want to sneeze—nerves, of course—and that makes your face look tense. I lifted his arm to feel his pulse and—"

"Was there any pulse?"

"I don't know! Great Scott, I'm not a doctor. I've taken a first-aid course like everybody else, but I never can find any of the pulse and pressure points when I want to. I just pretended to feel his pulse tonight. I didn't really feel it."

"You shouldn't have lifted his arm," said Basil. "You're more likely to find the pulse when the arm hangs down. Was the arm a dead weight?"

"It was relaxed. He was supposed to be limp. That's part of the play."

"But it wasn't stiff?"

"Oh, no."

"Was his skin warm?"

"Yes."

"And then?"

"I pushed up his right eyelid. The way doctors do."

"And still you can't say whether he was dead or not!" Foyle was sarcastic.

"It's difficult to tell whether a man at the point of death is alive or dead," Basil reminded the Inspector. "Even doctors who are looking for signs of death can make mistakes at such moments. A layman who thinks he is dealing with a live man pretending to be dead could easily be mistaken one way or the other. A man may be alive and still have no perceptible pulse. The skin of a live man suffering from a chill may be cooler to the touch than the skin of a dead man who has just died of fever." Basil turned back to Rod. "Did the eyeball move? Or the pupil expand?"

"I don't think so. I remember thinking he was trying to keep as still as possible."

"And after that?"

"I called for hot water and pretended to write a prescription. Then I opened the surgical bag and took out that probe you had told me a real surgeon would use. I pulled the bed quilt down just to his collar bone and pretended to dig a bullet out of his neck. Then I put a dressing on his neck where the wound was supposed to be—just a square of gauze, no bandage. That was the point where I left the alcove to consult *Grech*. A few moments later I returned to the alcove with the hot water and the prescribed medicine I had sent for, pretended to cleanse the wound, and made a more elaborate dressing. I fussed over him for a while, feeling his pulse again and pretending to let a few drops of medicine fall on his tongue. I didn't really give him anything. Finally I went down stage right and announced that he was dead."

" 'Downstage right?' " queried Foyle.

"Downstage is up near the footlights," explained Rod. "Right is stage right—my right as I face the house on stage. In other words, stage right is house left."

"Naturally," Basil smiled. "The stage is the other side of the mirror held up to nature where right is left and up is down. We'll remember that when you say 'right' you mean stage right. Did you go near *Vladimir* again?"

"No. I just stood there until the curtain fell. Then I took the first curtain call with Wanda and Leonard and—you know the rest."

"According to your story, *Vladimir* did not move once when you were near him. Can't you remember a single gesture? A flicker of an eyelid? A twitching of mouth or finger? A reflex flinching when you touched him?"

Rod closed his eyes for a moment. Suddenly he opened them flinging his head back. "Don't go by what I say! It's like trying to remember a dream. The image is so faint, and you're trying so hard to grasp it that before you know it, you're inventing instead of remembering. I don't believe he moved, but I can't swear it. I wasn't paying close attention, and I won't guess because—if he didn't move—that would mean that Wanda or Leonard did it before I went near him, and I would be swearing away their lives!"

"Very altruistic of you," said Foyle, coldly. "But what about your own position? You carried a bag of surgical knives on stage. The entire audience saw a knife in your hand when you leaned over *Vladimir*. Of the three people who had the opportunity to stab him you alone are known to have had a weapon at hand."

For the first time Rod looked frightened. "But one of the knives was stolen from me . . . " He turned to Basil.

"Is this the one that was missing?" Basil indicated the knife the medical examiner had left on the table.

Rod looked and winced as he saw the dark stains on the blade. "It looks like it." He lifted his eyes to Foyle. "There wouldn't have been a knife missing if—if—I—"

"On the contrary," answered Foyle. "If you were the murderer the most obvious way to divert suspicion from yourself would be to pretend one of the knives was stolen before the curtain rose. Now will you tell us the truth?" Foyle leaned forward, chin out-thrust, hands still behind his back. "I don't ask you to guess, and I don't ask you to swear to anything. But I do ask you to give us your honest impression: Was *Vladimir* alive the first time you touched him?"

Rod dropped his eyelids. His mouth settled in a tragic line. His response was dragged from him. "Yes."

"And was he alive the last time you touched him?"

This time the response was even more reluctant.

"I think so, but that's just a guess."

"How many people approached him after that?"

"One."

"And that was?

"Miss Morley."

"Thank you, Mr. Tait. That will be all for the present."

Rod rose and stumbled toward the gap in the wings like a drunken man. Suddenly he halted. Pauline was standing there in the shadow of the proscenium arch. Basil wondered how long she had been listening. Rod stared at her as if he didn't recognize her.

"Rod!" She plucked at his sleeve, face turned up to him. "Don't look like that. Everything's going to be all right. I'll take you home now in my car."

"What do you think I am? A baby? I can take myself home, thank you!" His voice rasped hoarsely and he stalked away toward his dressing room.

For a moment Pauline stood still looking after him. Then her head drooped like a wilting flower on its stalk. Basil rose and went toward her. "Pauline!"

"Oh, it's you." She lifted her head slowly as if it were too heavy for her neck to support. "Are you running with the hounds now?"

"I'm trying to get at the truth. That's the best cure for everything. Why don't you help?"

"What can I do?"

"Now, you're a costume designer. You must understand clothes and textures and colors. We want someone to look all through the theater—dressing rooms, lockers, everywhere—for a long cloak or overcoat or dressing gown that would envelop an average figure from head to foot and look black after dark. Will you do it?"

"I suppose I might as well." She turned away listlessly.

Foyle had listened to this in astonishment. "Don't you know the lieutenant put a man on that job the minute he heard your story of the figure on the fire escape?"

"She needs something to do," answered Basil. "And it's always interesting to get two reports and compare them."

III

Leonard Martin still wore the dark wig, padded shoulders, and high-heeled boots of *Grech,* the Russian police officer, but he was no longer *Grech.* The quiet voice and deprecating smile that acknowledged Foyle's greeting were those of Leonard Martin himself.

"I enjoyed your performance," said Basil. "Sardou left *Grech* a lay figure. You made him a neat sketch of a policeman on the job."

Leonard was pleasantly surprised. "I'm glad you liked it. Most people prefer lay figures on stage and screen—especially if they have nice legs."

"Wish I'd seen you." Foyle grinned. "I might have picked up a few pointers. Let's see if you're as good a policeman off stage as on. Mr. Tait who played *Dr. Lorek* can't even feel a pulse! Do you recognize any of these objects?"

"No."

"Ever see this before?" Foyle held out the cigarette lighter.

But Leonard did not touch it. Hands resting easily on his knees, he bent his head forward to look at it. "No, I can't say I have."

Foyle put it back on the table. "Let's see—you approached *Vladimir* twice, didn't you?"

At mention of *Vladimir* Leonard lost his good humored smile. The hands that lay on his knees shook slightly. He must have seen them himself, for suddenly he thrust both hands in his hip pockets.

"The first time was your first entrance." Foyle was looking at the lieutenant's notes. *Enter Grech, brusquely, from single door at left. He rushes excitedly to double doors and throws them wide open* . . . "Well? What happened?"

"Nothing." Leonard answered in a low voice—strained, yet under control. "The alcove was empty. *Vladimir* was lying on the bed. The candle was burning in front of the icon. I stood there for a moment pretending to examine him with my back to the audience. Then I went downstage right to speak my next line."

"The second time you approached him was just before your first exit," Foyle read again from the lieutenant's notes of the play. *Grech rises from desk and goes to bed in alcove.* "What happened that time?"

"I looked at *Vladimir* for a few moments standing with my back to the audience again. Milhau's direction —so Wanda could hog the scene as usual. Then I took a revolver out of my pocket and crossed the stage saying: *Come on, men, we'll get him now!* After that I exited at left."

"Now, think carefully. Was *Vladimir* alive or dead the first time you looked at him?"

"I don't know."

"And the second time?"

"I don't know."

"Come now, Mr. Martin! You must have noticed something. According to Dr. Willing who saw the play from the fourth row center, you actually fumbled with the bedclothes both times. Was there no sign of blood? No hump under the bedclothes where the knife handle protruded from his chest?"

"I didn't notice anything of the sort at the time."

"If there had been anything of that sort at the time, wouldn't you have noticed it?"

The question seemed to startle Leonard. Something stirred behind his eyes.

Foyle pursued the advantage. "Even if you have no observed fact you can cite to prove *Vladimir* alive or dead, you must have some opinion of your own—a general impression based on small things noticed but unremembered. After all, you were close enough to touch him—closer than I am to you now. You might not realize he was dead or dying at the time when you assumed he was acting the part of a dying man. But now you know that he was really dying at some point during the first act of the play. Can't you look backward in the light of this new knowledge and tell us when that point occurred? Surely you are not less observant than Mr. Tait?"

Leonard looked up in amazement. "You mean to say —that Rod said he knew—when—?"

"He did his best to give us an honest report of his impressions. I want you to do the same thing as honestly as he did."

"This is dreadful! There were only three of us who went near *Vladimir* on stage tonight and—we're all friends!"

The Inspector waited patiently.

"All right!" Leonard flung the words at him. "I'll give you my opinion for what it's worth. At the time, of course, I assumed *Vladimir* was all right. Now that I look back on it in the light of what has happened—I think—"

"Yes?"

"I know he was alive when I opened the alcove doors.

I can't say why—I just know it. But the second time—well, he could have been dead or dying."

"Why?" The word was soft and insistent.

"I can't say why. It's just an intuitive feeling—a hunch, I guess."

"How many people approached *Vladimir* in the interval between your two visits to the alcove? asked Foyle.

"Two."

"And they were?"

"Wanda Morley and Rodney Tait."

IV

When Leonard had gone, Foyle looked at Basil wearily. "Right back where we started! Rodney and Leonard cancel each other out. If Rodney's right about the moment death occurred, Wanda is the murderer. If Leonard's right, it could be either Wanda or Rodney. Is one of them lying? Or just mistaken? We can't tell! We have three witnesses right on the spot when a man was stabbed and none of them is any good. Rodney is throwing suspicion on Wanda, and Leonard is throwing it back on Rodney and Wanda. Question: Is this deliberate or unconscious?"

"It may have been done reluctantly," answered Basil. "But hardly unconsciously. An actor would not be likely to forget the topography and sequence of events in a scene acted so recently and rehearsed so often."

Foyle yawned and rose. "Well, I guess that's about all for the present. Or have you any aces up your sleeve?"

"No aces, just deuces and treys. But before I call it a night, I'd like to see the actor who played *Siriex* and the actor who spoke to *Vladimir* when he crossed the stage to enter the alcove before the curtain rose."

Seymour Hutchins as *Jean de Siriex of the French Embassy* looked the way princes and ambassadors ought to look and rarely do. Age had blurred the noble lines of his profile without destroying them entirely. Dark eyes, brilliantly intelligent, looked out of a white face under whiter hair. It was impossible to imagine Wanda or Leonard following any other profession than the stage, but Basil had an impression that Hutchins was a man of parts who would have succeeded in almost any calling and who had just drifted onto the stage through force of circumstance or youthful inclination. According to the programme notes, he had once been a successful leading man himself, and even in his old age producers were glad to entrust him with supporting roles as important as *Siriex*.

"You come on stage with *Grech* when he makes his first entrance and remain there all during the rest of the first act," said Basil. "Can you recall noticing anything wrong with *Vladimir* at any time?"

Hutchins considered the question carefully before he answered. "Toward the end of the act I had an impression that *Vladimir's* portrayal of a dying man was overdone. At the time I thought his dying was unreal because he was overacting. Now, I think it seemed unreal because it was the real thing—which always seems out of key in a world of make-believe."

"That's interesting," said Basil, "because I had the same impression; and when two witnesses reach the same conclusion independently it's apt to be the truth. Can you say at what moment his overacting began?"

"I'm afraid not. Can you?"

Basil shook his head ruefully and took something out of his overcoat pocket—a manuscript bound in blue paper. "Do you recognize this script, Mr. Hutchins?"

"I believe it is Miss Morley's."

"As *Siriex* you have a line to speak on page 19 of Act I." Basil read aloud from the script: *"He cannot escape now, every hand is against him!* Did you underscore that line in Miss Morley's script?"

"Certainly not." Hutchins was candidly puzzled.

"Did you underscore it in your own script?"

"No, I checked all my lines lightly in red ink. I didn't underscore any of them."

"Can you think of any reason why anyone else should wish to call attention to that line of yours in Miss Morley's script?"

"No, I can't." He frowned, considering the question. "Of course, this is a revision as well as a translation of the original *Fedora*. We had some trouble finding a copy of the play. We tried various booksellers and libraries, both public and private, without discovering it. They had other plays of Sardou's, but not *Fedora;* and Miss Morley had set her heart on doing *Fedora*. Finally at a music publisher's we found a libretto of the opera Giordano wrote around Sardou's play. It was in Italian, and Milhau had a translation made with a good deal of adaptation and modernization. Some superfluous characters were cut out; and in the course of the re-shuffling this line of mine was transferred from the end of the scene to the beginning, and the wording was altered. Originally it read: *He cannot escape now, all the shadows are converging.* It refers, of course, to *Vladimir's* murderer when the police are closing in on him. But it is not a vitally important or significant line in the play, for as you doubtless recall, *Vladimir's* murderer does escape at the end of the first act. The line has nothing to do with Miss Morley except that she as *Fedora* is listening to *Siriex* when he delivers it. I see no reason why Miss Morley or anyone else should mark that line in her script. I can see no reason why anyone should underscore it in any script unless—"

"Unless what?"

Seymour Hutchins' fingertips brushed his eyes as if he were pushing away something that obscured his vision materially. "In view of what has happened could this marked passage have been a message of some sort? A warning? Or a threat?"

"A warning to whom?"

"I don't know. It was just . . . an idea . . ."

V

The last of the five witnesses interviewed that evening faced Basil and Foyle with a certain truculence. His streamlined, bullet-shaped head was too small for the fleshy throat, thick wrists, and muscular forearms revealed by an open-necked short-sleeved shirt. Close-cropped, reddish hair grew so low on his forehead that it looked like a fur cap. His reddish-brown eyes were shrewd and impudent.

"Are you Dr. Willing, the psychiatrist?" he demanded.

"Yes."

"Then maybe you can help me with my play. It's about a nymphomaniac, and I was wondering—"

"We are here to investigate a murder," interrupted Foyle, in his harshest voice. "Your full name is Derek Adeane, and you are an actor?"

"That's my stage name. My real name is Daniel Adelaar—too long to put up in lights."

Basil wondered if length were really the only objection to professional use of this Teutonic name at the present time. The bullet-shaped head suggested Prussian blood and Adeane seemed to have a little of the unimaginative Prussian's inflexible insensibility to the reactions of others. He had already rubbed Inspector Foyle the wrong way, and now he proceeded to do so again. "I'm not really an actor," he said arrogantly. "I'm just acting temporarily until I can find a producer for my play. The first act takes place in a waterfront saloon, and—"

Again Foyle cut him short. "Interesting as the play may be, I'm afraid we'll have to postpone its discussion to another occasion."

"Sure. Any time you like." Adeane was impervious to irony.

"I understand you were one of the domino players on the stage before the curtain rose this evening?"

"That's right. I play *Nicola,* one of *Vladimir's* servants."

"And you saw *Vladimir* when he crossed the stage to enter the alcove just before the curtain rose?"

"Uh-huh." Adeane's restless eyes followed the fly still banking and diving like a miniature plane above the knife on the table. Transparent wings folded, and the fly alighted on the handle. Again the Inspector slapped at it. Again it buzzed angrily as it soared into the air. But it didn't go far away. It circled twice and returned to the handle of the knife.

"Suppose you tell us just what happened," said Foyle.

Adeane yawned. Basil had an impression that Adeane became bored whenever a conversation shifted from such interesting subjects as himself, his career, and his play. "He came through that gap in the wings and crossed the stage," said Adeane. "The double doors were closed. He opened them and went inside, shutting them behind him."

"How did he look? Normal in every way?"

"Yeah." Adeane's eyes were still following the fly. His brow puckered as if something puzzled him. He seemed to be giving Foyle the lesser part of his attention. "Of course, he was all made up for the part of *Vladimir*—a white·face with blue shadows around the eyes, mouth, and gray lips. But you could tell it was just make-up. He crossed the stage with a firm step, rather briskly because he was a bit late. The curtain was due to rise in three minutes, and he had to get settled on the bed before it rose, so there wouldn't be any noise from behind the double doors after the first act began. Those doors are pretty flimsy—plywood and ground glass. If he'd moved around in the alcove after the curtain rose the audience could have seen his shadow on the glass panels."

"How was he dressed?"

"Black socks and trousers, white shirt open at the throat."

"Did anyone else enter the alcove afterward?"

"Not until *Grech*—that is Leonard Martin—threw open the doors during the first act. He and Wanda and Rodney Tait all had to enter the alcove in the course of the play."

"According to others on the stage at that time, you were the only person who spoke to *Vladimir* when he crossed the stage. What exactly did you say?"

Adeane frowned as if he were trying to recall his words. Suddenly he laughed. "Good God, it sounds funny now!"

"What does?"

"What I said." He laughed again, with apparently genuine amusement. "I said: 'Hello, so you're the corpse!'"

VI

When Adeane had gone, Foyle ambled back to his chair meditatively. "Sure is a queer set-up. I'm pretty good at reading emotions in faces and behavior. I have to be. But actors are trained to fake their emotions in every detail—eyes, face, voice, carriage, hands, feet, everything! And they can do it off stage as well as on. It is a world of make-believe—false names and false faces! How can I tell which one of these is playing a part?"

"That's not the only thing that makes a stage murder difficult," replied Basil.

"Hell, is there something else?"

"Timing."

"Timing?"

"In a play, every line and gesture and bit of action has to be timed so accurately that the performance will last a certain period, each actor will get his cues at certain fixed moments and the whole thing will have pace and co-ordination. Most people have no idea how long it takes to do any specified thing—to walk across a room or carry on a conversation. But actors learn to think of their speeches and gestures and actions in terms of time. I suspect that this murderer knew exactly how long the action of stabbing would take and that he timed that action to fit smoothly into the chronological mosaic of the play. Many murderers are caught because they make some mistake in timing. An actor turned murderer is not likely to do that."

"This is a streamlined murder!" exploded Foyle. "Only three suspects and no clues, no alibis, no fingerprints, no footprints, no motives, no telltale looks or gestures! How can anyone crack a case like that?"

"We have just three points of departure," returned Basil.

"And they are?"

"The three things that no murderer can ever quite eliminate: the victim, the weapon, and the psychology of the crime. First, the weapon. It is the one tangible thing we possess that we are absolutely certain has been in contact with the murderer. Second, the victim. We don't know who he is now, but as soon as his identity is established it should tell us something about the identity of his murderer. Third, the psychology of the murder—the subtle traces of character that are left behind in all acts of criminal behavior. This murderer has been clever about eliminating all the usual clues. But there has to be a victim, there has to be a weapon, and there has to be a mind behind that weapon. Perhaps the mind is our best bet. Every murder committed is in itself a clue to the nature of the mind that conceived it, and a mind is almost as individual as a fingerprint. Our job is to find out which of three people has the sort of mind that would act as this murderer has acted."

"I don't see how the weapon is going to help us." Foyle picked up the knife again. The fly shot into space at a tangent. "Anyone in the theater could have taken it from Rodney Tait's dressing room, including Tait himself. Anyone could have sharpened it in the knife-grinder's workshop next door. And fingerprints don't show on that grooved handle." With a sigh, he laid it back on the table. The fly hovered over the blade for an instant; then it swerved and sank to the handle.

Basil drew near the table—so quietly that the fly did not move. "That's queer."

"What is?"

"There are bloodstains on the blade, but this fly keeps going back to the handle. It hasn't settled on the blade once in all the time we've been here."

The fly rocketed once more as Foyle picked up the knife by the handle. "Feels kind of sticky. What is there besides blood that would attract a fly? Gravy?"

"Yes. Or a sugar bowl." Basil was conscious of a teasing, fugitive fragrance as he bent over the knife—something like the air in a walled orchard. "You might ask Lambert to test that handle for traces of sugar."

Lambert was the city toxicologist who had made a name for himself identifying chemical ingredients in the smallest bits of matter—grease spots on a waistcoat, grime under a fingernail, the accumulation of dust in the welt around the sole of a shoe.

"Why sugar?" asked Foyle.

"Just an idea," responded Basil. "Probably a foolish one. I haven't worked it out yet."

"Am I interrupting?"

It was Pauline. She came through the wings her hair in a misty disorder, her eyes like wilted bluebells. "I should get a bonus from the Police Department for this! It's hard work." She dropped into a chair Basil had pulled back for her. "And I don't believe I've found your black cloak after all. I've made a list."

"Let's hear it." Foyle was a little wary of this amateur assistant. Basil stood behind her chair looking over her shoulder at the paper in her hand.

"Well, in Wanda's dressing room there's a yellow satin housecoat and a dressing gown of *chartreuse* wool *crêpe*. Neither of those would fill the bill. *Fedora* doesn't wear any coats or cloaks in the rest of the play, so that was all. Leonard wore a spring overcoat to the theater this evening—pale gray herringbone tweed. The uniform he wore on stage as *Grech* is dark blue, with silver braid and buttons that would shine in the dimmest light. His dressing gown is a clear cardinal red. There's no other wrap in his room, and—" She hesitated, frowning.

"And Rodney Tait?" prompted the Inspector.

"I knew he was out of it before I started to look. Otherwise—" She smiled, "I wouldn't have looked. The overcoat he wore to the theater is of beige camel's hair. His dressing gown is light blue flannel. The long Russian overcoat he wore on stage as *Dr. Lorek* is black but it is fur-lined with a collar of silver gray squirrel. That collar would look pale in any light, and anyone can see the fur was sewn to the cloth by a professional furrier. It couldn't have been removed and replaced quickly by an amateur like Rod, just as Leonard couldn't have removed and replaced the intricate silver braiding on his dark blue coat. And that's the lot. I looked all through the dressing rooms. I even looked in Milhau's office. I looked through the lockers the stagehands use in the recreation room under the stage. There just wasn't any long black cloak or even a darkish overcoat or dressing gown that would look black in a dim light."

"What about the sable cloak Wanda wore in the first act?" asked Basil.

"Oh!" Pauline was startled. "I never thought of that.

It wasn't in her dressing room. I suppose she's taken it home with her already."

"It was a very dark brown," went on Basil. "It enveloped her from head to heels, and it even had a hood. If she wore it over the house coat would the yellow satin show?"

"I suppose not." Pauline's smile had faded. She looked utterly spent. "I don't like Wanda, but I don't believe she would commit murder. Think what this means to her—wrecking her opening night, ruining her play. . . . Well, here's the list, Inspector. I've done my good deed for the day—or was it a bad deed? Anyway, I'm going home."

"I'll take you home," said Basil. "There's nothing more to be done here tonight."

VII

The street outside was almost empty now. Basil hailed a taxi, and they drove to Pauline's apartment on the upper East Side.

"What shall I say? *Thank you for a lovely evening, Dr. Willing? I did so enjoy the murder—we must do this again!*" She smiled ruefully and held out her hand.

"It was you who supplied the tickets and the murder! My idea of an evening's entertainment is much less ambitious. . . ." He took her hand and turned it over. The palm of her white glove was still streaked with black. "How did that happen?"

"Oh!" She looked down at her glove with a fastidious grimace. "I must have done that on the backstage fire escape. The dust of ages has sifted all over it in a fine black powder."

"Were you star-gazing?"

"No, there were no stars tonight. My watch stopped at seven-thirty, and I wanted to reset it. That fire escape is the only point in the theater where you can see the Tilbury clock." Her laughter bubbled. "Are you suggesting that I was the mysterious dark figure on the fire escape?"

"No. Your coat and dress are both light blue, and blue is the last of all the colors to darken when light fades. That's why a cloudless sky looks blue even at night if there's any light at all."

Pauline snatched her hand away. "So you did think of me! Basil Willing, what a nasty suspicious mind you have!"

He laughed.

"It isn't funny. Good night!"

It was some time after midnight when Basil got back to his own home—an old-fashioned brownstone house on Park Avenue below Grand Central. As he fumbled in his pocket for a latch key, his glance happened on the floor of the vestibule—a tessellated pavement of black and white stone.

That brought back one detail of his wanderings backstage that had been lost in the excitement and confusion of later events. Like a miniature moving picture in vivid technicolor, his memory unreeled a vision of a woman in a black and white dress and a black cloak opening double doors to cross a dim, firelit stage and brush past him in the wings. Those double doors must have been the doors to the alcove. *Vladimir* might have been already on his bed in the alcove at that moment, for the curtain rose only a few minutes afterward, and Adeane had seen

Vladimir enter the alcove three minutes before the curtain rose.

Were there four suspects instead of three? There was nothing to prove that *Vladimir* had been alive at any moment during the first act. He could have been stabbed before the curtain rose. He could have lain there dead all during the silly posturing and mummery of the first act without anyone on stage or in the audience suspecting it. . . .

CHAPTER FIVE

Leading Juvenile

BASIL'S HOUSE was at its best early in the morning when eastern sunshine flooded the principal rooms. The street was wide, the buildings opposite low; so the front windows had daylight all day and a segment of starry sky at night just as if they overlooked a small town instead of a skyscraper city. He had selected this house in the first place because it reminded him of his father's home in Baltimore, and a home was what he wanted after years of wandering from one set of students' lodgings to another in Paris and Vienna. It had high ceilings, thick walls, and deep fireplaces built for fires that would heat a whole room. Living room and dining room had cream paneled walls. Firelight painted them with apricot highlights; sunshine washed them with lemon yellow.

The original colors of the rugs had dulled to quiet shades of buff and brown, like dead flowers pressed in a book; and the whole place was faded, and comfortable as an old bedroom slipper.

The next morning in the sun-splashed dining room, Basil glanced at the daily paper as he started his grapefruit.

MURDER ON STAGE

Man Stabbed at Morley Opening

Only the barest outline of the crime had caugh the night shift of the morning paper in time for this edition. Basil turned to the theatrical page. For once a dramatic critic had paid some attention to what was occurring on the stage.

WANDA MORLEY *in* *FEDORA*

Reviewed by Milverton Trowbridge

The sensational discovery of a murdered man on the stage of the Royalty Theatre last night interrupted Sam Milhau's production of *Fedora* starring Wanda Morley, at the end of the first act. If such an incredible event had occurred in the action of the play, the writer would have condemned it unhesitatingly as a stale theatrical contrivance—a piece of pure ham, mechanical and impossible. But it is scarcely the function of a dramatic critic to subject reality to the same austere standard of criticism as make-believe. Suffice it to say that the impossible did happen last night at the Royalty, and it is now a story for the news section rather than an occasion for comment in this column. The identity of the murdered man, a super playing the walk-on part of *Vladimir,* has not been established. Apparently he was an amateur who had no connection with the stage. That is one of the many inexplicable features of the case. Many of us have felt on occasion that murdering an actor would be justifiable homicide, and there have been plays that would have justified the murder of the playwright; but it is difficult to understand why anyone would launch a murderous attack upon an inoffensive super who was apparently unknown to anyone else on the stage.

Everyone in the theatrical world will feel deep sympathy for Miss Morley who must have suffered a severe shock when she discovered the body. Judging by the first act alone her *Fedora* was a warm, highly colored interpretation, breathing new life into the lath and plaster of Sardou's creaky old melodrama. When will our theater provide Miss Morley with a vehicle worthy of her great talent as an actress? She is wasted on this pinchbeck stuff that Huneker used to call "Sardoodle."

Leonard Martin turned in one of his usual smooth performances as *Grech,* the police officer. Rodney Tait, making his debut on Broadway, was decidedly miscast as the elderly *Dr. Lorek.* Unfortunately there was no opportunity to observe him in the possibly more congenial role of *Loris Ipanov* as *Loris* does not appear until the second act.

There will be no performance of *Fedora* this evening. At the moment, it is uncertain whether or not the play will be resumed later this week.

This review irritated Basil. He had read it hoping to glean some significant sidelight on the murder. But, possibly through force of habit, the critic treated the murder the way he treated everything else that occurred on stage—as a peg on which to hang his own rather tepid "cuteness"—so Basil learned nothing.

Juniper came in with bacon and eggs. "Yo' coffee's gettin' cold, Doctah Willin'," he said, almost as grimly as a wife.

"I like my coffee cold—sometimes!"

The front doorbell rang.

"If that's a bomb insurance salesman or a man from the Society for the Suppression of Red Nail Polish with a petition to be signed, just say that I died last week and was buried yesterday."

As a rule Juniper was a blandly impenetrable obstruction to all casual time-wasters. This morning he met his match. As soon as the door opened, there was a rush of feet in the hall, and Pauline appeared in the doorway with Rodney Tait.

"Basil! You must help us!"

Astonished, Basil was on his feet already. "What can I do? What's wrong?"

"You can find out who killed that man last night and you must—please! If you don't, they'll arrest Rod. I know they will. They've been questioning him for hours."

Basil looked at Rodney. His eyes were puffy and red, as if he had been up all night. His jaw was set with a new firmness.

"I'm afraid we oughtn't to have barged in like this at breakfast—" he began.

"Not at all," interrupted Basil quickly. "Suppose you both sit down and tell me all about it. Coffee?"

"No, thanks. But we will cadge cigarettes."

They sat on either side of him, opposite each other. Pauline was trim in the same neat suit she had worn yesterday. She faced the sun fearlessly. But Rod sat with his back to it, his eyes veiled in shadow. There was a V-shaped frown between his brows. His hands were restless.

Apparently last night's quarrel was healed. Pauline looked at Rod, though she was speaking to Basil. "You're a policeman, aren't you?"

"No."

"Well, you're an Assistant District Attorney or something official. That Inspector Foyle behaved as if you were his bosom friend. All the police did."

"Officially I'm a medical assistant to the District Attorney, specializing in psychiatry. They only call me in when they want to determine the sanity of a witness or a suspect."

"But you've done all sorts of things unofficially. You're supposed to advise them on psychological aspects of a case, aren't you? And this case has psychological aspects. The police will never get the hang of it unless you help them. There are only three people who could have killed that man, and Rod's one of them. The police are playing eena, meena, mina, mo. They've counted out Wanda and Leon already. They're going for Rod. You must help. Please!"

Tranquilly, Basil poured a second cup of coffee and lit his first cigarette of the day. "What makes you think that?"

"I don't think it. I know it. Partly because of the knife. They just can't get over the fact that it belonged to Rod and came from a surgical bag he carried on stage. It would've been so damnably easy for Rod to carry the knife in the bag, slip it into *Vladimir* when Rod's back was turned toward the audience, and then go on with the play as if nothing had happened."

Basil drew on his cigarette. "I don't think you're being quite frank with me."

"Why not?"

"The police knew all this last night. There was no talk of arresting Rod then."

Pauline looked at Rod across the table. "Shall we tell him?"

"We have no business to bother you with all this, Dr. Willing," muttered Rod. "But Pauline *would* come and . . ."

Pauline cut him short and turned back to Basil. "They think they have a motive."

"Yes?"

"You remember Milhau said Bernhardt used to ask her 'boy friends' to play *Vladimir?* The police didn't miss that point. They think Wanda knew the dead man. They don't believe her denial. He could have been a lover . . ."

Basil turned to Rod. "Would that give you a motive?"

"No, it wouldn't!" Rod answered sharply. "But the police seem to think it would. And so does Pauline."

"How can I help it?" cried Pauline. "You're always with her! You brought her to that art gallery yesterday. There's been so much talk that the police got hold of it as soon as the case broke. And it would explain—a lot of things. . . ."

Basil turned back to Rod. "Let's hear your side of it."

Rod flushed uncomfortably and thrust his hands in his pockets. "I suppose you'd think me an utter heel if I said she ran after me, wouldn't you?"

Pauline's brows were daintily skeptical. "We should indeed! It was you who ran after her. I saw you."

"Well, I didn't." Rod appealed to Basil. "I know it sounds incredible as well as shabby, but she did come after me all the time. I didn't even like her."

"Do you mean she was in love with you?" demanded Basil a little ungently.

"No," answered Rod, surprisingly. "That's the funny part of it. I don't believe she cared a rap for me at all!"

"How modest!" murmured Pauline.

"Well, she never—er—made any passes at me!" Rod laughed. "I do sound like a maiden with reluctant feet, etc., don't I? But there was something queer about the whole thing. Whenever I was in a public place—a restaurant, or a theater, or an art gallery—Wanda was always there too, asking me to get her a cocktail or light her cigarette, or something, chattering away and rolling her eyes at me. She was always asking me to take her places, too. Somehow I just couldn't get rid of her—in public. But if we were alone together, her whole manner changed, and she let me alone. It was just the opposite of the usual thing. I couldn't shake her in public without being rude, and I couldn't be rude because I was dependent on her for my job as her leading man. She and Milhau were giving me my first chance on Broadway. If she had been in love with me I could have understood it better. But I swear she wasn't. It was an awful nuisance—especially when Pauline noticed it. And now, it's worse than a nuisance. If the police can establish that *Vladimir* was Wanda's lover, they'll assume I had a motive to kill him—jealousy. That, plus the knife, makes a pretty strong case against me. It would be a sweet mess to be accused of killing a man for the sake of a woman you've never cared a hoot about!"

"Wouldn't Wanda deny that you had been in love with her?" suggested Basil.

"Well, would she? That's the whole point. I don't

know what she'd do, because I don't know why she chased me."

"Rod!" Pauline was impatient. "Surely you've heard about the bees and flowers. You know perfectly well why she chased you."

"But it wasn't that at all! How many times do I have to say so before you'll believe it?"

"Anyway, that isn't the point," went on Pauline. "The point is that she's got you involved in a murder case. I don't know why I should care—but I do."

They smiled at each other. Something about that smile made Basil regret he had left his twenties behind him.

"Are you two engaged?" he asked bluntly.

A delicate pink color came into Pauline's cheeks. Rod dropped his eyelids.

"I seem to have said the wrong thing," went on Basil, "but I really can't help you unless I have some idea of the relationships involved."

Pauline crushed her cigarette in the ash tray. "Shall we tell him that, too?"

"I suppose we'll have to." Rod was embarrassed.

Pauline looked at Basil. "We were engaged until yesterday afternoon just before I ran into you at the art gallery. We're not engaged now, and we don't care anything about each other only—I don't want Rod arrested for murder."

Basil was beginning to understand why Pauline had looked so pale and tired yesterday. "Why was this engagement broken?"

"Oh, well—incompatibility—mutual consent and so forth—"

"What was the real reason?"

Pauline lifted her chin defiantly. "I wanted it announced, and Rod didn't. I stood that for a while; but when it dragged on and on, the best thing seemed to be a clean break."

Basil's glance shifted again to Rod. "And why didn't you want it announced?"

Rod's cheeks were cherry red. "Well—because of Wanda. I mean—I was dependent on her for my job and my chance on Broadway. I thought if I let her know, I was engaged before the play opened I—I might not get that chance after all. . . ."

"So you do admit she chased you for the usual reason?" cried Pauline, furiously.

"No, I don't. I have no idea why she was always after me. That's the honest truth. But, of course, I couldn't help wondering. I didn't want to complicate things any more than they were already—by suddenly getting engaged. . . ."

Basil's eyes rested on Rod's face seriously. "I suppose you realize that this may be far more dangerous for you than the fact that the knife belonged to you?"

"How?" asked Pauline.

"It's the nearest approach to a motive the police have had so far. Assuming that the man who played *Vladimir* was a lover of Wanda's, the police will concentrate on you immediately.

They were both silent for a moment. Then Rod's temper exploded. "How ridiculous!"

"Not at all. You admit you were seen with her everywhere."

"But good heavens! That doesn't mean anything. I was engaged to Pauline at the time."

"But you didn't want it announced—because of

Wanda. And finally it was broken—because of Wanda. The police may say that your engagement to Pauline was a clever move to conceal your real affair with Wanda and your motive for stabbing *Vladimir*."

"Why—it sounds as if someone had planned it!" There was awe in Pauline's breathless voice.

"It does rather." Basil held Rod's eyes with his own. "Do you really mean it when you say Wanda seemed almost bored when you were alone with her? Think carefully, for it's important. Didn't she ever show any sign of personal interest in you, however subtle?"

"By 'personal' I suppose you mean 'erotic'? No, she didn't. And—well, it's silly, but though I didn't like her I was human enough to feel a little piqued about the whole thing. It is rather insulting to have a woman always seeking your company and yet remaining entirely impervious to your existence as a man. I'd got so I almost hated Wanda and then—this happened."

"Hell knows no fury like a man scorned," murmured Pauline, but there was no malice in her voice.

"Possibly Wanda felt she was the woman scorned?" ventured Basil. "You weren't very responsive, were you?"

"There was nothing to respond to! So she couldn't have felt that way."

Pauline's eyes were dancing. "Basil, you are interested. I can see you are! You will help us, won't you? There's nobody else who can. If somebody did plan all this, you're the one to find out who and why. It might be Wanda herself. Suppose she knew this was going to happen to *Vladimir*? Suppose she chased Rod all these weeks just so suspicion would fall on him when it did happen? It was she who wanted to play *Fedora* in the first place. It was she who got Milhau to give Rod the part of the surgeon who carries a knife on stage. And I'm sure *Vladimir* was not a stranger to her. I'm sure he was the friend she invited to play *Vladimir,* even if she did deny it afterward."

"In other words, you believe that Wanda murdered *Vladimir* herself?" asked Basil. "And planned the details of the crime to throw suspicion on Rod?"

"Isn't it pretty obvious?" retorted Pauline. "Milhau had no reason to lie about knowing *Vladimir.* He isn't a suspect—he wasn't even on stage during the murder. Milhau must've been speaking the truth, and that means Wanda must have been lying. *Vladimir* must have been someone she had got to play the part, just as Milhau said. That means *Vladimir* was someone Wanda knew— perhaps someone she loved. There's nothing to suggest that anyone else on stage ever saw him before, so Wanda must be the one who killed him."

Rod was tilting the sugar bowl back and forth as if he needed some occupation for his hands. Basil didn't wonder that he was embarrassed—the position of a man pursued by a woman he doesn't like is hardly a graceful one.

"When did you first meet Wanda?" asked Basil.

"A year ago. In Chicago."

"How did it happen?"

"Wanda had taken one of her New York successes, a Guitry play, out there. Leonard Martin was playing opposite her when he fell ill suddenly. They had to get someone else in a hurry. I was in Chicago with a road company that had just been stranded. I applied to Milhau for Leonard's part and got it—largely because no one else was available. Wanda coached me herself, and I did fairly well."

"You made a smash hit!" interpolated Pauline.

Rod smiled at her enthusiasm. "It was pure luck; the part happened to suit me, and Wanda's coaching was a big help. Overnight I jumped from playing small parts in road companies to the male lead in a company fresh from Broadway. I was grateful, but I didn't fall for her. That's what made things so hard when she started behaving as if she'd fallen for me."

"You're not just being chivalrous when you say she didn't care for you?" inquired Basil.

"No, that's the truth. I'm never chivalrous."

"Indeed you aren't!" put in Pauline.

"And you've remained with the company ever since?" went on Basil.

"By the time we reached San Francisco, Sam Milhau put me under contract to play the lead in *Fedora* on Broadway this autumn." Some lumps of sugar fell out of the bowl. Rod's restless fingers arranged them in rows like dominoes.

"But *Dr. Lorek* is not the male lead in *Fedora*," objected Basil.

"No," agreed Rod, without looking up from the sugar lumps. "The big male part is *Loris Ipanov;* but he doesn't come on until the second act so I played *Lorek* in the first. Milhau's a thrifty producer, and as I'm just a beginner—glad of the chance—I couldn't very well refuse to double in both parts. *Lorek* was a bad role for me, but *Loris Ipanov* might have been the making of me. Now—" He shrugged. "This murder may push me right back to where I was when I started a year ago."

"When did Leonard Martin rejoin the company?"

Rod's wall of sugar lumps toppled, and he began piling them up again. "Milhau was still casting *Fedora* when Leon turned up in New York a few weeks ago, quite recovered and raring to go. Of course, he wanted to play *Loris Ipanov*. He's been Wanda's leading man in lots of plays. But Milhau had already signed me for *Ipanov,* and most of the other good parts like *Siriex* were already cast. The best Milhau could do was to give Leon the part of *Grech*. He was game enough to take it and make a good job of it. He deserved a better break. He doesn't just mug like the rest of us; he really acts."

"You don't mug!" protested Pauline. "You're good! Really good!"

"You think so?" Rod eyed her with pleasure. For a moment they both seemed to forget Basil.

"Have you told the police about this gossip linking you to Wanda?" inquired Basil.

"N-no." Rod frowned.

"You think we should?" cried Pauline.

"They're sure to find out. They always check on the personal history of everyone involved in a case. They may miss some of the subtleties; but they never miss a matter of general knowledge, and anything concealed makes them suspicious. You'd better forestall them by letting all the skeletons out of the cupboard now before the bones begin to rattle."

"But what is there to tell them?" Rod had the grace to flush. "I can't say: *See here, Inspector, Wanda Morley was always chasing me, but I didn't care a hoot about her, and I'm sure she didn't care a hoot about me. So if you hear any gossip, it's just smoke without fire. That* isn't the sort of thing you can say to anybody, least of all a policeman. He'd never believe it, would he?"

"I see your point." Basil smiled. "The police might agree with Pauline: *Hell knows no fury like a man scorned*—especially when he has a chance to stab a successful rival on the stage."

"Basil!" cried Pauline. "Don't say such things—even in fun!"

"Pauline, dear," said Rod, gently. "He's only anticipating what the police will say."

"I know what to do!" Pauline turned to Rod. "We'll tell the police you're engaged to me!"

"But I'm not—"

"You can be—if you want to."

Rod shook his head. "You know I won't drag you into this!"

"Why on earth not?"

"Because." Rod pushed his sugar lumps into a star pattern. "Just think what fun the more scurrilous tabloids would have with all three of us if we told the truth."

"Three of us?"

"You and I and Wanda—the good old triangle."

"You forget *Vladimir*," put in Basil. "That would make it a quadrangle."

"I don't care! If there's any question of your being accused of murder I'm going to say you're still engaged to me! Then they couldn't say that you were jealous of Wanda's affair with *Vladimir*—if there was one."

"Oh, yes, they could!" returned Basil. "They could say that you loved Rod, but that he didn't love you. And they would say it if they heard you had broken your engagement to him yesterday."

Tears stood in Pauline's eyes. "Then you'll have to find the murderer—as I said in the first place. The police wouldn't listen to us, but they would listen to you. Last night that Inspector treated you as if you were a little tin god!"

Basil laughed. "That's only because I have the District Attorney's ear." He looked Pauline in the eyes. "Are you quite sure you want me to find the murderer?"

"Sure? Why, of course!"

"Suppose it should be Rod after all?"

The tears that had gathered in her eyes slid down her cheeks unnoticed. Rod laughed awkwardly. "That's frank anyway!" There was a brick-red flush on his face.

Pauline looked at Basil as directly as he had looked at her. "I know Rod has nothing to fear from truth. Go as far as you like!"

Something stirred in Rod's eyes as he looked at her.

Basil hesitated. How young Pauline was! Only the very young had such faith that truth could not harm them or those they loved. He spoke briskly to scatter his own thoughts.

"All right. I'll do what I can." His eyes went to Rod's hands. "Are you in the habit of that?"

"Of what?" Rod looked down at his hands. "Oh." His flush deepened. He swept the sugar lumps together and dropped them into the bowl. "I'm sorry. I'm afraid I do fiddle with things."

"Especially sugar lumps at table." Pauline eyed him with almost motherly indulgence. "It's a filthy habit. And he'll have to get over it, now that sugar is being rationed."

Basil pushed back his chair from the table. "Suppose we adjourn to the next room. There's something there I want to show you."

They crossed the hall to another long, narrow room with cream paneled walls washed primrose by the eastern sun. Basil went to a desk and took out Wanda's script of *Fedora*.

"Recognize this?"

Rod turned the pages. "It's Wanda's."

"You're sure it didn't belong to the actor who played *Siriex?*"

"Of course not. I've seen this script in Wanda's hands at every rehearsal. Seymour Hutchins, who played *Siriex,* had his script all marked up with notes in red ink."

"Have you any idea why a line spoken by Siriex should be marked in Wanda's script?"

"No, unless it was the cue for some bit of business she had worked out."

"It couldn't have been that," cried Pauline. "She had no bit of business at that point in the first act."

"Last night Milhau told the police that the running time of the first act was supposed to be forty-eight minutes," went on Basil. "Did it run exactly that time last night?"

"Well, it may have been off schedule a minute or so either way," admitted Rod. "But no more than that. Milhau's very strict about timing."

"Do you think you could make out a rough timetable of the principal incidents in the first act?"

"Such as?"

"Entrances and exits of *Vladimir,* Wanda, Leonard, and yourself. Also the occasions when any of you went near *Vladimir* on stage. If you can time the duration of such incidents it would help."

"I can try." Rod sat down at the desk and studied the script, jotting figures on the margin. After a few moments he drew a sheet of notepaper toward him and scribbled. "Is this what you want?"

Basil and Pauline read the time table over his shoulder.

Vladimir enters left and goes into alcove, closing doors:	8:35
Curtain rises:	8:40
Wanda enters left:	8:46
Leonard enters left and opens alcove doors:	8:51
Leonard near *Vladimir*:	8:51–8:52
Wanda near *Vladimir*:	8:53–9:00
Rodney enters left:	9:01
Rodney near *Vladimir*:	9:02–9:03
Leonard near *Vladimir*:	9:04–9:05
Leonard exits left:	9:06
Rodney near *Vladimir*:	9:07–9:24
Leonard re-enters:	9:24
Wanda near *Vladimir*:	9:25–9:28
Curtain:	9:28
Vladimir discovered dead:	9:30

"Of course you understand that's only a rough estimate," said Rod. "Based on my memory of about how long each scene ran at rehearsal."

"Even if the timing isn't accurate to the split second, it gives me an idea of the continuity of events on the stage," replied Basil. "And that's what I want."

"That's simple," said Pauline. "Characters in order

of their approaches to *Vladimir:* Leonard, Rod, Wanda, Leonard, Rod, Wanda. But I hope the police don't get Milhau to make them a time table like this. Those seventeen minutes of Rod's show up too clearly!"

"And that's when I was holding the knife over *Vladimir* pretending to probe for a bullet!" Rod sighed wearily. "To hell with realism! I'll never take a knife on stage again as long as I live."

"I don't believe you've allotted enough time to Wanda," cried Pauline. "All during your scene with *Grech* and *Siriex* she kept edging up stage near the alcove to draw the attention of the audience away from you. Her scene-stealing gives her a longer time near the alcove than she would have had if she'd followed Milhau's direction exactly."

"But she wasn't actually in the alcove!" insisted Rod. "She couldn't have stabbed *Vladimir* from where she was."

"N-no." Pauline's tone was grudging. "But she might have seen something . . ."

Basil was seeing the stage again in his mind's eye—the actors coming and going as they had last night. "What about gloves?" he asked suddenly. "I seem to recall that Wanda came in carrying a muff without gloves, while you and Leonard both entered with gloves and pulled them off before approaching *Vladimir* in the alcove. Was that done on the spur of the moment? Or was it part of the direction of the play?"

"That was Milhau's direction," answered Rod. "The way we disposed of our wraps was supposed to indicate our characters in the play: Wanda, the great lady, careless of valuable furs; Leonard, the brisk and businesslike man-hunter, tearing off his gloves to get his hands free; I, the methodical professional man who won't be hurried, piling everything neatly on a chair."

"Then if any one of you had worn gloves on stage during the first act it would have attracted notice?"

"It would!"

"And it would have been impossible to put on gloves in the middle of the first act without drawing the attention of the audience, to say nothing of Milhau in the wings and the other actors on the stage?"

"Of course!"

Pauline's eyes widened. "Were there fingerprints on the knife handle?"

"No."

"Then why—?"

Basil cut her short. "One more question. Did you happen to notice a woman crossing the stage last night just before the curtain rose? She passed us in the wings."

"No. What sort of woman?"

"A hard, plain suntanned face and brown hair about the same color. Eyes light—gray or blue. She wore no make-up but lipstick, and last night she wore a rather striking dress—diagonal black-and-white stripes—under a long, black velvet cloak. Is there any woman in the cast like that?"

Rod shook his head. "There's only one other woman in the cast besides Wanda, and she's a fluffy little blonde with curls."

"Light eyes in a brown face and hair the same color?" repeated Pauline. "And a black-and-white dress. That sounds like Magpie."

"Who is Magpie?"

"Oh, she's just a woman you see around town at

night clubs and so forth. Her real name is Margaret Ingelow. People call her Margot to her face, and Magpie behind her back, because she always wears black and white. She lives near Philadelphia—Huntingdon Valley, I think—but she has an apartment in New York. Her husband, John Ingelow, is working on some sort of war job in Panama. He inherited an engineering company. She was the daughter of a Washington surgeon, but there was nothing to distinguish her from hundreds of other girls until she married him. She's a good horsewoman. She used to ride other people's horses at the Horse Show here. That was where she met Ingelow. I have a vague idea they're separated now."

"Was she educated in France?" asked Basil.

"No, but I believe her husband was. Why?"

Basil let that question slide. "What would she be doing backstage at the Royalty?"

"I suppose she knows Milhau or somebody in the cast. She's been stage-struck for some time."

"I see." Basil reflected a moment and then smiled. "How convenient it would be if we were in a small town instead of New York. Then I could stroll down to the village post office or the drugstore soda fountain and be reasonably certain that Margaret Ingelow would drop in sooner or later, so I could have a glimpse of her without deliberately seeking her out or getting the police to do so for me."

Pauline was amused. "Basil, where do you spend your spare time in New York?"

"I don't have much spare time. I suppose I spend most of it in libraries or theaters or the homes of people I know. Why?"

"It's high time you got out of your rut," returned

Pauline. "If you don't look out you'll develop into an old fogey. Don't you realize that modern New York is a small town with a completely village mentality? Haven't you ever noticed that people in offices gossip around the water cooler just the way peasants in Syrian villages gossip around the village well? You wouldn't find Magpie in a post office or a drugstore even if she were in the country, but if you want to see her without seeking her, all you have to do is to lunch at Capri's in New York. She's there every day."

"Is she?" Basil was interested. "Then suppose you two meet me there for luncheon today. Shall we say one o'clock?"

"We'll be there." Rod rose. "This has been less of an ordeal than I expected. No association test—no lie detector—no psycho-analysis. You just ask ordinary questions like a policeman."

Basil seized his opportunity. "Would you like an association test? I'll give you a very brief one—a single word. You're supposed to answer instantly with the first word it brings into your mind. Ready?"

"Shoot!" Rod was grinning as if this were a parlor game, but Pauline looked anxious.

"Canary."

"Blood."

Basil's face was impassive. "Any idea why a canary should make you think of blood?"

"We had a pet canary at home when I was a boy. It got out of its cage one day and flew around the room. I tried to catch it, and I was pretty clumsy. I was only six or seven at the time. I caught it by one leg and—" He made a little grimace as if the memory were still an emotional sore. "The leg came off in my hand. The poor bird wilted and bled profusely, but it didn't die quickly. My father had to chloroform it. The dreadful thing about cruelty to animals is that they judge you solely by your actions—never by words. You can never apologize or explain to them that your act was unintentional. That was the first time I saw death and the first time I saw blood flow from an act of violence. The fact that it was inadvertent didn't make me feel any the less guilty, and I've always had a guilty feeling about canaries ever since."

Pauline was watching Basil's face. "That isn't the way a murderer would talk, now, is it?"

"Unfortunately, murderers have no special way of talking." Basil's equable tone made his words inoffensive. "It would make things much easier for us if they did."

When the pair had gone, Basil went back to the living room and turned over his file of recent newspapers until he came to a Sunday edition that devoted considerable space to stage and screen. He found what he was looking for in a picture section dedicated to churchgoers promenading on Easter Sunday, a few weeks earlier:

Miss Wanda Morley snapped on Fifth Avenue with her leading man, Mr. Rodney Tait. An engagement is rumored. . . .

It was a blurred action snapshot taken in bright sunlight. Wind molded Wanda's print dress to her body and pushed back the floppy brim of her wide spring hat. One hand held the hat; the other was linked through Rod's arm. They were looking into each other's eyes and laughing happily. For a young man who was engaged to another woman the pose seemed a little indiscreet. . . .

Frowning, Basil cut out the picture and put it away in his desk. Then he tucked Wanda's script of *Fedora* under one arm and set out for her house.

CHAPTER SIX

First Lady

WANDA MORLEY lived in a little house with a garden that went down to the edge of the East River. It was perfection in miniature—a doll's house for a child princess. The walls were white-washed brick, roof and shutters were green, and the door was painted yellow. A mulatto maid answered Basil's ring. He gave his name and waited in a shallow green and white hall, wondering if Wanda would receive him. The maid returned and led him up a flight of narrow, curving stairs to a long, pale drawing room with French windows that gave on a balcony overlooking garden and river. Though it was nearly noon, Wanda was at breakfast on the balcony—a Swiss breakfast of coffee with hot milk, hot buttered rolls, and honey. Her dark hair was gathered in a loose coil on the nape of her neck. She looked rested and comfortable in beautifully cut slacks of gray flannel and a yellow sweater.

The morning sun brought out lines in her face that Basil had not noticed before. Ordinarily he found the look of disillusioned maturity more interesting in women than the blank freshness of youth. But middle age had carved lines of slyness in Wanda's face that

were unpleasing in spite of her vivid coloring and
regular features. There was still a certain melancholy in
her eyes, but the morbid hysteria of last night was gone.
He had an impression that she was essentially a practical
person. As soon as the first shock of any disaster was
over, she would pick up the pieces and put them together somehow. She would never nurse a grief and
wallow in it for sheer emotional luxury.

"Dr. Willing, how nice of you to call! And how nice
of you to bring my script back!" She smiled, eyes narrowed against the sun. Their golden color was no trick
of eye shadow or indirect lighting. Here in the sun's
glare he could see the irises plainly, and they were a
pure, buttercup yellow without a trace of *chartreuse*
or hazel. He recalled a tale he had read years ago in
French because it was then considered too "daring"
for translation into English: *La Fille aux Yeux d'Or.*
Was Wanda as savagely sensual as Paquita Valdes? Then
he remembered that Balzac had wanted to call the story
La Fille aux Yeux Rouge and that it was his publisher
who had insisted upon changing the red eyes to
gold. . . .

"Everyone else has deserted me this morning," Wanda
was saying. "Sam, Rod, Leonard—not one of them had
the grace to telephone, let alone appear in person. Yet
Sam is my favorite producer, and Leonard and Rod are
my very best friends. Leonard gave me my first start
by introducing me to Sam and making him give me a
part, and I did the same thing for Rod. . . . Will you
have coffee?"

"No, thanks. I've had breakfast." Basil dropped into
a wicker chair. It was a day of cool wind and brilliant
sunshine, hard and clear as a diamond. Not a cloud

flecked the pure blue of the sky. The horizon was sharp as a line drawn with a ruler, and every detail of the landscape stood out precisely—flower-beds and fruit trees in the garden, barges on the river, even houses on the Long Island shore.

"This isn't a purely social call. Can you tell me when you last saw this script?"

"Last night when you showed it to me."

"And before that?"

"It was in my dressing room yesterday afternoon."

"Who could have taken it?"

"Why—anybody—" One by one, Wanda dropped four lumps of sugar in her coffee. "Everything was in confusion—the eve of an opening is always hectic. Everyone was running in and out of my dressing room all the time."

Basil watched her, feeling like a man who is about to pull the firing pin on a hand grenade. Of course, it might not go off, but . . .

"Miss Morley," he continued, "the police are bound to identify *Vladimir* as John Ingelow sooner or later. Wouldn't it be wise for you to anticipate them?"

Her eyes flashed in the sun, but the face, schooled to mask emotion, remained impassive. At last she spoke. "So you know. How did you find out?"

"Last night at the theater I saw a woman in a black and white dress. Pauline identified her from my description as Margaret Ingelow. Pauline's description of her husband John Ingelow fitted *Vladimir*."

Wanda seemed disappointed. "You mean you identified *Vladimir* on the strength of a physical description? That's just guessing! If I'd denied it—"

"Not a physical description." Basil shook his head,

smiling. "A psychological description. I had already seen *Vladimir* for a few moments and surmised or 'guessed' if you like, that he was an only son of wealthy parents, born in Philadelphia, educated in France and returned from Panama recently. Also that he was a horseman. Pauline's description of John Ingelow included all those details—too many to be coincidental."

"But if you only saw *Vladimir* for a few moments, how could you 'guess' so much about him?"

"I first saw him in a cocktail bar near the theater early last evening. He behaved with the immature arrogance Adler attributes to an only son or a younger son. He ordered an exotic drink—rum, gum, and lime. That is a favorite substitute for whisky and soda among junior officers of the Army in Panama. Rum, sugar-cane syrup, and lime juice are cheap native products. Only senior officers can afford to import whisky there. *Vladimir's* sunburn suggested the Panama visit had been recent. When he asked the bartender the way to the stage door, he said he'd been all 'around the square.' A New Yorker would have said 'around the block.' His guttural 'R' was Philadelphian. That suggested he had been born in Philadelphia—not that he just lived there, since accent is usually determined by birth, no matter how widely a man travels. After death, the medical examiner noticed that his legs were slightly bowed. In such a healthy, prosperous young man that suggested long hours in the saddle rather than rickets in childhood. The police found a slip of paper in his pocket which seemed to read: RT, F:30.

"Of course 'RT' suggested Royalty Theatre—a memorandum of his appointment with you that evening. Such memoranda usually include time as well as place, and it was just seven-thirty when I first saw him in the neighborhood of the theater, looking for the stage door. The ':30' was clear enough, but what about that 'F'? Then I remembered that the French always write the figure 7 with a cross bar—'F'—so it looks like a capital letter F in its customary hand-written form. It only remained to link *Vladimir* with you, and that was easy. When you opened the door of your dressing room to me last night, you smiled as if you were welcoming someone you expected. Then you saw my face, and the smile turned into a look of surprise. I wasn't the person you had expected, though at first glance you took me for that person. In the cocktail bar I had noticed that *Vladimir* was just my own height and dressed as I was. I had heard him asking for the stage door and I saw no one else backstage dressed that way. Obviously you had mistaken me for *Vladimir,* and that meant you did know him in spite of your denials. I suppose it was he who sent you the red roses at the end of the first act?"

"Yes."

"Do you know where he was between the time he left the cocktail bar and the time he reached your dressing room?"

Wanda was surprised. "Didn't he come directly to me?"

"He left the bar several minutes before I did. But you were still expecting him when I reached your dressing-room door, or you wouldn't have mistaken me for him."

Wanda had listened to all this with absorption. Now her smile was challenging. "I'm afraid of you, Dr.

Willing! You notice too many things. And you put them together too quickly. I'm glad I have no idea what you're thinking about me at this moment!"

"I'm thinking that you were most unwise to mislead the police last night by pretending you didn't know *Vladimir*. I suppose it was you who took the labels out of his clothing and destroyed the card in his wallet?"

"How dare you suggest—"

"You had the opportunity. He left his coat and other things in your dressing room. Your maid took you back there after your faint—before the police arrived. Why did you do it?"

"I was frightened. I didn't want the police to connect him with me. I hoped they wouldn't identify him for a long time. I flushed the labels and the draft card down the drain. I didn't know how to get rid of the clothes. My maid was going to put them somewhere else when the police arrived. What else could I do?" She leaned forward in her chair, tense and supple as a coiled spring. There was irritation in her voice and a hint of bitterness. "Everyone thinks I murdered him! Everyone hopes that I murdered him! Of all the people on stage I did have the best opportunity. That last scene where I clasped the body . . . and wept over it . . ." A trace of emotion shook her voice.

"As I recall it there were two scenes where you clasped the body and wept over it. The first was just after Leonard as *Grech* opened the alcove doors and *Vladimir* was discovered to the audience. The second was at the end of the first act just after Rodney as *Lorek* announced *Vladimir's* death. Those two occasions bracketed the first act—one at the beginning, one at the end. Both times you actually touched *Vladimir's* cheeks and lips with your lips, as well as your hands. The shock of a stab wound should have made his skin cool to the touch, and lips are more sensitive to temperature than finger-tips. Did you notice anything different between the first time you kissed him on stage and the second?"

Wanda closed her eyes for a moment. Was she over-come with emotion? Or merely trying to summon the memory of last night as vividly as possible? Her eyelids lifted slowly, as if the weight of the heavy black lashes dragged them down. "At the time, I thought nothing was wrong with him. A stage kiss is different from an ordinary kiss. I barely touched his lips with mine. But now—as I look back in the light of what has happened —it seems to me that his cheek and lips were colder than they should have been."

"The first time? Or the second?"

"Both times."

"You realize that would mean he was stabbed at the beginning of the first act? And that only one person approached him on stage before you did?"

The golden eyes widened with horror. "What have I said! Poor Leonard would never do such a thing! It's ridiculous! What possible motive could Leon have? I was the only person in the company who knew John. When the police discover that they'll argue that I'm the only person who could have had a motive for stabbing him. That's why I lied about knowing him last night. It was just self-preservation."

"There is another possibility—Margaret Ingelow."

"But she wasn't on stage!"

"Not after the curtain rose. But she was seen leaving the alcove and crossing the stage just before the curtain rose. Apparently she left the alcove after *Vladimir* had entered it, and she was the only person to do so before *Grech* opened the alcove doors."

Wanda smiled her wry, uneven smile. "So there are four of us? Leonard, Rod, Magpie, and me! It could have been Magpie, I suppose . . ."

Basil noticed that Wanda preferred the derisive "Magpie" to the sedate "Margot" as a nickname for Margaret Ingelow.

"John could have been dying or dead all through the first act without one of us suspecting anything wrong. How awful!" Wanda shivered under her sweater in the warm sun.

"Are you sure no one else in the company knew Ingelow by sight?"

"I don't know." She flung out her hands in an almost Gallic gesture. "We had to be careful until his wife agreed to a divorce. Neither of us wanted scandal, and Magpie was being a little difficult. She hates me, because it was she herself who first introduced John to me. Magpie was stage-struck, and that was how we met. John didn't care for the theater or know any stage people until he met me. Of course, it was John who put up the money for *Fedora*. But I dealt with Sam Milhau myself. John was never inside the theater until last night, and so far as I know no one there knew him even by sight. He was just back from Panama, and I happened to tell him that old yarn about Bernhardt's friends playing the part of *Vladimir*. He thought it would be a lark to do the same thing. It was rather reckless under the circumstances, but we thought no one would recognize him in his corpse make-up; and taking a chance was what made it a lark. He always was a reckless devil. You should have seen him on a horse!"

"How did you happen to hear of the old legend about Bernhardt and Edward VII?" asked Basil.

"Oh, I don't know. I think from Seymour Hutchins who played *Siriex* last night. Do you mean you think that story was revived purposely just now?"

"It's possible. Pauline told me yesterday that you like to identify yourself with the great actresses of the past, by reviving their plays and even imitating their foibles. It was a 'probability you would ask Ingelow to play *Vladimir* when you heard that yarn. And that gave the murderer an opportunity."

"But Hutchins would never do that!"

"Perhaps the revival of the story didn't originate with Hutchins himself. He may have got it second or even third hand."

"How horrible!"

"Why do you say everyone 'hoped' that you had murdered *Vladimir?*"

"I could sense it in the theater last night. That was what frightened me. That was why I was afraid to admit I knew who the murdered man was. You have no idea how people hate me—how jealous they are of my success! Even Rod is sometimes a little resentful of my being a star when he isn't. And Leonard doesn't like playing second fiddle to Rod. Of course Leonard is the better actor—but he's been ill for a whole year, and I just couldn't keep the lead in *Fedora* open for him on the chance that he might recover in time—could I? And Magpie hated me because she knew I was going to marry John. . . . Do you realize that no matter who killed him or when, he must have been either dead or dying by the time I wept over his body at the end of the first act? For no one else went near him afterward. Don't you see what a horrible, spiteful thing that was? Whoever the murderer is, he or she was jeering at me then—making me go through a scene of mock grief for a stage lover mimicking death when he was really my lover and really dead though I didn't know it. You needn't tell me it wasn't planned that way! It was pure malice directed against me as well as John. It's as malicious as that French story of the man who walled up his wife's closet where her lover was hidden, pretending all the time he didn't know the lover was there."

"Then you suspect Rodney Tait?"

Her eyes widened. "He's not my husband!"

"But he would like to be?"

Wanda took on the preening, relaxed content of a cat that is being stroked along the spine. "Rod *is*—fond of me," she murmured. "Of course, he's only a boy . . ."

Basil was interested. "You really believe he is fond of you?"

"Well, he's always running after me. Sometimes it's quite embarrassing. All those items in the newspapers and magazines about us. John didn't like it at all; but I couldn't help it, could I? Oh, I know that in books written by men women are always held responsible for men falling in love with them; but in real life no woman can make a man fall for her if he doesn't want to, just as you can't hypnotize anyone who doesn't want to be hypnotized. I think even Rod himself would admit that I never did anything to encourage him!"

"Was Rod jealous of John Ingelow?" inquired Basil.

"He didn't know anything about John. And anyway, I just can't see Rod as a murderer, can you?" With another little shrug, Wanda returned to her rolls and honey. "I don't suspect anyone in particular, Dr. Willing, but I do believe that the murderer is someone who hates me, and that the whole thing was planned to hurt me as well as to kill John."

"Is there any way Rodney could have found out that you were going to marry Ingelow?"

"Well, if people listen at doors and windows they can find out anything. . . ."

"Does Rodney do that?"

"He never has but he might if he were jealous. . . ."

"I wonder you kept Rodney in your company—all things considered."

"You can't break contracts as cheaply as all that. Sam put us both under contract to play *Fedora* several months before Rod developed this silly infatuation with me. Sam was grateful to Rod for taking Leonard's part at short notice in Chicago when Leonard ran over that poor child and . . ." Wanda stopped as she saw Basil's astonishment.

"I thought Leonard Martin left the company in Chicago because he fell ill?"

"Oh, dear," Wanda sighed. "I *have* spilled the beans!"

"What really happened to Leonard?"

"I suppose you might as well know. I was in a hurry to get to a night club, and Leonard borrowed a car to drive me there. He ran over a little girl playing in the street. She was killed instantly. He had only had one highball, but the police insisted he was drunk. He was really just shaken and staggering from shock. His first thought was the effect on me and the show and his own career so, on impulse, he gave a false name—Lawrence Miller. He knew no one was likely to recognize him; all his published photos had been taken in stage make-up, and he had always played parts that required him to alter his appearance. It's always a shock to his fans when they discover that he's bald off stage.

"He pretended he had no driver's license to avoid showing them one with his name on it. That was another charge against him—driving without a license. He was tried in Chicago for manslaughter and sentenced as 'Lawrence Miller' to one year in prison. I paid his legal expenses so he wouldn't have to give away his real name by signing checks. Of course, I kept quiet about it for my own sake as well as Leonard's. The theater is a profession that depends on popular favor, and running over children is not a popular thing to do—especially if there's any suggestion you were drunk at the time. The fact that I had been a passenger in the car was quite bad enough for the show as it was. The newspapers were told that Leonard left the company because he was ill, and they never caught on. Only a few local police reporters attended the trial, and none of them knew him by sight without his make-up. The day I testified there were a few men from the news services there, but Leonard sat with his face in his hands all the time they were in the courtroom.

"This spring, when Leonard turned up in New York after his year in prison, he looked so thin and sick he had no trouble making people believe he really had been ill."

A voice spoke from the French window. "Don't you think you're being a little indiscreet, Wanda?"

Leonard Martin was standing in the window behind them. Basil wondered how long Leonard had been listening. Outwardly he showed no ill effect of last night's disaster—largely because his long, sober face had always suggested strain and weariness off stage. It was hard to realize now that this sickly, quiet, almost shy man was the actor who had made the part of *Grech,* the police-man such a robust characterization last night. On stage, wig and costume, and, above all, vigorous bearing had made Leonard seem younger and taller. Now, his bald head and dull, sallow face seemed colorless—a blank page upon which any message could be written. The muscles around his mouth looked stretched and tired, like rubber that has been pulled and pushed into so many different shapes it has finally lost its resilience. The skin on his high forehead was a mottled bronze, drawn tight as a drum head over his unfleshed skull. Perhaps he had always suppressed his own personality that he might never develop mannerisms to interfere with his portrayal of characters on the stage.

Basil tried to reassure him. "Miss Morley hasn't given anything away that I hadn't surmised already. I sus-pected from the beginning that you had served a prison term. I'm glad it was only a traffic accident. I was afraid it might be a deliberate crime."

Leonard stared. "Why did you suspect?"

Wanda laughed thinly. "If you have secrets, Leonard, prepare to shed them now! Dr. Willing is practically *clairvoyant!*"

"Are you?" Leonard fixed a direct gaze on Basil.

"Not in the least. Any rookie cop would have recog-nized you as an old lag. Inspector Foyle is probably try-ing to get hold of your record at this moment, though the false name will make it a little harder for him. Last night when you were pacing up and down Rodney's dressing room you went just five single paces either way before you stopped and turned. That's about twelve feet for a man of your stature, but there was a vacant space in the center of the room fifteen or sixteen feet square. No obstacle barred your path, for all furniture was pushed back to the walls. I've seen other men do that after spending months in a cell twelve feet square. Habit surrounds them with invisible walls wherever they go long after they are free. Last night you also recognized and avoided a simple fingerprint trap rather pointedly when Inspector Foyle handed you the dead man's cigarette case of polished silver for identification. As a rule, only the man with a police record has the wish to hide his fingerprints and the experience to know a police trap when he sees one—especially at such a moment when we were all shaken by the discovery of the murder. Rodney Tait fell into the same trap immediately without realizing it was one. Foyle would never have tried such a simple trick on you if he'd realized you were an ex-convict.

"You even showed your police record in your characterization of *Grech,* the policeman in the play. It was an amusing satire on police mannerisms, obviously contrived by an actor who had a grudge against policemen in general."

Leonard's astonishment yielded to pleasure—the pleasure an artist takes in his own craftsmanship. For a moment the murder was forgotten. "Did you like my *Grech?*" he cried eagerly. "I'm glad! I always try to be as lifelike as possible in every detail of a characterization, and I thought some of the points I made last night were pretty good! The change in my voice between the moment I said: *Who is that woman?* and the moment I said: *The Princess!* And the bit of business where I pick up *Fedora's* cloak and stroke it as if I were admiring the quality of the fur. Sam didn't want me to do that, but I insisted it was essential. Contrasted with my rudeness to *Vladimir's* servants it gives a perfect picture of a greedy beggar-on-horseback using a murder case as a stepping stone—"

"Leonard, darling, Dr. Willing isn't interested in stage technique!" Wanda's shoulders were shaking with laughter.

"But I am!" insisted Basil stoutly. "For instance, I noticed last night that even when you weren't in the alcove you were up stage or near it. Was that Milhau's direction, Miss Morley? Or your own idea?"

Leonard answered before Wanda could speak. "She's always up stage, and it's entirely her own idea."

"Did you see anything unusual going on in the alcove when you were near it?" continued Basil.

Wanda was no longer laughing. "I wasn't even looking at the alcove!" she protested a little shrilly. "I was entirely absorbed in playing my own part."

"You can rely on the latter statement absolutely," murmured Leonard.

"Why don't you sit down, Leonard?" said Wanda in her most wheedling tone. "Have some coffee?"

"Thanks. Milk, but no sugar, please."

"Rolls? Honey?"

"No, thanks."

"It's rose honey from Guatemala."

"You know I have no sweet tooth, Wanda!"

"A break for Leon Henderson!" murmured Wanda.

Cup in hand, Leonard's idle gaze followed a tugboat plowing sturdily through the wind-whipped water.

"The police are certain to discover the truth when they get your fingerprints and check with the F.B.I.," said Basil. "But your secret will be safe enough with them unless its publication proves necessary to the conviction of the murderer."

Leonard sat down on the wrought-iron railing of the balcony and sipped his *café-au-lait* with his back to the river. "I wouldn't make a secret of it if I felt guilty. But that child ran right out under the wheels of my car before I could stamp on the brake. It was the police charge of drunkenness that prejudiced the jury against me. A medical test for drunkenness would have cleared me, but they didn't bother with that. They just got up on the witness stand and swore that I had been drunk at the time. That was enough for judge and jury. As I wasn't drunk, I felt I didn't deserve a prison sentence. It ruined my health—I lost over twenty pounds in prison. But I'm not going to let it ruin my career too—if I can help it."

Wanda wiped her hands on a napkin. "Honey is like a ripe mango," she announced. "It should only be eaten in the bath tub. Tell me, Leon, how long were you standing in that window just now?"

"Only a few moments. I did hear about John Ingelow. I won't tell the police, but," he smiled, "I hope you will."

"How can I, without drawing suspicion on myself?"

"I don't believe anyone will suspect you seriously," argued Leonard. "It's so obvious that you had no motive. A woman doesn't kill an attractive young man of great wealth whom she expects to marry in a few months when there's no cause for jealousy, unless he's made a will in her favor; and Ingelow didn't do anything like that, did he?"

With an angry gesture, Wanda tossed the cigarette

she had just lighted down into the garden. "If you must know—he did."

If Leonard wanted to revenge himself for Wanda's revelation of his prison sentence, he had certainly succeeded. She looked at him with exasperation. Then she turned to Basil. "I suppose it's all bound to come out now! John wanted to make a financial arrangement with his wife before she went to Reno, so all that business need not be discussed in court. He was going to settle a lump sum on her in lieu of alimony. Of course, his old will was in her favor. He just had it altered in my favor yesterday. The police are certain to regard that as a motive, absurd as it is that I would kill John for money."

"Men have been killed for money," returned Basil, "and Ingelow had rather a lot, hadn't he?"

"Yes, he had." Wanda sighed. "That was the only serious obstacle to our marriage."

"Obstacle?" Basil was feeling his way cautiously in this conversation, like a man groping in the dark.

"I do so hate a life complicated by luxury and formality," explained Wanda gravely. "I often told John that I would have felt much safer about our chances of happiness if he had been a simple bookkeeper or salesman making about thirty or forty dollars a week. You see, Dr. Willing, I am a frightfully simple person myself with very plain, ordinary tastes. If I had married John, I would have had to lead a much more elaborate life than I've been used to—two big households in New York and the Huntingdon Valley, a villa in Florida, a huge staff of butlers and maids and chauffeurs, a great deal of entertaining—it would have been a dreadful responsibility and, to be quite frank, an awful bore. If

I hadn't loved John very much indeed, I just wouldn't have been able to put up with all that tinsel and sham. I have a beer and hamburger mentality—I detest caviar and champagne. So you see, I'm the last person in the world to commit a horrible crime for the sake of money."

"I see."

This was Basil's second encounter with Wanda's favorite line, and his first realization that it had any bearing on the murder. He wondered how the police would take it, now that Ingelow's will gave Wanda a possible motive for murder, providing she was not immune to the normal human desire for money. He allowed a flavor of irony to invade his voice as he remarked: "When I noticed that simple, little fur cloak you were wearing last night it never occurred to me you had a beer and hamburger mentality."

"Oh, that. It was a present from John, and I wore it on the stage because it did suit the part of *Fedora.* I never really liked it though—so ostentatious and vulgar."

"Let me see, it's mink, isn't it?"

"Oh, no! It's not mink at all—it's Russian sable!" For a woman who cared nothing for luxury and ostentation, Wanda's response was a little too heated.

"Seems dangerous to keep such valuable furs in the dressing room of a theater with everyone coming and going all the time."

"It wasn't there 'all the time,'" returned Wanda. "I had it stored in February, and I had some trouble getting it out again in time for the opening. A bonded messenger brought it to the theater in the nick of time—after the curtain rose just before I went on stage."

As Basil took his leave of Wanda a last question occurred to him. "Yesterday afternoon at the art gallery you said something about cutting some lines spoken by a character named *Desiré*. Did that make much difference in the action of the play?"

"No real difference," she answered. "Of course it did telescope the action a little in that first scene where *Grech* comes in and throws open the alcove doors. Didn't you notice that, Leonard?"

"I can't say I did." Leonard smiled sardonically. "You could cut half the lines out of a Sardou play without damaging plot or action at all."

He followed Basil toward the door into the living room.

"Not going already?" cried Wanda.

"I just stopped in to see how you were," responded Leonard. "But you can take it. I leave you with a clear conscience."

Wanda went indoors with them. Basil's glance swept the long, pale room with its velvet carpet and curtains in faint shades of gray, lime and lemon. It was silken and cushioned, as a case for jewels or wedding silver. There was a hint of the *boudoir* about the *chaise longue* of tufted, oyster-white satin with its heap of pillows in fresh laundered slips of fine lawn and lace, its fleecy coverlet of pale green wool neatly folded at one end. Surely this was not the room of a woman who scorned pleasure and ease for the sake of a robust simplicity? Basil's glance came to rest on an elaborate birdcage that hung from a stand in the sunshine by a window. Cage and stand were wood, painted gray and carved with little flying birds in low relief picked out in bright colors. Inside on the central perch two small green birds, something like parrots, sat side by side, beaks touching in a parody of a human kiss.

As he drew near the cage the birds did not flutter or even turn their heads. With a little shock, he realized that they were dead birds, stuffed and mounted by a taxidermist.

"Love birds?" queried Basil.

"They were pets of mine when they were alive, and after they died I had them preserved like this."

Basil had once known a woman who did the same thing when a favorite horse died, but the idea did not appeal to him.

"That parrot green is a little crude for the rest of the room." His gaze went to the lemon yellow hangings. "Why not . . . canaries?"

Wanda lifted both hands, crossed them against her throat as if something were choking her. "Because I hate canaries!" Her voice quavered out of control. "That bilious yellow. Those ugly, raw, peeled-looking pink legs—ugh!"

The two men stepped through the doorway from the sunlit room overlooking the river into a dim, window-less hall. As they turned the sharp curve in the narrow stair, they looked back and saw Wanda standing in the doorway watching them, one hand braced against the lintel, the other still clasping her throat. The tall, slim figure outlined darkly against the light of the room beyond might have been a girl of nineteen or twenty. In contour Wanda was still a young woman; only the tex-ture of her skin and the expression of her face betrayed her real age. The dimness of the hallway veiled her face now, and her pose was arresting and eloquent.

Leonard turned his head. Basil rather expected some

expression of sympathy for Wanda. But Leonard said: "What a wonderful gesture that was—when she clasped both hands across her throat. I must remember that. It would be most effective on the stage. If ever I have a part that calls the same emotion into play, I shall use it."

"And just what is that emotion?" asked Basil.

The question seemed to surprise Leonard. "Why, fear—of course!"

II

They were in the lower hall now. Daylight streamed through a lunette fanlight thinly veiled in white muslin. The mulatto produced their hats and opened the door for them.

"A charming house," mused Leonard as they went down the steps. "It always reminds me of Becky Sharpe's little slice of house in Mayfair. You remember the cramped little stairway, and how all the great personages of the day crowded into it? To me there is always something fascinating about a little house—particularly when it's a town house, luxurious and complete to the last detail, but all on the smallest possible scale. And there must be a pretty woman nestling inside like a jewel in a plush-lined box."

"Doubtless it is charming," agreed Basil. "But not precisely the home of a beer and hamburger mentality."

Leonard's sudden, harsh laughter sounded loud in Beekman Place, quiet and shady as a courtyard with the two big apartment buildings and the double row of small houses enclosing it almost entirely on four sides. "You mustn't let Wanda's inverted boasting confuse you!"

"Inverted boasting?"

"That's what it is. Didn't you notice how she got in all her points in the very act of deprecating them? Sable, not mink; two homes and a villa in Florida; a huge household staff; etc. She couldn't have told you more if she'd been bragging about those things instead of deploring them, now could she? You see, luxury is the breath of life to Wanda. Years ago, as a child, she was starved of comforts and even necessities, and she's always trying to get the chill of that early poverty out of her bones. When she first came to New York, green and raw from a factory town, she used to admire quite openly everything that glittered. She would go to the most elaborate trouble to drag the conversation around to mention of some well known person she had met. If you gave her an orchid or an opera ticket she would tell everyone she knew all about it. Her snobbery was so transparent it was innocent and childlike. I thought it rather attractive for that reason. But others did not agree with me. She was well and truly snubbed. After a year or so she developed the formula you heard today as protective coloring, to wit: a cruel fate has imposed a life of luxury and ostentation upon her, but she remains a simple soul at heart who longs for nothing so much as hard work and obscurity. Since the modern mind is as prudish about snobbery as the Victorians were about sex, this blatantly phony, pseudo-democracy of Wanda's has made a big hit with everybody. She is no longer snubbed by the rich and famous, for she tells them to their faces that she loathes their riches and despises their fame; and they are impressed by her righteous scorn for them as they would be impressed by nothing else. As for the poor and obscure—well, you can imagine how they eat it up. Her personal popularity dates from the day she had a poor-little-rich-girl inter-view published in one of the women's magazines. *Wanda Morley says that the poorest housewife rich in a home and babies is far happier than a woman like herself who has nothing but the hollow joys of fame and glamour.* . . . I really believe Pauline is the the first person who's ever said to Wanda: *Well, if you don't like this sort of life why not give it up?* That was hitting below the belt!"

They turned into East 51st Street past old slum houses converted into prosperous dwellings with gaily painted doors and arty brass knockers.

"Why does Miss Morley hate canaries?" inquired Basil.

"Because she used to be a canary herself."

"She—what?"

" 'Canary' is jive slang for a girl who sings with a hot band. Wanda got her start as a canary. Those were her leanest years. It wasn't just that she went hungry. She had no professional dignity; no one took her work seri-ously. She doesn't like to be reminded in any way of the time when she sang for her supper. I remember one eve-ning we were at Sam Milhau's house in the country, and a pet canary he had began to sing. Wanda screamed at it: 'Stop that noise!' No one but me knew her well enough to know why."

"You've known her a long time?"

"Ever since she first joined one of Sam's companies." Leonard smiled reminiscently, almost sentimentally. "She was a regular little guttersnipe in those days—or shall we be polite and say *gamine?* But there was some-thing attractive about her—a black-haired, yellow-eyed alley kitten, a scrapper tough as they come, all legs and bones and claws. I liked her better then than I do now. She was real then. Of course, the reality is still there; but it's buried under layers and layers of egoism. I don't suppose she can help it. We all worship our creator, and so the self-made worship themselves. It isn't ordinary selfishness—it's the occupational disease of the successful. Wanda shows it in a thousand little ways, from taking the largest piece of candy in the box to talking the way she did just now about the murder. You heard her say that the murder was committed in order to hurt *her* feelings and *her* career? That the murderer was mocking *her* when he planned his crime so she would weep over the stage death of a stage lover who was really her lover and really dead without her knowing it? Of course, the truth is probably that the murderer was not thinking of her at all. But she transposes everything into terms of its effect on herself. She hardly seemed to think of Ingelow at all. He was just the poor sucker who got murdered. The only important thing about his murder was its effect on Wanda Morley—her reputation, her fortunes, her future."

"You must have been standing in that French window for some time before you spoke!" remarked Basil.

"It was far too interesting to interrupt," returned Leonard. "I particularly enjoyed the way she scattered suspicion right and left on Rod and me and even on Mrs. Ingelow. That wasn't malice—just selfishness. If only four people could have committed the murder and Wanda was one of the four, then the police must be made to think that one of the other three is guilty; even if two of them happen to be close friends of hers. So she hinted—with the most beguiling air of inadvertence— that her affair with Ingelow had made Mrs. Ingelow jealous; that Rod was in love with Wanda, and, therefore, jealous of Ingelow; and finally, that I was a dangerous character who had served a prison term for manslaughter."

"You revenged yourself promptly," said Basil. "That shot about the Ingelow will went home."

"A shot in the dark. But I had to do something in self-defense."

At Madison Avenue the two men parted. Leonard went on west toward the theater. Basil entered a hotel and found a telephone booth. He called Inspector Foyle at his office.

"Have you traced *Vladimir* yet?"

"No dice," returned the Inspector crisply. "One of the newspaper boys says *Vladimir's* face is familiar, but he can't place it. He's combing the morgue now—newspaper morgue."

"Tell him to look under I—Ingelow, John."

"Who's that?"

"Engineer—young—wealthy—just back from a war job in Panama. Had an apartment in New York and a home near Philadelphia—Huntingdon Valley. His wife can identify the body. She might be at the New York apartment. She was backstage last night. I didn't know who she was then, but I saw her leave the alcove and cross the stage to the wings just before the curtain rose."

"Was *Vladimir*—I mean, Ingelow—already in the alcove then?"

"I don't know. It's possible."

Foyle whistled under his breath. "Did anyone but you see her leaving the alcove?"

"Adeane and the other actors playing *Vladimir's* servants were already on stage at the time. Even if they didn't know who she was, they must have noticed her dress—black and white stripes—rather striking. Have you anything from Lambert on the knife yet?"

"He's going to drop in my office tomorrow about five o'clock. You'd better come, too. He says he's on to something."

CHAPTER SEVEN

Character Part

THE CAPRI RESTAURANT is on West 44th Street. As Basil passed the Royalty Theatre its dark masonry, impressive in artificial glare, looked dingy and corrupt in the clean sunlight. Several idlers were staring at the dead electric bulbs that still proclaimed:

OPENING TONIGHT

WANDA MORLEY *in FEDORA*

Already the wind had torn a strip loose from one of the posters that displayed a sketch of Wanda. Like a pennant it flapped and rippled in the breeze. The box office was closed. There was no sign of life about the theater. A sturdy policeman paced the sidewalk and urged the idlers to move on.

Basil paused as he came to the alley. Like the playhouse, it was disenchanted by daylight. Now he saw that it was a blind alley blocked by the rear of another big theater building. Fire escapes at either end were linked by long balconies of wrought iron at each landing. Had the iron work been only a little lacier—more fanciful—

it would have brought to mind back alleys of New Orleans.

Basil surveyed the fire escape of the Royalty at his right. Would he have had the nerve to climb it last night had he been able to see how high it went? All the iron-work was coated with a thick crust of black dust that at the slightest touch flaked off fine and powdery—"the dust of generations," Pauline had said. Basil lifted his eyes. The tangled cluster of skyscrapers against the pure blue of the sky were as gray and bleak as bald mountain tops. He could see part of the Tilbury building from this point, but another skyscraper barred his view of the clock. He did not envy air-raid wardens their job of de-ciding which building was in which street if ever they had to enforce a real blackout.

Last night Basil had assumed that the alley could only be entered through 44th Street. Now he realized there were five other ways of entering or leaving it—the two fire escapes of the two theaters, their respective stage doors, and the kitchen door of the cocktail bar.

A slight noise drew Basil's attention to the shack half-way down the alley. A man had just come out of it into the alley, and he was struggling to close the door against the wind.

Basil approached him. "Mr. Lazarus?"

"Yes?" The man looked at him sidewise. Like the mother of François Villon, he was "little and old and poor." But his voice was surprisingly round and reso-nant—the voice of an actor.

"My name is Willing. I happened to read something in the papers about a burglar breaking into your work-shop."

"Yes?" Lazarus was cautiously noncommittal.

"I couldn't help being interested. According to the newspapers, the burglar stole nothing; yet he released a canary from its cage. Newspaper reports are often careless and inaccurate. Is that what really happened? Or did the reporter color the story to suit his fancy?"

Lazarus considered. "You are from the police?"

"No. I'm attached to the District Attorney's office, but this is not official. I'm just curious."

"So." Lazarus lost some of his caution. "After what happened at the theater last night I shouldn't think anyone would be worrying about my burglary! It happened just the way the paper said. So far as I could see nothing was stolen. And the canary was set free."

"May I see the canary?"

"Why not?" Lazarus unlocked the door he had just locked. Basil followed him inside. The shack was so tiny that there was hardly room for two men as well as the big grindstone and the chair in front of it. Shelves against the wall were piled with scissors, knives, and saws, all dull, many rusty. There was also a portable radio, an oil lamp, a glass, and a pitcher of water.

"From the cocktail bar," explained Lazarus as his glance followed Basil's. "They are very kind about letting me use their washroom, and the bartender often brings me sandwiches for my luncheon. You see, I don't live here. I have a room uptown. I did have a wagon when I was younger, but all my customers are theater people in this neighborhood, and when I got older I began to think: "Why not have a workshop and stay in one place? So I sold the wagon, and here I am."

"You were lucky to find such a suitable place," said Basil.

Lazarus smiled wisely. "Sam Milhau built me this

shack when he bought the Royalty Theatre. His father and I were friends years ago in Posen where we were born. In those days I was an actor too. In Warsaw I played *Hamlet* once—in Polish. But now . . ." He smiled. "I call Sam *Dives*, because, you see, I am *Lazarus* —almost a beggar and always at his gate. But it is better than one of those homes for old actors. Here I am free and independent. I pay my own way—all I get from Sam is this shack, rent free. I have work to do, and I hear all the theatrical gossip when stage people bring me their knives and scissors. And when they don't, I have my own tenor to sing to me!"

Smiling, he turned toward the cage.

It was made of brass wire, roomy and clean. There were the usual wooden perches and swinging trapeze; the usual white porcelain cups of seed and water fitted into the wire at either end, and a bit of cuttlefish bone for sharpening a small beak. On the shelf near by was a bird bathtub and a package of bird seed.

Eyes like tiny jet beads blinked at Basil from a ball of yellow feathers. Frail, pink claws curled around the central perch.

"Half asleep now," said Lazarus. "But he's lively in the early morning when the eastern sun comes through the window. He sings nicely then. Imitates the radio if it's turned on. He always joins in when I get Bach, but he doesn't like modern music."

"A discriminating bird," Basil was amused. "What's his name?"

"Dickie."

This was disappointing—like meeting a *dachshund* called Hans or an Aberdeen terrier named Mac-something.

"When I passed your window last night I happened to look in, but I didn't see Dickie. Was he here?"

"Yes, but the cage was covered with burlap so he would sleep from sunset to sunrise. I always do that when I work late by artificial light."

"Why do you keep the bird here instead of at home?"

"My 'home' is a room on a court with no sun. I'm only there at night when Dickie should be asleep. It never occurred to me that anyone would break in and molest him if he were left here alone at night."

"The cage seems comfortable." Basil surveyed the freshly sanded floor, the clean water cup, the full seed cup. "Have you any idea why anyone should want to let a bird out of a nice cage like this?"

"No, I haven't," admitted Lazarus. "I was puzzled by the whole thing."

"You're sure nothing was stolen?"

"There's nothing of value here—unless it is the radio. It wasn't taken, and I couldn't find anything else missing. I can't imagine why anyone would break in at all. You can tell from the outside of the shack that there's nothing worth stealing here."

The bird was awake now. He hopped up to his trapeze, and his weight swung it gently back and forth like a pendulum. "Cheep?" he demanded with a rising inflection.

"Hello, Dickie," said Lazarus, conversationally.

"Cheep!" responded the bird in exactly the tone of a human being responding: *Hello there yourself!*

Basil's glance wandered to the grindstone. "Do you think it possible that someone could have used your stone to sharpen something—say a knife?"

Lazarus grew interested. "It's possible. I hadn't

thought of that. If I had, I would have examined the stone more carefully when I first discovered the burglary yesterday morning. Of course, it's too late now. I used it myself last night and this morning. But why should anyone take all the risk and trouble of burgling a shop in order to sharpen a knife? My prices are not high!"

"Suppose this person didn't want any witnesses to his possession of the knife."

"So. We'll never know now." Lazarus smiled at the bird. "Only Dickie can tell us what the burglar did, and he's not talking. You should come back on Christmas Eve at midnight when all animals are supposed to talk!"

Standing before the cage, Lazarus whistled the opening bars of the *Unfinished Symphony*. Dickie took up the strain and repeated it. Then he added some frills of his own and wandered off into a maze of musical improvisation.

"That bird!" exclaimed Lazarus fondly. "He is like the man who wanted to finish the *Unfinished Symphony!* He cannot let well enough alone! Once I had a steam kettle here, and he used to sing with it whenever the water boiled. Once when I was ill he spent a few days in Sam's office, and when he came back, what do you think he did? Made a little clack-clack-clack sound in his throat like a typewriter!"

"Could a scalpel be sharpened on your grindstone?"

"Ah! I begin to understand you, Dr. Willing!" No man could have been as wise as Lazarus looked when he smiled. "You think my burglary and what happened at the theater last night are all one crime?"

"We know the scalpel was sharpened somewhere. It belonged to Rodney Tait, and he admits that it was blunt a few days ago."

"But why?" Lazarus' face grew sober. "The murderer could have bought a knife already sharp."

"And left a record of the sale."

"He could have taken this scalpel to a knife-grinder far away—in some suburb or neighboring city."

"And left a record of the transaction, just as he would if he had bought a grindstone. An ordinary whetstone would not have done. The knife was large.

"Could the police trace the purchase of a grindstone so easily?"

"That's the sort of thing they're particularly good at. There are many of them, and they are all dogged, patient, and trained. They would question every shopkeeper who sells grindstones for miles around, if they thought they could trace a murderer that way. But this way there is no clue to the person who wanted to sharpen the scalpel except the fact that he or she set your canary free. If it hadn't been for Dickie, the burglary would never have got in the papers. It would have attracted so little attention, it might never have been connected with the murder at all."

"If it hadn't been for Dickie, I might never have known there was a burglary, and I might never have reported it to the police!" cried Lazarus. "It was only when I saw the door of the cage open and Dickie flying around the room that I noticed the broken window latch and realized someone must have been in here."

"That makes it more curious than ever." Basil frowned. "Could the wind have blown open the window and then the cage door?"

"It might blow the window open but not the cage door. Try it for yourself."

Dickie fluttered his wings and retreated to the farthest

corner of the cage as a strange face approached him. Basil tugged at the door of the cage and opened it with some difficulty. The latch was stiff. "No, it wasn't the wind," he said as he closed it again. "You're sure you latched it when you left for the night?"

"Oh, yes, I remember that clearly. Dickie had moulted a feather, and it got caught in the hinge. I pulled it out and latched the door very carefully."

Basil surveyed the rest of the shack. "You're sure there were no clues of any kind when you first came in yesterday morning?"

"None whatever," answered Lazarus. "But there is one thing: it must have been someone who knew this neighborhood. Only the people around here know my shop."

"Unfortunately all our suspects are familiar with this neighborhood, so that doesn't help at all." Basil sighed. "So far, there is just one clue to your burglar's identity."

"What?"

"The canary was let out of his cage. Why? There must have been a reason, and that reason is a clue."

"But, heavens, what could it be?"

"I don't know. The cage is large, clean, and comfortable. There seems no reason for it at all. And yet it was done, and everything that a human being does has the motive power of some reason or emotion back of it, consciously or unconsciously. Otherwise, it wouldn't be done."

"But sometimes people do things for no reason at all," ventured Lazarus. "A whim . . . a caprice . . ."

Basil smiled. "Do you dislike modern psychology as much as modern music? In modern psychology even a whim is supposed to have a motive. Even an involuntary act, like stammering or stumbling, and a neurotic act, like sleep-walking, is supposed to have some motive, even though the neurotic or the stammerer himself does not know what makes him do such things. Your burglar moved his arm and hand and fingers to unlatch the door of the cage and pull it open. The latch is stiff, and it takes quite a lot of muscular effort to get it open. Muscles just can't be set in motion unless there is some emotional spark plug in brain and nerves to start them off. Whether that action was rational or whimsical, there must have been some emotional impulse behind it. In some way, for some reason, it gave him or her satisfaction to get that bird out of its cage. If only we could discover why, we would have a clue to the identity of the murderer."

Basil's earnestness seemed to impress Lazarus. "Could it have been cruelty?" he suggested. "A bird that is used to being caged is often bewildered when it is set free suddenly. Such a bird may injure its wings or legs attempting to fly around an unfamiliar room with unused wings."

Basil pondered a moment, then shook his head. "If it were cruelty, wouldn't the bird have been injured? Or at least let out the window into the night where the cold or a dog or cat or another bird might have killed it?"

"That sounds reasonable. But—" Lazarus smiled his wise smile. "If this burglar is a murderer you are surely not suggesting that he or she was moved by compassion? A sentimentalist might take pity on a caged bird and imagine it would be happier if it were free. But a man or woman who kills with a knife in cold blood is not likely to take pity on a bird!"

"You've raised a tricky point," answered Basil. "It

doesn't seem likely and yet—the most curious thing about human nature is the way people keep their kindness and cruelty in separate, airtight compartments. The Nazi leader, Julius Streicher, who is notoriously sadistic toward his fellow human beings, is said to have wept like a child when his pet canary died. On the other hand, a Spaniard may be kindness itself to his family and friends and yet wallow in the bloody brutalities of the bullfight. In some people cruelty is so impersonal that they will pay a victim good money to submit to a flogging. Perhaps they are more honest than the political, moral, and religious fanatics who only torture others for the most refined ideological reasons. The kind have their cruelties; the cruel, their kindnesses. And both emotions seem to be rigidly canalized by social custom. Though it may not be likely that this murderer took pity on Dickie because he was a caged bird, it is possible.

"Some feeling, conscious or unconscious, guided his hand when it opened the door of that bird cage, but what? We can't even tell if it was the act of someone who loves canaries . . . or the act of someone who hates canaries . . ."

Lazarus sighed. "In that case, the murderer's action in freeing Dickie tells you nothing about the murderer at all?"

"I wonder . . ." Basil's eyes were on the canary. It was trilling happily now as it hopped from perch to trapeze and back again. "I wonder . . ." he repeated softly. "I'm going to give you my address. If you discover anything more about the burglary, I'd be grateful if you'd let me know."

CHAPTER EIGHT

Enter Rumor, Painted Full of Tongues

CAPRI'S RESTAURANT was below street level. From the entrance, a flight of steps led down to a dim, cavernous dining room decorated in red and black. The dark paneled walls were enlivened with mirrors and framed caricatures of theatrical personalities. A plush carpet made every footfall stealthy. Tables were ranged around the walls in front of upholstered benches. In the center a *buffet* displayed all sort of delicacies—cold smoked turkey, squabs in aspic, hot-house strawberries, and a huge cake with green icing soaked in rum. In the foreground was a small horseshoe bar. It was there that Basil discovered Pauline and Rodney.

Their glasses were empty. The ash tray in front of Rodney was piled with cigarette stubs. Pauline had her sketch pad on her knee, and her restless pencil was tracing profiles—always a sign of anxiety in her.

"Hello," she greeted Basil. "Margot Ingelow hasn't put in an appearance yet."

"I don't believe she'll come," he answered. "Shall we find a table?"

They got one facing the entrance. Pauline and Rodney sat on the bench; Basil took a chair opposite. A mirror above Pauline's head gave him a clear view of the entrance and most of the room. They ordered the beer and club sandwiches for which the place was famous.

"Why isn't Mrs. Ingelow coming?" asked Rodney.

Basil's eyes were on the mirror as he told them about his visit to Wanda's house. "And," he concluded, "she identified *Vladimir* as John Ingelow."

"Oh!" The exclamation was torn from Pauline.

Rodney seemed equally astonished.

Color flooded Pauline's cheeks. "Then—if Wanda was really going to marry Ingelow . . ." She turned a radiant face to Rodney. "Can you ever forgive me?"

He smiled at her. Watching the two young faces, Basil hated to sound a note of warning. "This makes it all the more curious that Wanda should have been so . . ." He sought a euphemism. "So interested in Rodney."

Pauline's gladness faded like a mirror tarnished with a breath. "Maybe she just craves admiration from every man she meets."

"Possibly." Basil was studying Rod. Was this young man as frank and open as he appeared? Was this really the first time he had heard that Wanda planned to marry Ingelow? He had been seen so often with Wanda in the last few weeks, and she had seemed so certain he was infatuated with her. . . .

Rod grew uneasy under Basil's scrutiny. "Do the police know about Ingelow?"

"Yes. It's in the early editions of the evening papers."

"Then of course Margot won't come," cried Pauline. "She's as bold as brass and hard as nails, but even she would hardly lunch in public the day after her husband's murder!"

154

"It seems unlikely," agreed Basil. "The police are probably questioning her now."

"Could she be the murderess?" suggested Pauline. "You saw her leaving the alcove. That gives her both motive and opportunity."

Basil laughed. "Opportunity, yes—but is marriage alone a motive for murder?"

"They were estranged. They were going to be divorced."

"Why risk your neck by murdering a husband when you can get rid of him by divorce and secure a handsome financial settlement besides?" returned Basil. "Today, marital murders are confined to sadists and those stern moralists who believe murder more virtuous or at least more respectable than divorce."

"But she knew him." Pauline was fighting to the last ditch for her theory. "That's more than anyone else did —except Wanda."

Basil turned to Rod. "Can you prove that you didn't know Ingelow even by sight?"

"Well, no." Rod's restless fingers began tilting the salt cellar back and forth. "How can anyone prove a negative like that?"

"You can't. You were seen everywhere with Wanda, and Ingelow was her lover. The police will assume that you knew who Ingelow was, and they will consider that a motive. So would a jury drawn at random from the citizens of a big city. One woman plus two men equals jealousy."

"But it's such damned nonsense!" exploded Rod. "Going about now and then with a woman you met casually in your daily work doesn't mean you're in love with her.

And no man would risk his neck for anything less than love!"

Basil nodded, but there was doubt in his eyes. Wanda was an alluring woman. Rod was too young to be very experienced. A certain boyish naïveté was part of his charm. Suppose he had got beyond his depth with Wanda and then discovered she was playing with him while she planned to marry Ingelow? Men have been killed for less. . . . And such a killer might return to Pauline afterward in order to hide his motive from the police. . . .

"There she is," said Basil quietly.

"Who?" They turned back to him as if they were coming out of a fog.

"Margot Ingelow."

Evidently it took more than the murder of a husband to keep Margot away from her favorite restaurant at lunch time. She paused at the head of the stairs. Her gray eyes looked almost white in her smooth, brown face; her thin lips were firmly set together. She wore shepherd's plaid taffeta with white doeskin gloves and patent leather sandals. Jaunty white wings decorated her small black hat.

"Who is the man with her?" murmured Rod. As the pair descended the stairs, he answered himself. "Good Lord, it's Sam Milhau!"

The headwaiter seated them with a flourish and took their order himself. Milhau fussed and fluttered over his guest, arranging cushions at her back and taking her jacket. Margot received homage as calmly as an empress holding court. Other men began pausing at her table on their way in or out of the restaurant. She welcomed them with a smile that discovered a deep dimple in one cheek. It was hardly the smile of a brokenhearted widow, nor were the men who spoke to her mourners consoling the bereaved. Evidently she ranked already as a *divorcée*. But that didn't quite explain the attitude of these men toward her. As Basil watched the pantomime in the mirror, he felt that these were not the poses and gestures of gallants flocking around a pretty woman. For one thing Margot was not pretty; for another, the men were all a little old for gallantry. Like Milhau, their manner was oddly deferential, pathetically eager.

At one end of the *buffet* were some live lobsters on ice. Milhau got up to select the ones he wanted.

"Now's your chance," whispered Pauline.

Basil rose, but he didn't go to Margot's table. He joined Milhau at the *buffet*.

"Oh, Dr. Willing!" Milhau's plump face sagged unhappily. He lost interest in the lobsters. "Those'll do." The waiter took them away.

"Isn't this devotion to Mrs. Ingelow rather sudden?" suggested Basil.

Milhau's eyes were round and black and beady, like the canary's eyes on a larger scale. "Well, business is business, Dr. Willing. I'm in rather a hole. My show is broken up, and my star is on the verge of a nervous break-down. I stand to lose about eighty thousand dollars unless I do something and do it quick. I've got a lot of people under contract, and I've got to put on another show as quickly as I can." Milhau contemplated the lobsters that remained on their bed of ice with a deep sigh. "Mrs. Ingelow has always been nuts about the theater so —I'm trying to promote a little first aid to my bank account by getting her to back my next show."

Basil was surprised. "Can Mrs. Ingelow afford that?"

"Can she?" Milhau's eyes gleamed hungrily. "I'll say she can! With all that Ingelow money!"

"I thought the money went to Miss Morley now."

"That's what Wanda thought!" said Milhau curtly. "But she thought wrong. I've just been down to Police Headquarters this morning and they've got the facts straight from Ingelow's own lawyer. That new will leaving everything to Wanda hadn't been signed yet. The whole fortune goes to 'my beloved wife, Margaret Adams Ingelow' as it says in the old will. Poor Wanda!"

"Then if Ingelow had lived to sign the new will, Mrs. Ingelow would have got nothing but her divorce settlement?"

"Sure. Oh, I know it's a motive, but she wasn't on stage last night, so she couldn't—"

"One moment." Basil stopped him. "Mrs. Ingelow was on stage last night. I saw her leaving the alcove shortly before the curtain rose."

Milhau swore under his breath. "What are you trying to do? Railroad the only prospect I've got to the Tombs for murder? My God! If Wanda had to kill somebody why, oh, why, did she pick the fellow who was backing her show?"

"You think Wanda did it?"

"Well . . ." Milhau shuffled his feet. "I don't know. But . . . who else?"

"Rodney? Leonard? Or Mrs. Ingelow herself? They all had the same opportunity as Wanda."

"I don't see Rod or Leonard as a murderer, do you?" Milhau's eyes narrowed shrewdly. "They're both ordinary, everyday fellows, and Mrs. Ingelow didn't need the money that badly. She had a big divorce settlement."

"Did Wanda need money?"

"She always needs money."

"I think you'd better introduce me to Mrs. Ingelow," said Basil.

"O.K." Milhau was reluctant.

At close range Margot's hard, smooth brown face looked as if it had been carved from wood and polished. The pale eyes and white teeth were like the ivory eyes and teeth set in dark fetish masks from Africa. Any other woman in the world would have shown some trace of embarrassment in her situation. But Margot did not. A man was talking to her as they approached. She dismissed him with a smile. When she saw Basil, the smile faded. As Milhau mumbled an introduction, she stared at Basil with blank insolence.

"No doubt you've forgotten me," he said. "But I remember you clearly. We passed each other backstage at the Royalty last night."

Eyelashes the same light brown as her skin flickered under the impact of this. "Won't you sit down?" She ignored Milhau as he slumped on the bench beside her. "Then it's you who told the police I was at the theater last night?"

"Dr. Willing is the police," put in Milhau woefully. "At least, he's hand in glove with them. He's in the District Attorney's office."

"Oh." Margot thawed a little. "An inspector came to my apartment just as I was leaving for the theater this morning. He kept me nearly an hour. I can't understand why. Isn't it obvious that that woman did it?"

"What woman?"

"Why, Wanda Morley, of course!"

Basil matched her directness. "You had motive and opportunity yourself."

"Motive? Oh, the will. How sordid! Do you really believe I would kill my husband to prevent his signing a will leaving everything to another woman?"

"It has been done."

"But I didn't have to do it."

"No?"

The waiter brought broiled lobsters. Margot waited until they were served. When the waiter was gone, she resumed. "You see, Dr. Willing, John was never going to sign that will leaving everything to Wanda."

"Why not?"

"John and I were reconciled."

"Rather sudden, wasn't it?"

"No doubt it seemed sudden to Miss Morley." Margot's thin lips curled contemptuously.

"Was there any special reason for it?"

"I told John I was going to have a baby."

"Oh."

Basil's expression amused Margot. She laughed aloud. "My dear Dr. Willing, you didn't suppose I really was going to have a baby did you?"

"Wouldn't it have been a little embarrassing when the expected heir did not appear?"

"Oh, I should have had one afterward. I was a fool not to have had one before, but I never realized that John cared about that sort of thing."

"Why didn't you come forward to identify *Vladimir* as John Ingelow when the morning papers carried the story of *Vladimir's* murder?" asked Basil.

"It's one thing to be innocent and quite another to appear innocent," retorted Margot. "I knew the first suspect in the eyes of the police would be whoever inherited the Ingelow fortune. That happened to be I. So I hoped the police would never learn that I had been in the theater last night or even that I knew John was playing *Vladimir*. I felt sure someone else would identify him in a short while."

"When did this reconciliation take place?"

"Last night. That's why I went backstage. I was desperate. I had to do something to keep John from making a fool of himself over Wanda—a woman nearly twice his age. He had refused to see me again, but I knew he was playing *Vladimir* the opening night of *Fedora*. I tried to see him when he got back from Panama a few days ago, and I overheard him discussing the *Vladimir* business with Wanda on the telephone. It seemed a unique chance to have a word with him. I bought a ticket and bribed an usher to show me the way backstage."

"By way of the fire escape?"

"Of course not! What ever made you think of such a thing? I went through the box-office door and then through the door that leads backstage from the orchestra seats. I waylaid John just as he was coming in the stage door. We stood there talking for about twenty minutes. Then he went on to Wanda's dressing room."

"So that was what delayed Ingelow," said Basil. "And then?"

"He promised to give up Wanda and come back to me. You see how silly it is to talk about my killing John for money. I was to have all the money and John too."

"But now you have all the money without John. Perhaps you prefer it that way. There are many wives of rich men who would."

Margot considered this without emotion. "I won't

pretend I was madly in love with him but—I was sort of used to him. I wouldn't have stabbed him just to get rid of him."

"And what were you doing on stage when Adeane and I saw you leave the alcove?"

"After John left me, I suddenly decided I wanted him to take me home after the first act was over. The sooner I got him away from Wanda's influence the better. So I crossed the stage to the alcove and waited for him in there. But when the actors began to gather on the stage I was afraid I might be caught there when the curtain rose. So I left the alcove before he came and crossed the stage to the wings in order to go round in front. That must have been when you saw me."

"Then according to you, Wanda Morley had no motive for stabbing Ingelow. When he saw her in her dressing room after his interview with you he must have told her that he was going back to you and that his new will would never be signed."

"No, he didn't," put in Milhau. "The police have been all over that with Wanda's dresser. By the time Ingelow got to Wanda's dressing room, she was fully dressed and there were several people there—her press agent, some boys from my office, and so on. She was worrying about her sable cloak—it hadn't been delivered on time—and Ingelow had no chance to talk to her privately. Her dresser daubed his face with that corpse make-up. Everybody assumed he was some friend of Wanda's playing *Vladimir*, but nobody knew who he was, and nobody paid any particular attention to him. You know how it is backstage on a first night—regular madhouse."

"Wanda had every reason to believe he had signed the

new will leaving everything to her," insisted Margot. "And that's why she killed him. It's as simple as that."

"It might be," admitted Basil. "But of the two motives, yours is the more solid; for you did get the money, and she didn't."

"Does a motive have to be solid?"

"Not necessarily."

"Then it was Wanda." The pale eyes caught Basil's and held them. "Dr. Willing, take my word for it. Wanda is the murderer. Everybody on stage saw John enter the alcove. He was alive, and the alcove was empty. The doors weren't opened again until after the first act had started. Only three people approached John during the first act—Wanda, Rodney Tait, and Leonard Martin. The two men had no motive for killing John—they don't even know him by sight. I introduced John to Wanda a few months before he went to Panama. He's only been back three days, and last night was his first visit to the theater. Wanda was his only link with these people. She must have killed him—either because she believed he had signed the new will leaving everything to her, or because she had some reason to think he was tired of her and ripe for a reconciliation with me."

"You can't have it both ways."

"No, but it might be either way."

"Did anyone overhear your talk with Ingelow back stage?"

"Of course not."

"Then we only have your word for it that there was a reconciliation. It's equally possible that Ingelow refused to come back to you and that you waited for him in the alcove and stabbed him before the curtain rose, knowing that if he lived he would sign the will leaving everything to Wanda Morley and you would have nothing but your divorce settlement."

"But I left the alcove before John entered it."

"Can you prove that?"

Margot was relieved by the approach of the waiter. She pushed away her lobster without finishing it. *"Omelette au rhum,"* she said to Milhau. "And coffee." She lit a cigarette and drew on it as if she felt the need of solace.

"It's all the fault of that wretched Morley creature," she went on almost passionately. "If she hadn't run after John, all this would never have happened. It was such a silly infatuation of his! He never really cared for those sexy women. My God!" Margot's eyes widened until a rim of white showed around the iris. She was staring beyond Basil. "Has the woman no shame? There she is now!"

Basil turned his head. Wanda was standing at the head of the stairs. Characteristically, Margot Ingelow thought it was all right for herself to lunch at Capri's the day after the murder but all wrong for Wanda Morley to do so.

Blue flame flickered in a spoon as a waiter ladled burning rum and sugar over Margot's omelette, but she had lost all interest in food. Her eyes were still on the stairs.

Wanda looked excessively thin in black from head to toe relieved only by topaz earrings and clip. Her freshly made up face was composed in an expression of interesting melancholy. Leonard was in attendance, quiet and self-effacing as he always was off stage.

Everyone waited to see if Wanda would pass Margot's table. Basil saw Pauline's little face, white and tense.

Rodney was folding and unfolding his napkin quite unconscious of what he did.

Wanda reached the foot of the stairs. The head waiter tried to lead her to the other side of the room. She looked at him haughtily. "I want my usual table, Gennaro!" She swept down the left side of the *buffet*. She came face to face with Margot. Lines sprang into being as the muscles of her face grew taut. Milhau and the men who had flocked about Margot were not the only people who had heard the rumor of her newly acquired wealth. There was a gleam of savage hate in Wanda's yellow eyes. She was no longer the famous actress or the charming woman—she was the *gamine,* grown old, but still redolent of the gutter.

Milhau half rose from his chair. "Wanda, I—I can explain. I need backing for your next show, and she's just inherited the Ingelow fortune; and—"

"So I've heard!" Wanda flicked him with a glance, and his voice died. The hush became breathless. Leonard moved forward to Wanda's side. She might have been transparent for any sign Margot gave of seeing her. That was too much for Wanda. Her hand darted out like a snake's tongue. She snatched Milhau's glass of liqueur from the table and dashed the contents into Margot's eyes. She put all her trained power of expression into one word:

"Murderess!"

Margot rose with her hand over her eyes. She gave no sign of pain. She ignored Wanda. She ignored Milhau. "Will you get me a taxi, Dr. Willing? This is disgusting."

Wanda burst into loud sobs. Leonard tried to comfort her, wiping her eyes with his own handkerchief.

Milhau looked after Margot with a moan. "There goes my eighty thousand bucks!"

In the taxi, Margot looked at Basil. For the first time he saw uncertainty in her eyes. "You know she spoke as if she really thought I did it. That would mean that she didn't do it. But then . . . who did?"

Basil made no answer. He was wondering if Margot Ingelow might not be a better actress than Wanda Morley. . . .

II

The taxi moved up Fifth Avenue in a stream of cars that stopped and started for red and green lights as uniformly as if they were all controlled by a master switch. To a Martian who didn't know the significance of traffic lights and one-way streets, it would have seemed as if some great game were being played on a chessboard with city blocks for squares and cars for chessmen, so strictly were the length and direction of each move prescribed. Margot sat leaning against the back of the seat, eyes closed, face blank as a mask carved in wood. Basil wondered why John Ingelow had been drawn to her in the first place. Just because she was different from most women? A young man of such wealth would get more than his share of feminine attention. He would soon grow tired of the simpering sweet, the fluffy frivolous, the austerely noble, and the lusciously earthy. To such a man satiated with the sickly sweet scents of the *boudoir* Margot might seem as refreshing as a sea-breeze. But what had driven him from Margot to Wanda and . . .

"Why Magpie?" asked Basil aloud.

She opened her eyes wide in surprise. The inner lids were still red with inflammation. "What *do* you mean?"

"Why do some people call you 'Magpie'?"

"I didn't know they did." She stroked the rustling black and white silk skirt that billowed over her knee. "A magpie's plumage is black and white, and I'm fond of the combination. I suppose that's why. It saves time and trouble shopping to confine yourself to a few colors. And it impresses your personality on people."

So her effects were deliberately contrived. She must realize that in a ruffled dress with permanented hair and china doll make-up she would be not only plain but commonplace. It was the severely straight hair, the sun-browned skin, and the crips dresses with their emphatic contrast of the darkest and lightest of colors that made her a personage. "Is that the only reason?"

"For what?"

"For the nickname Magpie."

"Of course." Her eyelids dropped. "What other reason could there be?"

"I don't know. I wondered."

"My friends call me Margot, and Margot means Magpie in French. John was the first to call me Margot. His mother was French, you know. She came to America as a governess. John's father was a friend of her first employer and a good many years older than she. John was an only child, and between them they spoiled him."

"How did his affair with Wanda Morley start?"

She shrugged with a twisted smile. "How do those affairs always start? John and I were quarreling a good bit. I had become interested in the stage. I met Wanda somewhere, and she said she would help me to get a start. I invited her to the house and . . . it wasn't long before she was John's friend instead of mine. He even talked of backing her plays. But as she was still theoretically my friend seeing him in my home and in my presence, no one suspected an affair between them at first, and later they were very careful. They even tried to hide the affair from me, so I wouldn't bring counter charges and demand big alimony. Before he went to Panama he said he wanted a divorce from me. I wasn't supposed to know he meant to marry Wanda; but I had guessed, and I refused. I tried everything I could think of to get him back but—we had quarreled too much. We no longer had any illusions about each other. Something that had been between us was gone, and you just couldn't bring it back again."

"What did you quarrel about?"

"Oh, nothing . . . everything . . ." She looked down now, playing with the gloves in her lap. "When a man gets tired of a woman any pretext for a quarrel will do."

"Was one of the pretexts money?"

"Money?" Her light lashes flared back again and the wide, pale eyes stared into his. "No. I could have had all the money I wanted. But I didn't want money—I wanted John. If only I'd realized sooner that he wanted children . . ." She spoke in a cold, level voice without apparent feeling. Basil wondered if it were really John she had wanted or the prestige and power of being his wife.

The taxi stopped in the shadow of a skyscraper apartment house towering against a sky that looked hard as a gray-blue stone.

"Won't you come in?"

He followed her into the lobby. An express elevator rocketed twenty-three stories and they stepped into a vestibule made of glass walls. Through the glass they could see a living room, spacious and impersonal as a hotel lounge. It was surrounded by a terrace on all four sides. Each window framed a slice of garden chairs and shrubbery, parapet, and gray-blue sky. Awnings kept the living room shady and cool. It was furnished in the modern manner—an enormous, velvety rug all one color; plump davenports that seemed capacious enough to seat a regiment; radios that looked like tables and tables that looked like radios; little groups of book shelves with few books; and a great many bits of modern glass and pottery in unexpected corners. The whole thing was done in soothing, unobtrusive shades of cream and tan. The sober colors and stripped, functional lines expressed Margot's nature perfectly. Had it expressed John Ingelow's too? Or would he have preferred something more flamboyant—like Wanda's drawing room?

There was no glossy display of silken luxury here. The magnificence of the place lay in its space and privacy—dearest of all luxuries on Manhattan Island.

"Wonderful place for children or pets," said Basil.

"And I have neither!"

"Not even a canary?"

"Not in New York. I have a pair of Irish setters at Fernleigh and a whole stableful of saddle horses. I believe there are some canaries in the conservatory there. I never paid any attention to them. They belonged to John's mother."

With a crisp rustle of taffeta skirts Margot crossed the broad, shady room to the sunlit terrace. Far below the city lay wide and flat as a parti-colored carpet between its twin rivers. The clarity of the noon horizon had gone. The west was blurred with streamers of cloud. Glass and brightwork on cars and buildings glinted in the sun through a smoky blue haze.

The terrace was gay with spring flowers nodding to a brisk breeze. Margot dropped into a wicker armchair and touched a bell attached to the arm. It must have been a pre-arranged signal, for almost at once a maid appeared with a tray of Tom Collins'.

"There is a gentleman to see you, ma'am—Mr. Adeane."

"I don't believe I know a Mr. Adeane." Margot cocked an inquiring brow at Basil.

"He played one of *Vladimir's* servants last night."

"Oh." Margot considered this. "Perhaps I'd better see him."

The maid disappeared into the living room. After a moment they heard the elevator doors sliding open once more. Apparently there was a reception room on the floor below. Without a sound of footfalls on the velvety rug the maid reappeared in the doorway and announced: "Mr. Adeane."

He was hatless, and once more he wore a Byronic shirt open at the neck, but without a Byronic profile the effect was spoiled. His hairy tweed jacket had an unfortunate mustard tinge and brought out all the yellow undertones in his reddish hair and freckled skin. He was carrying a pipe and a bulky manuscript bound in green paper with brass staples that glittered in the sun. A shaggy dog was all he needed to look exactly like the standard publicity still of a Great Author.

He was obviously surprised to see Basil. It was to Margot he turned.

"Good afternoon, Mrs. Ingelow. I'm afraid you don't remember me; but I met you this morning in Sam Milhau's office, and I was on stage last night when you left the alcove."

"Yes?" Margot's voice tinkled coolly as the ice cubes in her glass.

But it took more than mere coolness to daunt Adeane. He sat down without waiting for an invitation to do so and went on completely at his ease. "The police were asking me about it this morning. I told them you left the alcove before your husband entered it, so—" Adeane used a pause to emphasize his next words. "You couldn't possibly have killed him."

"That's true."

"Sure, it's true, but—" A small, unpleasant smile played around Adeane's mouth. "I'm the only witness you have to prove it."

Margot looked at him contemptuously. "Did you come here to remind me of that?"

"Oh, no." Adeane looked quickly at Basil as if he realized this was perilously close to blackmail. "I just want to say I'm sorry about your husband's death, and all you've been through; and I have a suggestion to make. Sam Milhau says you're interested in the theater. Now, you're going to inherit the Ingelow fortune, so why don't you back a play? I thought you might like to read mine."

Margot stared at him speechless. Basil was reminded of the super-salesman who wrote: *Dear Mr. Smith, I am very sorry to hear of the sad death of your mother, and I wonder if you would be interested in our new line of comic valentines?*

"Take a look at it, will you?" Adeane thrust the thick manuscript into Margot's hands and leaned back in his chair complacently as if he had conferred a favor upon her.

Margot seemed a little dazed by this frontal attack.

Mechanically she began to turn the pages of the manuscript with one hand.

Adeane turned to Basil. "It's called *Destroying All Twigs.*"

"Why?" asked Basil.

"Why not?" murmured Margot.

"That's a quotation from Spender," explained Adeane.

"And it means—well, it means any great social upheaval that sweeps all minor things aside."

"Torn from the context, it sounds a little like *Calling All Cars,*" remarked Basil.

"Do you think anyone will know what it means?" added Margot.

"Why should they? Nobody knew what *Dear Brutus* meant at first. Or *Cynara.* Or *Of Mice and Men.* By getting an obscure, trick title you get people puzzled. They have to look it up, and that starts them talking about the play. My first scene is laid in a waterfront dive. There are three characters on stage when the curtain rises— Lulu, Rat-face, and Bugsy."

Margot made a small gesture of distaste. "Is this another gangster play?"

"Oh, no, nothing like that. It's more like *Tobacco Road*—only in New York."

Basil noticed how quick Adeane was to cite models, or at least precedents, for everything about his play. Whatever talent he had appeared to be derivative rather than creative.

"They're salty, down-to-earth characters," he went on. "Lulu is a procuress. Rat-face had his head crushed in an hydraulic press when he was three years old, and he's never been quite the same since. Bugsy is perfectly normal except that he has an overwhelming desire every now and then to taste human blood, and he has to kill somebody to gratify this impulse."

"I suppose he's the hero?" A spark of mischief danced in Margot's eyes.

"There isn't any hero." Adeane was aggrieved. "These are just weak, ignorant people warped by life in a smug, hypocritical society. I've shown them just as they really are—ugly and vicious and cruel—but human and pathetic. Squeamish people won't like the scene where Bugsy kills the crippled child, but if there are any realistic minds in the audience they will welcome such an honest, unflinching statement of fact. When the curtain rises, Bugsy is discovered in a drunken stupor. Lulu comes in and starts kicking him in the groin. He pulls out a handful of her hair, and—"

"It's no use, Mr. Adeane." Margot dropped the script on the table. "I'm not going to put on your play."

Adeane was astonished. "But you haven't read it!"

"No. I've made up my mind." Margot answered crisply. "There are enough horrors in real life, especially in war time. People don't want to see them on the stage as well."

"But—" Adeane began to bluster. "Putting on a play like this is a public service. It's the only way to show up life for the rotten mess it is. Besides—" He turned abruptly from the ideal to the practical. "People will pay real money to see that scene where Bugsy and Flo—just wait until I read it to you."

He stretched out a hand toward the manuscript, but before he could pick it up Margot was on her feet. "I have an idea," she cried. "I am going to back a play—but not this one!"

"You have another one in mind?"

"Yes. Wait a minute." She darted inside. They could hear her dialing a telephone.

Adeane looked at Basil and sighed. "If only she'd listened to that one scene. I got it out of a book on psychopathology—Krafft-Ebing—and—"

"That sounds rather second-hand," said Basil. "I thought realists got their stuff from real life. Why don't you try writing a play around something in your own experience?"

"But my life is so dull!" Adeane was appalled. "Nothing ever happens to me! I've never met a sadist or a nymphomaniac or even a murderer—"

"I wouldn't be too sure of that."

"Oh!" Adeane was startled. "You mean—last night? Funny, I didn't get any kick out of last night at all. Just hours of waiting for that inspector to question me, and then a few minutes of questioning, and then—home. Even murder is dull when it happens to me. Only one thing I saw seemed sort of interesting."

"What was that?"

"When you and the Inspector were questioning me, did you happen to notice that fly?"

"Fly?" Basil was startled. He had not credited Adeane with any powers of observation.

"Uh-huh." Adeane's eyes were on the horizon. The sun had gone. The gray clouds were massing and spreading. Already they darkened the whole sky and dulled the sparkle of the city below. "The knife that killed Ingelow was on the table, remember? And there was a house fly buzzing around. It kept settling on the handle of the knife instead of the blade. But there was blood on the blade. I thought flies always went for blood. It seemed sort of queer."

Margot's voice came through the open window. "Mr. Milhau, please. . . . Sam? . . . Yes, yes, never mind that. I don't care whether Wanda's sorry or not! The point is this: I want you to carry on with the production of *Fedora*. . . . Yes, I said *Fedora*. I'll back you to the limit. . . . No, I do not want to see a play by Granby Saunderson or anyone else! It's *Fedora* or nothing! And it must be played exactly the same way by the same actors. I'll send you a check. . . . Wanda needn't know who's putting up the money. . . . Nonsense! The murder will be good publicity. . . . Who'll play *Vladimir?* My dear Sam, that's your headache. . . ."

They heard the receiver click into place. When she came back her eyes were defiant.

"Mrs. Ingelow!" protested Adeane. "That awful romantic twaddle of Sardou's! It was only staged as a vehicle for Wanda. Nobody liked it. But *Destroying All Twigs* is stark reality. It has the makings of a smash hit!"

Margot's thin lips were set close in a taut smile. She looked at the sky. "Better come inside. It's going to rain."

The living room seemed shadowy now the sky was overcast. Margot stood at the open window for a moment, her back half turned toward the two men, her eyes on the sky.

"Just what is the idea of going on with *Fedora?*" demanded Adeane.

"Don't you understand?" She glanced back over her shoulder.

Basil answered for Adeane. *"The play's the thing with which to catch the conscience of the king?"*

175

"Exactly. John was killed during a performance of *Fedora* by one of three actors taking part in the play. I can watch all three every night and see which one really has the best opportunity to murder *Vladimir* during the action of the play. I'm reconstructing the crime—not just once, but every night as long as *Fedora* runs. Sooner or later as that scene is repeated over and over again the murderer's nerves will crack and he'll give himself away . . . or she . . ."

"But they might not play the scene exactly the same way they did last night," objected Basil.

"Actors tend to play a scene pretty much the same way night after night," argued Margot. "Habit is what makes it possible for them to remember a part. Milhau directed, and he'll see to it that they stick to his direction."

"You've forgotten one thing," put in Adeane. "Stage people are superstitious. You'll never get any actor in that company to play *Vladimir* again."

"Oh, we'll get somebody!" returned Margot airily. "Somebody who needs the money badly."

"Why don't you put on my play as well as *Fedora?*" insisted Adeane stubbornly. "Suppose I leave the manuscript with you, and when you've read it—"

"I don't want to back any play except *Fedora*," answered Margot. "Wanda Morley has cured me of all interest in the theater. I've had enough of the stage and stage people to last me all the rest of my life."

"You'll be sorry." Adeane sounded more like a defeated salesman than a disappointed dramatist. "You're throwing away a fortune. Sooner or later I'm going to get a backer for that play, and then just watch my dust! Where'd you leave the script?"

"I think it's on the terrace," Margot replied indifferently.

Adeane thrust his way past her and jerked open the terrace door. Wind hurled a handful of raindrops in his face. "Hey!" He sprang forward with the cry of a lioness who sees her cub attacked. The wind was tossing loose sheets of white paper about the terrace with the heavy playfulness of a gamboling elephant. There was typewriting on the sheets. They had come from Adeane's script.

Basil went to help him gather the scattered pages together. By great good luck not a single page had blown over the parapet, but all of them were blistered with rain. Adeane stuffed the sodden mass between the green paper covers. "How did that happen?" he muttered.

There was no sign of the brass staples that had held the pages of the script together. Each page was loose and at the mercy of the wind.

"But the wind couldn't have undone those staples!" Adeane's eyes were on Basil angry and puzzled.

"Are you sure the staples weren't loose?"

"No. I tightened them before I came out. I'm always afraid of losing a page or so."

A clear voice came through the window. "Something wrong?"

They turned to see Margot watching them from the doorway. Her cheeks were flushed, her pale eyes bright as winter sunshine.

"The staples have fallen out of Adeane's script," Basil turned back to Adeane. "Are they on the terrace?"

"No." Adeane was on his knees looking under the porch chairs. "They're gone. Maybe that maid—"

"Why? Staples are scarcely valuable."

"Maybe the wind . . ."

"Maybe." Basil was unconvinced.

They went inside closing the French window against the rain. Basil looked thoughtfully at Margot. Was she capable of such a small act of cruelty? Could she have done it when she stood at the window overlooking the terrace near the garden table where she had left the script? Granted the play was silly, granted Adeane was callous and impertinent, it still seemed a petty, mean revenge for her to have taken. . . .

Damp and sulky, Adeane tucked the script under one arm. "I guess I'd better be going . . ."

"I'll go with you," said Basil.

"Don't go, Dr. Willing!" Margot ignored Adeane. "At least wait until the rain is over. We can have tea or a cocktail."

At that moment it was a tempting invitation with a dark, wet, unfriendly world outside, and everything warm, dry, and cushioned inside. But Basil wanted to see a little more of Adeane.

"Thanks, but I really must go."

When the two men were in the elevator, Adeane spoke morosely. "You know, I don't believe that woman likes me."

"You chose the wrong moment to approach her—just after her husband's death."

"They were separated, weren't they?"

"Perhaps she doesn't want to be reminded of that now."

"I don't know what's the matter with me." Adeane seemed genuinely concerned. "I don't know how to get on with people. I just haven't any tact."

"It has been said that tact is love," returned Basil. "No amount of intelligence can replace sympathy when it comes to putting yourself in another person's place."

"I should sympathize with a woman like that who's got everything I'd like to have!" cried Adeane bitterly. "Old Hutchins says I'm an egoist. Sure I am. Why not? How's a guy going to get along if he doesn't keep looking out for himself?"

"It didn't get you very far this time, did it?" said Basil.

The doorman whistled up a taxi for them. Adeane asked to be let off at the theater. "Tact!" He brooded over the word resentfully "I don't know anyone who can afford to back plays. My script has been knocking around producers' offices for two or three years. I've tried and tried to break into the theater, and it's been like trying to scale a wall of glass—high, cold, slippery and smooth, without a toehold anywhere. Talent counts for nothing. It's all done by pull. I'd just about given up hope when Sam Milhau introduced me to Mrs. Ingelow at the theater this morning. They were going out to luncheon together, so I couldn't speak to her then; but I'd heard she was stage struck, and I'd heard the rumor about her inheriting all this money, and she does owe me something for telling the police she couldn't have killed her husband."

"Does she?"

Again Basil discovered that irony was lost on Adeane. "Sure she does. I'm the only witness who testified she came out of that alcove before Ingelow went in."

"And did she?"

Adeane's eyes grew wary. "I should stick my neck out

lying to the police for a dame like that! It's the truth, but she still owes me something as I see it. I saved her a lot of grief. It seemed like a chance, so I followed it up. And what do I get? The cold shoulder! Because—you say—she's upset by her husband's death—a guy she was on the point of divorcing! I said I was sorry he was dead, didn't I?"

Basil gave it up. Adeane was unteachable.

"If only she'd read that scene where Bugsy and Lulu gang up on Flo!" went on Adeane. "It's stark realism—a slice of life raw and bleeding. I got the idea out of Krafft-Ebing." He looked up suddenly. "You know, doc, you might be a lot of use to me."

Basil had an instant impression that Adeane classified everyone he met by their possible usefulness to himself. "I'm afraid I couldn't afford to back a play—"

"Oh, I don't mean that. But you're a psychiatrist, aren't you? And all the characters in my plays have something the matter with them—usually psychopathic. You could tell me a lot about symptoms and things like that. For instance, take Bugsy, the sadist, in *Destroying All Twigs*. It would be possible for him to be a simple, friendly fellow when he wasn't actually tasting human blood, wouldn't it? I mean, psychologically possible."

Basil disliked having his brains picked. "You ought to look it up at the medical library."

"What medical library?"

"The one at Fifth Avenue and 103rd. Once you learn your way about there you can find anything. They have books you won't find in any of the public libraries or even at Columbia."

Adeane pouted. "It's pretty hard for a layman to find

out about these things in libraries. You spend hours looking something like hay fever up in card indices. It'll say *Hay Fever* see *Fever* and then *Fever, Hay* see *Hay*. That's what they call a cross-reference! When you finally run down the definitive work on the subject under *Sternutatory Diseases* see *Nasal Passages* you find it's either in Choctaw or at the bindery or it only deals with *Hay Fever* as it affects Eskimos transplanted to the tropics."

"What you want is a general reference book," advised Basil. "A sort of medical encyclopedia that'll give you a bird's-eye view of the symptoms, treatment, and so forth, for each disease. Then you can fill in the rough outline with your own characters and local color, I suppose?"

"Uh-huh," responded Adeane. "If I could find a book like that it would keep me busy for years."

"Then your best bets are Barr, Tice, and Cushny." The taxi swung into West 44th Street. Basil wondered if posterity would thank him for putting still more pathology into Adeane's plays. "Each one has written, or rather edited, a pretty inclusive survey of disease in several volumes. With three of them to check on each other you can't go far wrong. If you want more details, they always give bibliographies."

"What are those names?" Adeanne drew out a stubby pencil and scribbled on the cover of his wilted script. "Barr—Tice—Cushny. Thanks a lot."

Adeane backed out of the cab gracelessly. "So long, doc. And thanks for the lift." He turned and swaggered down the stagedoor alley, a ridiculously cocky figure with his reddish hair and mustard tweed jacket exposed to the rain.

Basil gave Seymour Hutchins' address to the cab driver and leaned back in his seat with closed eyes. Again he was seeing Adeane as he had first appeared on the terrace—coming up to Margot so insolently, the script in one hand, its brass staples gleaming in the sun. . . .

CHAPTER NINE

Aside

IN THE WEST FORTIES there is a small shabby hotel. To people from out of town it looks exactly like all the other small, shabby hotels in the theatrical district. Only dyed-in-the-wool New Yorkers who know the various planes and facets of their city well realize that this particular hotel has been for years the headquarters of all those stage people who cannot afford to live at clubs or luxury hotels. Young actors on their way up and old actors on their way down pass each other at this half-way house between success and failure. Seymour Hutchins had lived there before he became a star and returned there now he had ceased to be one. According to Milhau, who gave Basil the address, Wanda and Rod had both lived there in their salad days, but not Leonard, who always occupied a little attic room at the Players when he was in New York, no matter how much money he was making.

There were only three people in the shallow lobby, yet Basil recognized each face as one he had seen on the stage that season in a minor part. He gave his name at the desk and asked if Mr. Hutchins could see him. The message was relayed through a switchboard operator, and a moment later he was in a rheumatic elevator creaking up to the twelfth floor and room 1243.

Perhaps nothing is more revealing of character than the condition of a hotel room when you descend on the occupant without warning. Hutchins passed the test with flying colors. It was a large double room with a bay window and bathroom. There was no kitchenette and no evidence of those furtive attempts at housekeeping with a small electric stove in defiance of the Fire Department that most elderly women living alone in hotel rooms seem unable to resist. Nor was there any pathetic assumption that a bedroom can be turned into a living room accessible to both sexes without impropriety by keeping combs and brushes in a bureau drawer and substituting a hard, narrow couch with a dingy cretonne cover for a wide, comfortable bed with an immaculate white counterpane and pillow slips. The moment Basil saw that bed he concluded that Seymour Hutchins was a man who had an intelligently selfish interest in his own comfort and a refreshingly candid indifference to the comfort of others. He had supplied himself with one large armchair, a case for his own books, and a powerful radio. But there was no armchair for visitors, and Basil was not offered any such feminine amenity as weak tea hastily brewed in the bathroom or any such bachelor refreshment as rye whisky in a tooth glass.

The window opened on a courtyard, but it was high enough to look over the roof of a lower building opposite to a wide view of skyscrapers massed irregularly which seemed oddly familiar. The rain had stopped now, and the sun was already far down the western hemisphere of the sky in a pool of saffron light that washed the tall buildings with a roseate glow making them unnaturally radiant under the dull, gray clouds overhead. Basil had seen the same appearance in the mountains at sunset on a rainy day, and once again he realized how closely the skyscrapers approximated a range of hills in their scenic effect.

"I hope I'm not intruding," he said to Hutchins, "but there are some things I can learn from you in this case that I could not learn from anyone else involved."

"Not at all." With his usual ambassadorial dignity, Hutchins waved Basil to the lone armchair beside the bay window and perched himself on a narrow window seat. "I'm glad to help you if I can. But frankly I can't imagine how. If it's that line of mine about *Vladimir— He cannot escape now, every hand is against him—* there's nothing more I can tell you. I've thought it over carefully, and it has no special significance for me."

Basil took a sheet of paper from his pocket—the time table of the first act that Rod had prepared for him that morning. "There's one thing I forgot to ask. Have you any idea of the approximate time when you spoke that line?"

Hutchins bent his white head as if he were looking down into the question. "I can only give you a very rough approximation," he answered finally. "Curtain rises at 8:40, I go on at 8:51. That line comes about twenty minutes later—about four or five minutes after nine."

"Well, an approximation is better than nothing." Basil jotted down the hour on the margin of Rod's time table.

"You can do better than an approximation." Suddenly Hutchins lifted his eyes, searching Basil's face. "Have you heard that Sam Milhau is going to go on with

Fedora? He's called a rehearsal for tomorrow morning at nine-thirty. If you'd care to come to the theater as my guest—" Another touch of ambassadorial urbanity— "you can time the whole thing exactly yourself."

"I'd like to very much." Basil saw that Hutchins was troubled. "You don't like the idea of a revival?"

The answer came in a roundabout way. "Have you ever heard of the doctrine of 'eternal recurrence?' "

"You mean the idea that time has latitude as well as longitude?"

"Roughly, yes. We all think and speak of the length of time, but some philosophers have suggested that it may have width as well—that there is more than one twentieth century and that we recur in all of them, repeating all the mistakes and misfortunes in our lives throughout eternity."

. Basil smiled. "That idea of lateral time is an amusing intellectual exercise, but I doubt if the universe is organized in quite that way. Certainly, I hope not. A hell of fire and brimstone would be a cozy summer resort in comparison, and it makes the annihilation of the atheist seem like Paradise."

"Perhaps. But such an idea must appeal to an actor, because he spends so much of his life doing the same thing over and over again. No one understands better the enormous impulsive force of habit."

"It has a certain appeal for a psychiatrist, too," admitted Basil. "The Viennese School collected a good bit of evidence suggesting that a man who fails to meet one situation in life adequately will go on through his whole life repeating the same failure each time he is confronted with a similar situation. In most cases habit is far stronger than the lessons of experience, possibly because the psychic factors that formed the habit in the first place are always there to support it and continue it. Of course this tendency to repeat is even more marked in neurotics and criminals."

"And in murderers?" Hutchins' smile had a fine edge. "Now you see why I don't like the idea of going on with *Fedora*. I certainly wouldn't care to take Ingelow's place as *Vladimir!*"

"I understand that *Vladimir* will be played by some actor who was not in the original company," replied Basil. "That ought to eliminate any motive for a second murder, and it would certainly involve great risk to the murderer."

"That's entirely reasonable but—I still don't like the idea. People say we stage folk are superstitious. How can we help it when our success depends so much on chance? You can never predict whether a play will succeed or not until after the first night, and sometimes not even then. It's all a gamble, and we all have a gambler's psychology."

Basil saw an opportunity to ask another question without appearing to attach much importance to it. "It seems all the more strange that Milhau should revive *Fedora* this season," he said in his most casual voice. "So far as I could tell from the first act, the play has nothing in it to appeal to a modern audience. Do you know what first put it into his head?"

"I believe that Wanda wanted to play the part." Hutchins answered as if he saw no significance in the question. "I don't know just where she got the idea. But I don't agree with you that the play is dead. I think it has far more vitality than some of the modern amorphous tripe—" He stopped himself with a smile. "I don't suppose tripe can be called amorphous." His glance went to Basil's hat lying on the bed. "What do you call that?"

"A gray felt hat."

"Yes, and what else?"

"A soft felt hat."

"And?"

Basil laughed. "A *fedora!*"

"Exactly. That gives you some idea of how popular the play was originally. If you could have seen Bernhardt do it you might understand."

"Was it you who told Wanda Morley the anecdote about Edward VII playing *Vladimir* to Bernhardt's *Fedora?*"

"Yes." Hutchins' face sobered. "Leonard Martin had heard it from someone, and one day at rehearsal he asked me if it were true. Wanda overheard us talking and asked about it. That must be how she got the idea of having Ingelow play *Vladimir*. In a way it makes me feel responsible for what happened. Dr. Willing, I wish you'd persuade Sam Milhau to give up this idea of going on with *Fedora*. Have you any idea why he insists on it?"

"Partly because he's found a backer," explained Basil without naming the backer. "And he wants to recover the money he's invested in costumes, scenery, salaries, and so forth."

"Is there any other reason?" demanded Hutchins shrewdly.

"I think he imagines it's the best way to safeguard the reputation of his cast—particularly Miss Morley's reputation. The official story as it appears in the papers by grace of his publicity department seems to be that Ingelow was just a casual acquaintance of Miss Morley's and that his murder has nothing to do with her or any members of her company. The best way to prove that is to have her go on with the same play as if nothing had happened."

"But obviously some member of the cast is the murderer!"

Basil shrugged. "So long as the murder is unsolved everyone is presumed innocent. Perhaps Milhau has some idea that going on with the play will keep the actors psychologically steady—like sending an aviator up in a plane directly after an accident."

"If I know anything about Milhau he has no such altruistic motive," returned Hutchins, bitterly. "His only idea is to make money out of the morbid curiosity of the general public, and he will. People will flock to see the first act that was performed when Ingelow was killed just because they'll be reasonably sure that one of the actors on the stage is Ingelow's murderer. This is more of Milhau's literal realism. What a thrill to see a *real* murderer on the stage in a murder play that led to a *real* murder! But it won't be very pleasant for us on the stage to know that we're rubbing elbows with a murderer, especially when we don't know which one he or she is."

Basil decided not to tell Hutchins that there was a fourth suspect—Margot Ingelow. And that again she would have access to the stage—this time as backer of the play.

"Do you think any actors will resign from the cast?" queried Basil.

"None of us can afford to break a contract with a producer as influential as Milhau, but—" A cold light shone in Hutchins eyes. "He has nobody under contract to play *Vladimir,* and he'll have a hard time getting any-body. He'd never use a dummy. Not realistic enough. *Vladimir* may put a stop to the whole thing. I hope it does."

"Mr. Hutchins," said Basil. "You've known most of these people for some years. You may be able to tell us more about them than anyone else. Just what is your opinion of Derek Adeane?"

"'A louse in the locks of literature,'" returned Hutch-ins promptly. "An intellectual parasite. Whenever a play is a hit he immediately writes one as near like it as possible. He calls it 'following a trend'; I call it plagia-rism. He did have a play produced once—a faint carbon copy of *Our Town* called *Your City.* It ran exactly four nights. Now he's going in for the hard-boiled cult—a round denial of human virtues and an unctuous sym-pathy for human vices. As soon as another point of view becomes fashionable he'll adopt that with equal enthu-siasm. Some men have great talent and no ambition; Adeane has colossal ambition and no talent. There are a good many like him, and some more successful than he. To them the arts are simply an easy way of earning a living. Easy because they never go through the agonies of creation that afflict a real artist."

"Is Adeane monstrously stupid?" asked Basil. "Or simply insensitive?"

"He's not stupid in the ordinary sense of the word. I should say he had intelligence but no intellect, cun-ning but no wisdom. And, of course, he has none of the sympathetic qualities—no charms or graces. That's the real reason he hasn't been more successful. He has never learned to conceal his egoism as most of us do, so he is heartily disliked."

"Would he lie if he thought the lie would help him to get a play produced?"

"I should imagine he would."

"And what is your opinion of the three under suspicion—Wanda Morley, Rodney Tait, and Leonard Martin?"

"Leonard is a sterling actor of the old school who can play any part. Wanda and Rod are products of the modern type-casting idea—artless naturalism reduced to an absurdity; you have a part for a handsome young man, so you get a handsome young man to play it. Disgusting! I can remember the days when an ugly old man could act the part of a handsome young man with far more dash and conviction than any of these toothpaste-ad boys who walk through their parts being themselves. There was Gregory Lawrence—ugly as sin off stage—who used to get torrents of fan mail and even presents of gold cigarette cases and jeweled cuff links from matinée girls because he could re-create the spirit of a handsome young man on stage. That's art—the sort of thing Rod does isn't even artifice!"

Basil smiled at the way Hutchins had answered his question by describing the acting ability of the three suspects instead of their moral or emotional attributes. If Hutchins were called as a character witness he would probably devote his testimony entirely to saying whether or not the accused was a true artist or a product of type casting. It would not be surprising to hear Hutchins say that an actor who would "walk through" his part was capable of homicide, arson, sabotage and any other crime in the calendar.

"One more thing." Basil was watching Hutchins' face closely. "Does the word 'canary' suggest anything to you in connection with any of these three people—Wanda, Leonard, or Rodney?"

"No."

Hutchins looked so puzzled that Basil explained. "We have reason to believe that the murderer sharpened the knife he used in Lazarus' workshop. Before leaving he released a pet canary from its cage. It seems a wanton, capricious thing to do, but there must have been some reason for it. Think over the past lives of these people and see if you can suggest any reason for it."

"I'm afraid I can't," answered Hutchins, after a moment. "You think it might be a symbol or signal of some kind?"

"Frankly, I don't know. Of course, all criminals are neurotic. Indeed, crime in most cases is really an exaggerated form of compulsion neurosis. That's why criminals, like neurotics, delight in symbolism and fetichism. I could cite you hundreds of cases—burglars who always leave a colored napkin at the scene of a crime and so on."

"But what would a canary symbolize?" Hutchins' lively intellectual curiosity was aroused. "Maybe the dictionary will help!" He went to his bookcase and took out the first volume of a large dictionary. "Let me see—" He looked like an elderly scholar as his hoary head bent over the huge book on his knees. He began reading aloud; abbreviations and all:

Ca-na-ry, a. Of or pertaining to the color of a canary; of a bright yellow color.

Ca-na-ry, n; pl. ca-na-ries. (Sp., canario, a bird, a dance; from L. Canaria insula, canary island, so-called from its large dogs; L. canis, a dog.)

1. Wine made in the Canary Islands.
2. An old dance. (Obs.)
3. The canary bird or its characteristic color.
4. A word put by Shakespeare in its singular and plural forms into the mouth of Mrs. Quickly, (Merry Wives) which commentators differ in explaining. It is probably a blunder for quandary.

ca-na-ry, v.i. To dance, to frolic; to perform the old dance called a canary. (Obs.)

ca-na-ry-bird, n. An insessorial singing bird, a kind of finch, from the Canary Islands, the Carduelis canaria or Fringilla canaria of the finch family, much esteemed as a household pet, being one of the most common cage birds.

"Not much help I'm afraid!" Hutchins looked up with a smile. "A dog? An island? A wine? A dance? You have a wide choice. And here are a lot of derived words —canary-bird flower, canary-vine, canary-moss, canary-stone, canary-wood."

"That's enough!" cried Basil. "You're making it too complicated!"

Hutchins laughed and shut the book with a loud clap. Basil rose and picked up his hat. Lights in the windows of various buildings were beginning to glow through the early dusk. Suddenly he saw letters of fire: *Time For Tilbury's Tea!* Now he understood why the skyline looked so oddly familiar—it was the same scene he had observed last night from a different angle. "That wall with the fire escape must be the Royalty Theatre!" he exclaimed. "And the low building opposite us is the tax-payer beside the stage door alley!"

"Yes." Hutchins' gaze followed Basil's. "Amazing how

a little shift in the angle of vision can change the look of everything, isn't it? This hotel faces on 45th Street, but as my window is in the back it overlooks 44th. New York is full of these surprises. When you enter a building you can never tell from the front door view what unexpected sights you may see from a back, top-floor window. Over there is a physical culture school that has classes on the roof all during the day though nobody in the street knows anything about it."

"I should think that Tilbury neon sign would get on your nerves."

"One gets used to things, and I won't have to put up with it much longer. I understand Broadway is to be dimmed out in a few days, and before the war is over it'll probably be blacked out."

As Basil started for the door, Hutchins called after him. "One moment." Hutchins laid aside the book and came over to the door. His eyes were fixed on Basil's earnestly. "You know you said something important a moment ago."

"What?"

"You said I was making the canary business too complicated. Has it occurred to you that you are making it too complicated yourself?"

Basil smiled. "Maybe you have something there! It's one of my worst failings—to elaborate an idea with so many fine shadings of implication and potential meaning that I lose sight of the essential thing. The murderer's motive for releasing the canary is probably something extremely simple and obvious, and that's why I've missed it. I've been looking for something subtle and complex. I needed what I got from your window—a little shift in the angle of vision!"

As Basil went down in the elevator he made an effort to dismiss all the complexities and think of the simplest, most obvious significance implied in the act of releasing a canary from its cage. For a moment an idea seemed to flicker on the periphery of consciousness. But strain his attention as he would its color and shape still eluded him.

CHAPTER TEN

Rehearsal

IN THE EARLY MORNING the theatrical district looks as tawdry and disheveled as a woman caught by the dawn still wearing evening dress and make up blended for artificial light. This morning a sun glare as ruthlessly intolerant as youth itself searched out everything that was mean and ugly and false in the neighborhood of Broadway and West 44th: sidewalks littered with paper and cigarette butts; garbage cans in the alley at the rear of the cocktail bar; showy façades of varnish, glass, and metal camouflaging buildings of drab brick or dingy stone; and eddies of dust everywhere, the thick, black, powdery dust at the heart of the city. It was not pretty. It was the dance hall and gambling saloon section of a frontier town raised to the nth degree.

Yet Basil looked at the scene with a certain affection this morning, for it had suddenly become ephemeral—part of a world that might be destined to change beyond recognition. He no longer asked himself if the buildings were handsome or hideous, sanitary or insanitary, but if they were bombproof or non-bombproof. The Tilbury building towered against the cold blue sky with the arrogance of a structure confident in the strength of its steel frame and cinder-concrete roof and floor arches. The shabby walls of the theater looked defenseless and insubstantial as paper—brick walls without a steel frame that would crumble at the first blast.

A timid voice cut across these sentimental reflections. "Excuse me, but can you tell me the way to Mr. Milhau's office?"

Basil looked and saw a long, weedy youth whom any draft board would automatically classify as 4F on sight. His blondness was as wan as a faded water-color. He bore all the sad stigmata of the shabby genteel—worn suit carefully pressed, cracked shoes scrupulously polished. His manner was a blend of eagerness and anxiety. It was just for the purpose of keeping such perennial job-seekers out of their offices that big business men surrounded themselves with *cordons* of secretaries and receptionists. But Basil had always had a sneaking suspicion that this system kept out a good deal of grain along with the chaff, so he took a certain perverse pleasure in saying: "I'll show you the way. I'm just going there myself."

Milhau's office was on the ground floor to the right of the box office—two rooms as small, dark, and glossy as Milhau himself. The outer office was ruled by a houri with soft, improbably golden hair and hard, brown eyes. She recognized Basil whom she had seen with the police when Ingelow's death was first discovered. "Dr. Willing —go right in." Her stony gaze shifted to the youth. He winced and colored and mumbled something inaudible. A little regretfully Basil left him to his fate and went inside.

"Hello." Milhau at his desk waved Basil to a chair and pushed a box of cigars in his direction. "Hutchins says you want to see the rehearsal this morning. That's O.K. with me, but what's the big idea?"

Basil pushed the cigars back with a shake of his head. "Timing."

"Timing?" Milhau took one of the cigars himself and bit off the end. "I don't get it. Nobody has an alibi—I mean nobody that's under suspicion." He waited for Basil's explanation. None came. He went on in a lower voice. "Listen, Dr. Willing—no one knows that Mrs. Ingelow is backing this revival of *Fedora* except you and me and Adeane. He told me you knew. I'm relying on you not to talk about it, because—"

The door burst open and the houri plunged into the room. "A Mr. Russell to see you—from Carson's." She was excited.

Milhau's eyes narrowed. "So they got somebody?" he said in a level voice.

"Yeah. And he's been in hospital six weeks. Hasn't seen a newspaper."

"Oh." Basil was aware of some message passing from the girl's eyes to Milhau's. Then Milhau said: "You'll excuse me a minute, Dr. Willing?"

"Certainly." Basil settled back in his chair. Milhau looked as if Basil's presence hardly suited his programme but he dared not protest. He spoke to his secretary with resignation. "Send the guy in."

The weedy youth came in diffidently. "My name's Russell, and I'm from the Lemuel Carson agency. Mr. Carson said there was a small part for me in a play called *Fedora.*"

"Yeah." Milhau's voice was genial, but his gaze was coldly appraising. "It's a walk-on part. You only appear in the first act. All you have to do is to lie perfectly still on a couch in an alcove at the back of the stage. You're supposed to be dying."

The boy smiled. "I ought to be able to do that. I've been doing nothing else for the last six weeks. How many lines do I speak?"

"None."

The boy's face fell. Basil recalled that in minor parts an actor's salary bore some relation to the number of lines he spoke on stage.

Milhau went on in his level voice: "You'll get fifty dollars a week."

"Fifty bucks and no lines to speak!" Russell smiled nervously. "Seems as if there must be a catch in it!"

"I've had trouble getting anyone to play the part at short notice," answered Milhau. "As it is, you'll only have one rehearsal. Then—if you do all right—we'll sign a contract."

"That suits me." Russell was beaming as if he had just found the pot of gold at the foot of the rainbow.

Again the door burst open. It was not the secretary this time, but Rodney Tait. The doctor's bag in his hand looked incongruous with his tweed jacket and flannel trousers. He nodded briefly to Basil, ignored Russell, and marched up to Milhau's desk. He turned the bag upside down and dumped its contents on the blotter—a shining array of surgical knives.

"Listen, Sam. I want you to lock them in your safe in the presence of witnesses."

"But—" began Milhau.

"And give me a receipt!" continued Rod implacably. "If I've got to carry this bag on stage tonight I'm going to carry it empty. Nobody's going to say again that I was the only person seen on stage with a knife in my hand."

"All right, all right!" Milhau looked anxiously at Russell. "Some other time—"

"No, now!" Rod's voice was taut and brittle. "I'm not going to be put on the spot again."

"Oh, all right!" Frowning, Milhau got up and went to a wall safe. His thick fingers fiddled with the lock for a moment, and the massive door swung open ponderously. He picked up the knives by their handles and dropped them on the floor of the safe.

"All right," said Rod with a sigh of relief. "Now you can close the door."

Milhau swung the door back into place and fumbled with the lock again.

Rod held out the empty black bag to Basil. "I call you to witness that the bag is empty. Put your hand inside and make sure."

Basil obliged with a grin. The bag was empty.

Rod turned to Russell. "You, too!"

Russell looked inside the bag. "There's nothing there now. But—I don't understand—"

"I want everyone to realize that if anything happens tonight it has nothing to do with me!" explained Rod.

"Hello, Sam."

The three men turned and saw Pauline in the doorway. She looked like a schoolgirl, hatless, in low-heeled shoes, and a polo coat, with a portfolio under one arm. Her fresh young face showed no sign of the strains and shocks of the last few days. She nodded casually to Basil as she came forward and even more casually to Rod. "Here are the sketches for Wanda's new costume."

"Wanda's new costume?" Milhau lifted his hands in the air and shook them helplessly. "Is this an office or a madhouse? What new costume?"

"For the first act," answered Pauline quietly. "Wanda says she'll never wear that gold dress again."

"Why not? That gold dress cost money!"

"Well . . ." Pauline smiled slightly. "It did get rather crushed the other evening."

"Why can't she have it pressed?"

"Come on, Sam. Be human. Don't make it any harder for her than it is. After what happened she just can't wear that gold dress again. The associations are too unpleasant." Pauline opened her portfolio on the desk.

"I don't see why not." Milhau looked at the sketches cursorily. "What's this, no yellow? Wanda always wears yellow or gold because of her eyes."

"She wants it as different as possible this time," explained Pauline. "All white—ermine, velvet, and diamonds."

Milhau frowned. "Too high-keyed for those deep reds and blues in the background."

"I'm not so sure." Pauline was pleading. "I think it might be effective to have Wanda the one pale note in that dark scene. Ermine-and-diamonds does give a sort of ice-and-snow effect that's good with a Russian background, and it would set off her dark hair."

"How are you going to get this ready by tonight?"

"She has an ermine coat of her own and diamonds. Rosamonde has promised to rush the dress here by seven-thirty. It's perfectly simple—a few lengths of white velvet cut and stitched together."

"Oh, all right." Milhau waved her aside. "But do try to keep the cost down."

"Sam, are you busy?"

It was Leonard this time. His long, bronzed face was serious.

"Oh, no, I'm not busy! I'm a gentleman of leisure!" groaned Milhau. "What now?"

"I just wanted to make a suggestion about tonight." Leonard leaned against the corner of Milhau's desk. "Don't you think we'd all be a little happier if the fellow who plays *Vladimir* weren't made up quite so . . . realistically? You could have his head turned away from the audience you know."

The secretary stuck her improbable golden head around the door jamb. "Rehearsal, Mr. Milhau. Everybody's waiting for you on stage!"

Milhau groaned again, snatched a dog-eared copy of the script from his desk and rose. "Why did I ever go into show business?" he asked the universe. "Why wasn't I a bootblack or a truck driver?"

As he plunged through the lobby to the auditorium the others straggled after him. Russell fell into step beside Basil.

"Excuse me . . ." Russell's manner was more anxious than ever. "But—" His voice sank to a whisper. "There's something queer going on here. I don't understand it. Why does this man they call 'Rod' make such a fuss about carrying a knife on stage? Why does Miss Morley want a new costume when she only wore the other one once? And why is an old skinflint like Sam Milhau offering fifty bucks a week for a walk-on part that's not worth thirty-five?"

Basil looked at him almost as appraisingly as Milhau had done. "Is true you've been in hospital for six weeks without seeing a newspaper?"

"Yes. I had a touch of tuberculosis."

"You might as well hear the truth from me," went

on Basil. "You're sure to hear it from someone sooner or later, and I don't think it's quite fair to keep you in the dark. I suppose Milhau thinks that if he can just get you through one or two performances before you learn the truth you won't mind so much when you do learn it."

"Learn what?"

"Your predecessor who played the part of *Vladimir* at the opening night before last was murdered on stage."

"W-what?" Russell stood stock still in the middle of the center aisle. Basil stood beside him as the others went on down to the footlights. "He was stabbed with a surgical knife like those you saw in Rod's bag. It happened during the first act but his death wasn't discovered until the curtain fell."

"And no one noticed he was dying until then?"

"No, because he was playing the part of *Vladimir*— a dying man—all during the first act. He was even made up to look like a corpse."

The word "corpse" seemed to bring the thing home to Russell. "Who did it?" he demanded hoarsely.

"No one knows. Only four people had the opportunity. Three are actors who'll be on stage with you tonight: Wanda Morley, Rodney Tait, and Leonard Martin. The fourth is the wife of the murdered man, a Mrs. Ingelow."

"What's the idea of going on with the show?"

"It's the only way Milhau can get any return on the money he's already invested in it."

"Money." Russell grew thoughtful. "I could certainly use fifty bucks a week, but I don't much-like stepping into a dead man's shoes and a murdered man's at that.

. . . Do you think it would be—well—dangerous?"

"I don't see how," answered Basil. "You have no connection with anyone else in the cast or with the Ingelow family, have you?"

"No. I've seen Miss Morley and her company on the stage from a gallery séat, and I've been turned down by Milhau's secretary once or twice when I asked for a job; but that's the sole extent of my connection with any of them. I never even heard of this Ingelow and his wife."

"Then I should think you could enjoy your fifty bucks a week without worrying," said Basil.

"Coming, Russell?" called Milhau from the footlights.

"Yes, sir!" The boy hurried down to the stage.

Basil followed more slowly, taking in every detail of the scene. Instead of a shadowy auditorium with a single work light dangling from a wire on stage, all the lights were blazing. Evidently Milhau was a sufficiently shrewd practical psychologist to realize that his cast would see all sorts of ghosts in dark corners and shady vistas. Adeane was standing near the footlights at the edge of the stage with a new book in a fresh dust jacket tucked under one arm. As he saw Basil and the others coming down the aisle from Milhau's office, Adeane leaned forward to greet Basil. "Well, doc, have you found out who killed Cock Robin yet?"

As Basil disliked being called "doc" by anyone except Inspector Foyle, he did not reply in kind to Adeane's jarring laugh.

Adeane seemed in unusually high spirits. His freckled, usually sallow face was flushed, and there was a reddish glint in his hazel eyes. Had he been drinking? Or had something more subtle than alcohol intoxicated him? He called loudly across the footlights:

"It was I,
Said the Fly,
With my little Eye . . ."

"Is this a confession?" murmured Basil.

Adeane laughed again. "Oh, no—I didn't do it, and I didn't even see it done. But I know whom I'd make the murderer if I were writing a play about it."

"Who?"

"That's telling." Adeane rattled on. "I must thank you for sending me to that medical library. I got enough dope on disease there to last me twenty years. When I got home I had aches and pains in every part of my body —head, heart, lungs, stomach, kidneys, and I would have had a pain in the pancreas if I'd known where the pancreas is! I read a lot about diseases of the pancreas in your friends Barr, Tice, and Cushny. A bit too technical for me, they were. But I got hold of a book by Victor Heiser that was really something. A lot of stuff about native medicine in India and so forth that was very interesting . . . ve-ry interesting indeed!" Adeane smiled his slow, thick-lipped smile which Basil had found so unpleasant from the first moment they had met.

On stage the first-act set looked as if it had not been touched since the other evening. Already the actors playing *Vladimir's* servants were gathering around the domino table for the opening scene, only this time they were in shirts and slacks instead of high-collared Russian blouses. Adeane's reddish hair and mustard tweed jacket stood out among them as he thrust his way to his seat at the domino table. Russell crossed the stage to the couch in the alcove. Adeane looked up and drawled with almost impish malice the very words he had spoken to Ingelow: "Hello, so you're the corpse!"

Russell stopped short. There was a deathly stillness. Then Milhau called out: "That isn't funny, Adeane! Go in the alcove and shut the door, Russell. We're ten minutes late already."

His top sergeant brusqueness restored order. But it could not scatter the unpleasant aftertaste of that moment. Russell entered the alcove. The double doors closed slowly, hiding him from view.

Leonard's voice spoke in Basil's ear. "It's absurd, but I hate the look of those closed doors. After what happened last time I wish I weren't the one who has to open them. I can't help being afraid I'll find him dead, though I know it's entirely unreasonable. I wonder why I feel that way?"

"Suggestion," answered Basil. "A scene can revivify memory just as intensely as an odor or a musical phrase. Memory has more to do with the senses than reason."

Leonard turned away to take up his place in the wings ready for his entrance a few minutes later. Milhau was sitting with an assistant producer in the second row center. Basil took a place beside Pauline in the third row.

"I don't like this," she whispered.

"Been reading about 'eternal recurrence' like Hutchins?"

"No, it's just—"

"What?"

"Suppose that by taking the part of *Vladimir* and seeing the action of the play from *Vladimir's* angle of vision this boy, Russell, will discover something about the action of the play that proves only one person could possibly murder *Vladimir* during the first act? And suppose the murderer realizes this? Then the boy wouldn't be too safe would he?"

"You do have the nicest ideas," said Basil. "But I've been over the script thoroughly, and I don't see any way *Vladimir* could learn something that was not known to any other observer on stage or in the audience."

"Everybody ready?" cried Milhau. "Shoot!"

The orchestra lights were dimmed but the stage remained a brightly lighted box.

One of the servants moved a domino. *Four!*

Six! cried Adeane.

Rehearsal had begun.

The full force of all Hutchins had said about eternal recurrence came home to Basil in the next few moments. To a layman there was something uncanny and even a little frightening about the way the actors repeated every word and inflection and gesture of the other evening as if they had ceased to be human beings and become mechanical toys who always did and said certain things when you wound up their springs. While one part of Basil's brain kept his eyes on his watch and his hands busy with a pencil noting the time of each entrance and exit on the margin of Rod's time table, another part of his brain was considering that law of intertia that makes momentum or habit such a tremendous power in the physical and psychical worlds. Everything was a part of it—planets and electrons going round and round the same orbits; Hindu marriage ritual still performed though its significance is forgotten; the intricate instincts of insects who also performed elaborate rituals without knowing why; the child who had to repeat a poem from the beginning in order to remember the last line; the embryo that has to recapitulate the development of the whole species before it can turn a cell into a man. No wonder the most evil and the most ridiculous beliefs became sacred once they were sanctioned by tradition. No wonder that "thinking is hard work while prejudice is a pleasure." Obviously it was initiative in both act and thought which taxed the nervous system most exhaustingly and unpleasantly. But habit like a buoyant tide of psychic momentum bore the actors through their parts and enabled them to perform prodigious feats of memory repeating page after page of dialogue without mistake or omission.

Once more the domino game was broken up by the ring of the doorbell. Once more Wanda swept into the room saying: *Is the master away?* This morning her stage presence had the same quality that had held Basil's attention the other evening; but she was less imposing in her plain black dress, and her lines seemed to come a little more rapidly.

"Are they taking it at the same pace they did the other night?" he asked Pauline.

"A shade faster," she answered. "They're nervous. That's why Sam made them have this run-through. It'll break the ice so they'll be all right tonight."

Again Wanda was at the fireplace. Again the doorbell rang. Again Leonard rushed into the room crying: *The count's room—quickly!*

Even without costume and make-up he seemed another man on stage—taller and more robust as he strode to the alcove and threw the doors open.

Pauline gasped and caught Basil's hand. Russell was lying on the couch exactly as *Vladimir* had lain, head turned to the audience, one arm dangling. It was as if time had been turned backward. Leonard opened his mouth and closed it as if he could not remember his next line. No one else moved or spoke. Then Russell shifted the position of his head. Someone laughed. It sounded like Adeane's laugh.

"Steady!" Milhau used his top-sergeant voice again. "Russell!"

"Yes, Mr. Milhau?" The "corpse" sat up on the couch with a grin. Basil could almost hear the tension relaxing all around him.

"Be careful not to move at all after the doors are opened. Get into as comfortable a position as you can, and then keep perfectly still. I know it isn't easy; but it can be done, and you're supposed to be in a coma."

"Yes, sir."

"O.K." said Milhau. "We'll start at the beginning again."

Pauline dropped Basil's hand with a sigh. "That's the first time I ever saw Leonard blow up in his lines."

Wanda, Leonard, and Hutchins left the stage. The corpse rose and closed the alcove doors. The servants sat around the domino table again.

"Shoot!" said Milhau.

Four!

Six!

Is the master away?

The count's room—quickly!

Every word, tone, shade of meaning was repeated with mechanical perfection as if they were seeing a movie twice over. This time when the double doors were thrown back there was no longer the same feeling of horror. They had been through that scene once this morning and nothing had happened. The evil spell was broken. Already the memory of the other evening was beginning to fade, to be replaced by other memories. Psychologically this repetition of *Fedora* was the best thing that Milhau could possibly have done for the actors in his company.

Russell lay still as a log. Rod, in tweed jacket and flannel trousers, was even more inadequate than ever as *Dr. Lorek. An accident?*

Attempted murder.

Rod moved into the alcove and opened his bag. This time there was no flash of steel. He stood between *Vladimir* and the audience, so no one could see what he was doing.

Fedora was sobbing. *I pray you, as I pray God—save his life!* Suddenly *Fedora* turned her back on *Lorek* and walked down to the footlights. She was Wanda Morley now and she spoke in an angry voice without a hint of sobbing: "What are you doing here?"

Her gaze went beyond the row of seats where Basil and Pauline was sitting. They turned and saw Margot Ingelow calmly ensconced in the seat behind them. She looked remarkably cool and fresh in a white linen dress printed with large, splashy black poppies. She wore a small white hat, and her head was tilted slightly to one side, a smile curving her lips.

"What are you doing here?" repeated Wanda.

"Enjoying myself."

"I will not go on with this rehearsal as long as that woman is in the theater!" cried Wanda.

Milhau came up the aisle and spoke in a low voice to Margot. "You shouldn't have come; but as long as you did, you'll have to make your peace with her somehow."

"Isn't it she who should make peace with me?" retorted Margot. "I didn't throw a glass of *liqueur* in her face!"

Milhau stood still for a moment, his eyes narrow and calculating. Then he said: "The only thing to do now is to tell her you're backing the revival."

"But you said she'd never stand for that!"

"She'll have to. This is the only way to rehabilitate her career, and she needs the money."

"Wanda Morley needs money!" Margot laughed. "I thought she was the actress who always wanted to lead a simple life in the suburbs. This is her opportunity!"

"You'll have to talk to her—nicely. Or else give up the whole thing."

"I'm never 'nice,'" returned Margot.

But she followed him down the aisle to the footlights where Wanda was standing. Wanda leaned down to speak to them, her face ugly with anger. Soon that look gave way to surprise. Evidently it had not occurred to her that Margot was backing the revival of *Fedora*. Milhau did most of the talking, waving his hands eloquently. Margot was silent and smiling. Finally with a shrug Wanda yielded. Basil decided she did need money pretty badly or she would never have accepted Margot's backing.

Magpie returned to her seat, and this time Milhau let the company go on from the point where they had been interrupted. But Wanda's acting had lost fire and conviction. Evidently Margot's presence troubled her.

With ambassadorial unction, Hutchins delivered the line Basil was waiting for: *He cannot escape now, every hand is against him.* Basil glanced swiftly at his watch again and noted the time. Leonard left the stage to search for *Vladimir's* murderer. Rod announced *Vladi-*

mir's death solemnly. . . . *Madame, it is the end.* . . .

Leonard re-entered through the door at left: *Gone!*

Wanda ran to the alcove. *Vladimir! Speak!* She threw herself across Russell's body, cradling his head in her arms as she had cradled Ingelow's. *Don't you know me? Speak! Ah!* She sank to the floor. It was the end of the first act.

But *Vladimir* lay still.

On stage every face was strained and rigid. Wanda rose. A topaz ring winked golden as she put out one slim hand cautiously and touched Russell's shoulder. "Are you all right?"

"Sure." He sat up grinning. "Is that the end of the act? Nobody told me!"

Everyone began to talk and laugh a little too loudly. Milhau interrupted. "Second act, please."

The second act set was brought down from the flies to stage level, and the second act began.

Basil paid little attention to the second and third acts of *Fedora*. He was lost in calculating the timing of the first act. He had to allow for the minutes lost by each interruption during the rehearsal and its slightly more rapid tempo. But at last he had worked it out. On the opening night the *Siriex* line—*He cannot escape now,*—must have occurred at the very moment Hutchins had surmised—twenty-four minutes after the curtain rose, that is at 9:04 if the curtain rose at 8:40. The estimates Rod had made of the exits and entrances in his original time table appeared to be equally accurate, if you assumed that the rehearsal was a shade too fast.

When Basil put down his pencil the third act was drawing to a close. This scene represented the garden of *Fedora's* villa in the Bernese Oberland. There was a backdrop of Bernese alps. In the middle distance there was a glimpse of the village of Thun beside a small lake. Then came a gateway and in the foreground a terrace with a profusion of flowers. Stage sunshine brooded over the scene for it was supposed to be an afternoon in May.

Rodney Tait's portrayal of *Loris Ipanov* in this scene was just as wooden as his portrayal of *Dr. Lorek* in the first act; but at least he was young and tall and well proportioned, and all those qualities suited the part. Wanda's black dress looked absurd against the country background, but her acting had regained some of its authority and enthusiasm. It was she who was supposed to die at the end of this scene and she was putting a great deal of feeling into her last moments. *It's getting dark . . . Everything is fading. . . . But, Loris. I'm not sorry to die. Life and love are unjust . . .*

A boy wearing shirt and slacks of pea-green cotton crossed the back of the stage beyond the garden gate singing in a rather sweet tenor: *My girl of the mountains . . .*

"What's he supposed to be?" Basil asked Pauline.

"A Savoyard peasant. The beach costume does mar the effect, doesn't it? But he'll be in peasant dress tonight."

I'm cold . . . Wanda was still dying. *Loris, where are you? I can't see you now. . . .*

I'm here, my darling! responded Rod as ardently as a man reading aloud a passage from the *Encyclopædia Britannica. Here to give you my forgiveness!*

Loris! sighed Wanda. *I love you!* Their lips met in a kiss that looked like a real one—the first suggestion of realism Rod's acting had achieved so far.

"She made him do that!" whispered Pauline furiously.

Wanda's head fell back on the cushions of a garden

seat. Rod sobbed aloud—three sobs a minute carefully`
timed. Hutchins laid a flower beside Wanda's hand.
Other actors—supposed to be Italian servants—knelt
and crossed themselves. The electrician off-stage pressed
a switch and the sunshine faded into a beautiful lav-
ender twilight.

Again like an echo the voice of the singing peasant
was heard off-stage: *My girl of the mountains . . . will
never come back. . . .*

If someone had set off a charge of dynamite the effect
could not have seemed more devastating. Wanda, so
gracefully dead, sprang to her feet shouting. Basil would
not have believed her carefully modulated voice could
become so strident: "Damn it, what did you do that
for?" was the mildest expression she used. Rod was
equally furious. "Haven't you any sense at all?" Hutchins
plunged through the frail garden gate into the wings
and reappeared dragging the boy in pea-green slacks
with him. "You know you shouldn't have done that!"
Everyone began to talk so furiously that it was impossible to hear a word. Leonard and the other actors in
the orchestra seats were as excited as those on stage.
Only two people besides Basil himself seemed undis-
mayed—Margot and Adeane. Even Milhau was red with
fury. He ran up three shallow steps that bridged the
footlights to the stage and confronted the boy in green.
"Who told you to do that?"

"Nobody. I just didn't think. After all, it isn't an ordinary rehearsal. We've already had one first night."

This was not the happiest excuse he could have offered. At mention of that first night the gabbling
tongues died away in silence.

"You're fired," said Milhau bitterly. "Get your money and go."

"Lissen, Mr. Milhau. I got a contract, and—"

Basil leaned toward Pauline. "What is the trouble?"

Her smile was faintly ironic. "You may have heard that stage people are superstitious. One of their pet superstitions is that the last line of a play must never be spoken at rehearsal. I suppose they wouldn't mind quite so much if they hadn't been jittery to start with. After all, this production has had its quota of bad luck already."

"Didn't the boy in green realize what he was doing?"

"I suppose not. I suppose he thought having had the opening already . . . But that was only one act. The whole production has never been shown in public, so technically this is a pre-production rehearsal."

"Aw, gee, Mr. Milhau," the boy was arguing. He was a plump, swarthy youth who had evidently been chosen for the part because his large, moist, black eyes and oily waves of black hair suggested the coarse vitality of a peasant. "It's just a superstition . . ."

The cackle of voices rose again. A tall, thin figure pushed its way through the crowd of actors on the stage clustered around Milhau and the boy.

"Mr. Milhau!" It was Russell. His voice broke like an adolescent's. "I'm sorry, but I can't play *Vladimir* tonight. I just can't. Not after that."

"Well, now, Russell, it's just a superstition," Milhau took over the boy's own argument glibly.

"You may call it superstition, but I believe in good luck and bad. I'm not going to play that part tonight."

"A hundred a week!" snapped Milhau.

"No," retorted Russell. "There's something fishy going on around here, and I don't like it. Why didn't you tell me about the murder when I applied for this job? Why did you get a new man like me instead of getting one of the actors who only appears in the last act to play *Vladimir* in the first? Why were you all so scared when I didn't move at the end of the first act? No, thank you, Mr. Milhau, you can get somebody else to play *Vladimir*. I haven't signed a contract yet, and I'm not going to!"

There was complete silence as Russell stalked down the steps and up the center aisle to the exit.

Before anyone could speak, Adeane left his seat in the orchestra and lounged down to the footlights, hands in his pockets. "I never heard such blasted nonsense in all my life!" he drawled scornfully. "Anybody'd think you were a pack of kids or savages the way you fuss over your taboos. I'm not an actor, thank God—I'm a dramatist just doing a little acting on the side, so I'm not superstitious. I walk under ladders all the time and spill salt whenever I get the chance. I'll be glad to play *Vladimir* if somebody else will play *Nikola*."

Milhau came down to the footlights. "Thank you, Adeane. I won't forget this. You'll get the same salary you're getting now, and let me know if there's anything else I can do for you."

"How about reading some of my plays?" responded Adeane with the same smile he had given Margot when he told her she "owed" him something.

Milhau swallowed and steeled himself to make a real sacrifice. "O.K. Give them to my secretary."

Adeane looked as if he were patting himself on the back. "Thanks, Mr. Milhau. I'll do that!"

But the rest of the company was uneasy. Wanda spoke. "Sam, do we have to go on with *Fedora?*"

Margot answered her: "Of course we do! It's all settled. Mr. Milhau and I between us would make things very unpleasant for anyone who broke a contract at the last moment."

"You heard the lady," said Milhau curtly. "The box office is sold out for weeks ahead, and no silly superstition is going to keep me from seeing that curtain rise tonight at 8:40 sharp!"

"What about me?" The boy in pea-green slacks looked at Milhau impudently.

"Oh—go to hell!" Milhau hurried back to his own office—the rehearsal was over.

CHAPTER ELEVEN

Behind the Scenes

BASIL HAD ALMOST FORGOTTEN his appointment to meet Lambert, the toxicologist, in Foyle's office at Police Headquarters late that afternoon. A taxi took him downtown through a twilight that the overcast sky turned into night. All the office buildings were gay with lighted windows, but it was no longer a pleasantly decorative sight to those who realized how ships bringing oil and sugar to New York were silhouetted against the glow of these towers for the benefit of submarines many miles at sea.

As Basil entered the Inspector's private office he heard the hollow, dehumanized voice of a radio announcer: "When you hear the time signal it will be just five o'clock, Naval Observatory Time . . ." As the whistle tooted he looked at his own watch and found that it was nearly ten minutes fast.

At the radio controls stood Lambert himself—a short, chunky man with a porcine face who looked more like a stockbroker or an insurance salesman than a biological chemist. The Inspector was hunched over his own desk, his lean, sharp face twisted into a frowning knot as he read Lambert's report on the knife handle.

"Just wanted to get the war news," explained Lambert. "But there doesn't seem to be any."

"The city of New York will have a complete practice black-out tonight between 14th Street and 125th from nine-thirty to nine-fifty," said the hollow voice. "In discussing plans for the dim-out, which will be enforced in the near future, General Wilkenson said—"

Foyle got up and turned off the radio. "What with black-outs and dim-outs and *saboteurs* and television lectures for air-raid wardens this place is becoming a mere branch of the War Department, and we have no time for ordinary murders. But we're learning a lot about the physics of high explosive and the chemistry of poison gas. Being a noncombatant in a modern war is a liberal education!"

"Of course there's no time for murder," returned Lambert. "With scores of men dying at sea every day to say nothing of Europe, Asia and Africa why should we care who murdered this John Ingelow?"

"Force of habit," suggested Basil. "A sort of hobby to keep up our morale."

"Morale, what crimes are committed in thy name!" added Lambert.

Foyle greeted Basil sourly. "Your bright idea about the knife handle is a dud. Look at this analysis. It might mean anything!"

Basil glanced at Lambert's report. "Chlorate of sodium . . . chlorate of potassium . . . minute quantities . . ." He turned to Lambert. "What does that suggest to you?"

"Well, chlorate of sodium and potassium are ingredients of human perspiration."

"Sure, sweat is always salt, like tears!" agreed Foyle.

"Loss of body salt through sweat is what causes heat prostration. But you said this stuff tasted sweet!"

"If you will take the trouble to read the whole report carefully you will see that I also identified glucose on the knife handle," returned Lambert with dignity. "Of course glucose is sugar, and the explanation is childishly simple; the knife handle was grasped by a perspiring hand that had just been touching sugar in some form. Once or twice I caught a faint odor about the knife— sort of like baked apple—whatever that came from, there wasn't enough to identify it as a chemical compound."

"What earthly good does that do us?" asked Foyle. "Anybody might handle sugar. Probably it was apple jelly and that's why you got an apple odor."

"Not exactly apple," mused Lambert. "More generalized . . . sort of fruity like—like—a fruit salad!"

Basil looked at Foyle. "Have you got any more background material?"

"Lots, but nothing of value," retorted Foyle. "Just about what you'd expect. Wanda Morley is a stage name. Her real name was Wilhelmina Minton. She was born in Rochester in 1900 which makes her just forty-two. She attended public school and ran away to join a theatrical company at the age of fifteen. Her father was foreman in some factory there—glue, I think. He reported her disappearance to the police at the time, but they couldn't find her. She seems to have had a pretty tough time the next twelve years doing all sorts of odd jobs more or less connected with the stage. She appeared in burlesque in Chicago and as an extra in Hollywood. She also sang with a jive band. At twenty-eight she had her first small part on Broadway in a Milhau production of a Noel Coward comedy. The show was a flop, but her performance was praised. In three years she was a star, and she has been with Milhau ever since. Maybe there was some sort of affair between her and Milhau at first, and that's why he pushed her up the ladder. I wouldn't know," the Inspector added austerely. Basil had a theory that Foyle had developed his almost Puritanically strict moral sense as a reaction to his life-long association with crime.

"What about the others?"

"Rodney Tait is another type. Tait is his real name. He was born in Boston, went to a small private school and then to Harvard. Took all sorts of drama courses there and appeared in amateur shows given by some club or other. I forget the cockeyed name of it. When he was graduated he became an instructor in French literature there for a year, but he got fed up with academic life and chucked it for the stage. I gather there was consternation in the family. They all say they have absolutely no prejudice against the stage or stage people but —etc. All his pals say he's a nice guy, but the older actors, who saw him in stock and on tour before he reached New York in *Fedora* say he can't act. They have absolutely no prejudice against amateurs but—etc. They say he always plays himself on the stage. I gather he's a sort of male ingenue, always the nice guy if you get what I mean."

"And Leonard Martin?"

"Ah!" Foyle grinned reminiscently. "I never heard of him before, but according to the stage people he's tops and would have been a star by now if he hadn't dropped out of sight for over a year a few months ago. It seems he comes of old stage stock. His father and mother used to play Shakespeare, and he was actually born in a dressing room backstage during a performance of *Macbeth*. As a boy he played all sorts of child parts from the time he was carried on as a baby at the age of three. Apparently he never went to any school and his parents spent a lot of time dodging policemen who tried to enforce the laws about child labor and school attendance. Result, he may not be educated, but he can act. His first real acting part was in the Mary Pickford production of the *Good Little Devil*. He made his first hit as a young man when he played the lead in a road company of *Young Woodley*. You remember that play about an English schoolboy who fell for his teacher's wife? Awful muck I thought, but the highbrows went for it in a big way. Anyway, it made Leonard Martin, and he's played every sort of part ever since—old, young, good, bad, comic, tragic, everything from *Iago* to *Raffles*. According to Sam Milhau, Leonard Martin is really good, and he would have been great if the modern public had been educated up to his acting and if he'd been about three inches taller. His small size made it possible for him to play boys of fifteen in his twenties, but now he's reached his forties he's not quite tall enough for the important male leads. For all his talent, the managers feel he can't quite get it across without those few extra inches. Still, he would've been a star by this time if he hadn't dropped out for a year or so when that Chicago business came up."

"What was that?" asked Lambert.

"He was mixed up in a nasty motor accident and served a prison term for manslaughter under another name."

"I suppose you checked with the Chicago police?" put in Basil. "Was there any doubt about his guilt?"

"None whatever. A little girl was killed. When the police caught up with his car, five minutes later, he was still at the wheel. He swore then and all through the trial that he wasn't drunk, but the motorcycle cop who caught him smelled liquor on his breath. There were tire marks from his car beside the kid's body and bits of her hair and dress on the front wheels of his car."

"I'm surprised the evidence of his drinking was so well established," said Basil. "He still denies it, and he doesn't seem like the sort of man who would be a drunken driver."

"I dare say he isn't habitually," retorted Foyle. "He may not have been roaring drunk; he may just have had an extra highball. Drivers always deny they're drunk unless they're out cold. As I see it, the whole thing was just a tough break—the sort of thing that might happen to any man in a moment of carelessness."

"What about Milhau?" asked Lambert. "Any dope on him?"

"Usual stuff. Born on the East Side and reached Broadway via Coney Island side shows. Good business man. His shows are often panned by the critics, but I don't believe he's ever really lost money on any of them. Claims he can always tell whether a script is a money-maker or not when he reads it because he gets a sort of shiver down his spine."

"A new version of the divining rod," murmured Basil.

"So where do we go from here?" Foyle sighed and ran both hands through his graying hair until it stood up on his head like the plumage of a cockatoo. "Two nights ago everybody was sweet and innocent and loved everybody else. Nobody knew who *Vladimir* was, and nobody could think of any motive for murdering him. Now in forty-eight hours we've just scratched the surface, and we've already got three motives: 1 Wanda Morley murdered Ingelow so she could inherit his fortune under a new will in her favor which she believed he had signed; 2 Margaret Ingelow murdered Ingelow so she could inherit his fortune before he had time to sign the new will in Wanda's favor; 3 Rodney Tait murdered Ingelow because he was in love with Wanda and jealous of Ingelow's affair with her."

"Are you quite sure Rodney was in love with Wanda?" asked Basil.

Foyle returned his gaze quizzically. "Well, she thinks so."

"And he?"

"He's sort of cagey about the whole thing. Naturally because he realizes it's the key to his motive. But they were seen together all the time in public places, and there was a tremendous lot of gossip about them. What more do you want?"

"Suppose I were to tell you that Rod has been engaged to another woman all along—a particularly nice girl?"

"I'd say he'd got himself in one sweet mess," retorted the Inspector. "It isn't the first time that a good-looking young man has got himself into such a mess either—especially if he's good-natured as well as good-looking and enjoys pleasing women and keeping the social atmosphere at a warm temperature."

Basil decided this was not an auspicious moment to mention Pauline's name. "Sometimes I think a popular man's desire to please everybody does more harm than the worst vices," he agreed blandly.

"Then there are at least three motives," resumed Lambert. "And of course, that's just two too many."

"In other words, this murder follows the same pattern in motive as in opportunity," responded Basil. "At first we had too many people with opportunity to commit the murder, and now we have too many people with motives. All three of these motives were matters of general public knowledge—two were rooted in a will, a matter of public record, and one in the affair between Wanda and Rodney which was widely publicized. It seems to me we were meant to discover these motives. It's all part of the murderer's plan to diffuse suspicion among as many people as possible."

"But we still have one advantage," insisted Foyle. "Opportunity limits our suspects to four people."

"No," said Basil. "Three—providing we accept Adeane's testimony that Margot Ingelow left the alcove before her husband entered it. Only Wanda and Rod have both motive and opportunity. Leonard had opportunity without motive and Margot had motive without opportunity."

"Can't you break down the alibi Adeane is giving Margot?" suggested Lambert.

"Adeane is thinking only of himself," answered Basil. "It's hard to tell whether he's telling the truth about Margot or whether he only gave her an alibi in the hope that she would repay him for it by backing his play."

"What about finding a motive for Leonard?"

"This was a premeditated murder," answered Basil. "The weapon—the situation—everything was prepared beforehand. That means that the motive must be unusually compelling. Almost anyone may kill on impulse, but premeditated murder must have a motive strong enough to sustain a mood of cold fury that nullifies all fear of punishment. It must be a motive that makes every alternative to murder seem intolerable. So far we haven't learned anything about Leonard that suggests a motive of such intensity."

"I don't want motives!" exclaimed Foyle. "I want evidence. And I don't see how I'm going to get it."

"I can see several possibilities." Basil turned to Lambert. "Have you tried a spectrograph on that knife handle?"

"Is it as important as all that?"

"It never hurts to try."

"I don't suppose you could give me any idea what to look for?"

"If I were you, I'd look for the constituents of butyric acid."

This remark had no effect on Foyle, but it seemed to startle Lambert. "You don't mean—?"

Basil cut him short. "I mean that every possibility should be tested."

"Any little job for me?" queried Foyle.

"You might try to find out more about the dark figure on the fire escape that night. If it was the murderer— what was he or she doing there? Why was Wanda's copy of the script dropped? And why was that line spoken by Hutchins marked?" I don't believe it was anything so melodramatic as a warning or a threat. This murder was planned by a neat, ingenious mind—not a flamboyant one."

"I've assumed all along that the figure was the murderer," said Foyle. "But I suppose it could have been anyone."

"Anyone who had a black cloak at the theater that night," answered Basil. "Or a cloak that would look black in a dim light. I saw Wanda, Leonard, and Rodney so soon after that incident they wouldn't have had time to change. Wanda was in yellow, Rodney in pale blue, Leonard in bright red. After the murder, when we searched the dressing rooms, we found that the men had no dark coats or cloaks they could have worn over their light-colored dressing gowns and suits. Wanda had a dark brown sable cloak that enveloped her from head to heels, but she told me this morning that it didn't reach the theater until just after the curtain rose—a long time after the incident. Margot Ingelow was wearing a long, sooty, black velvet cloak at the theater that evening, and Ingelow himself was wearing a black overcoat and black trousers when I saw him at the cocktail bar just beforehand."

"But what would either of the Ingelows be doing on the fire escape with Wanda's script?" demanded Foyle.

"I don't know. At the moment it seems as if it must have been one of them, and yet that doesn't fit any other detail of the crime as I see it now."

"It would make Mrs. Ingelow the most likely suspect," went on Foyle. "Don't you believe it's possible that she is the murderer?"

Basil rose and turned toward the door. "I shan't accuse anyone seriously until I find out exactly why the fly was attracted to the knife handle, and why the canary was let out of its cage."

Lambert laughed. "He knows—or guesses—a lot more

than he's telling, Inspector. Butyric acid!" The words seemed to fascinate Lambert. "That's what I call neat!"

II

That evening Basil dined at home without company. Juniper, waiting on table, noticed that his master was silent and preoccupied. They had reached the cheese and fruit course when the telephone rang in the hall. Juniper left the dining room. Basil heard his voice muffled by the closed door. A moment later he came back. "There's a Mr. Lazarus on the telephone," he announced.

"Lazarus?" Basil looked up from his figs with a frown.

He reached the telephone in a dozen quick strides. The voice on the wire had a small, far away sound that gave the words uncanny emphasis. It might have been a disembodied spirit calling faintly across the Styx.

"Dr. Willing? This is Lazarus, the knife-grinder in the alley beside the Royalty Theatre. Excuse me for bothering you; but something has happened, and you said—"

"What has happened?"

"Well . . ." The voice was still fainter. "Someone has been in my workshop again."

"Was the door forced open?"

"No, that wasn't necessary, because the broken window latch hasn't been repaired yet."

"Then how do you know anyone has been there?"

"Because of Dickie."

"Dickie?"

"My canary. Don't you remember? He's been let out of the cage again. I don't see why anybody should do such a thing but—somebody did."

CHAPTER TWELVE

Encore

A THRILL OF EXCITEMENT poured through Basil's nerves. He had a sharp sense of something ominous and evil. His taxi seemed to crawl through the westward traffic. He left it at the corner of 44th and Fifth and walked the rest of the way to the theater.

He had to cross the street to get past the box-office door. There was a great turn-out for the "second first night" of *Fedora* as one of the critics called it. The sidewalk in front of the theater was black with people and car after car discharged its load of sensation-hungry men and women—the same type that haunts dreary court-rooms during a spectacular murder trial. Milhau's taste might be questioned, but his business sense was beyond reproach.

Basil slipped through the crowd to the mouth of the alley—an inconspicuous figure this evening in a light overcoat and a soft felt hat. There was a light in the window of the knife-grinder's shack. Lazarus opened the door himself. His time-worn face was always so grave that it was hard to tell now if he were really more troubled than usual. He led the way to the bird cage. Dickie had decided on the avian equivalent of a night

229

raid on the ice box. He was plunging his beak into his seed cup so vigorously that the seeds were sprayed all around the floor of the cage. His small, beady black eye rolled as if he were enjoying such unaccustomed late hours.

"Are you sure he couldn't have escaped by himself this time?" asked Basil.

"Oh, no. I went out to get a bite to eat, and I left Dickie in his cage with the door securely latched. When I came back the cage was empty, and the door was standing open. Dickie was flying all around the room. I had some trouble catching him—I was afraid I might hurt him. He seems all right now but—after this I don't like to leave him alone here tonight. . . ."

Basil saw that to an old man without a future, without a family, and perhaps without friends, this pet canary meant more than an ordinary man leading a normally gregarious life could understand. "If you'll wait here until the performance is over, I'll see if the bird can't be taken elsewhere for a while."

"Thank you, I'll be glad to wait." Lazarus sat down at the grindstone and took up a pair of shears. "I have plenty of work to do."

Basil's glance fell on a long, red mark like the scratch of a cat's claw across Lazarus' forefinger. "Have you cut your hand?"

"Oh, that." Lazarus smiled. "See the scars?" He held out his hand, and Basil saw a dozen faint, thin white lines across the forefinger. "If you ever find an unidentified corpse with scars like that on his forefinger you'll know he's a knife-grinder. No matter how careful a grinder is he always cuts that part of his finger every few months."

At the stage door Basil saw one of the assistant producers. "Where is Mr. Milhau?"

"In his apartment, Dr. Willing. I'll show you the way."

"I know the way to his office already."

The man grinned. "His apartment is something else again."

They passed down a dimly lit passage and went up a narrow, enclosed stairway to the top of the theater. To Basil's surprise he was ushered into a comfortably furnished living room.

"Hello, come right in!" Milhau was holding a champagne cocktail in one hand, and his plump cheeks were flushed a bluish pink. His thick, pale lips stretched in a rubbery smile, but his eyes were glazed and unhappy. "I live in the country so I don't use this place much," he confided. "And then only when I'm in town for the night. It was built and furnished by the former owner of the theater."

Through a haze of cigarette smoke Basil saw a group of men and women clustered around a *buffet* supper table. They were mostly assistants and secretaries from Milhau's office; but Basil caught a glimpse of Margot's splashy black poppies on their white ground surrounded by a group of men, and he saw Pauline's light brown curls bronzed by lamplight.

"Aren't you going to watch the performance?" he asked Milhau.

"Oh, yes." Milhau chuckled like Santa Claus with a surprise in his pack. "Grab a cocktail and a plate of creamed chicken, and I'll show you."

"I've just had dinner, thank you."

Milhau led the way to the end of the room where

Pauline and Margot were sitting. He stepped to the wall and touched a spring. A panel in the wall slid back noiselessly. Basil looked down through the opening into a brilliantly lighted world. The walls were painted red and blue and green. There was a silver samovar in front of a fireplace and a table set for dominoes in the center. It was an oblique of the stage.

"Mrs. Ingelow didn't want to appear in public this evening," went on Milhau. "So I told her we could watch the whole performance very comfortably from up here without anyone knowing she was in the audience."

Basil's glance circled the stage. "You can't see the alcove from this angle?"

"Only when the doors are open. Then we get a foreshortened view of it."

Basil told Milhau about the canary.

"That's too bad. Lazarus is attached to that bird. He's had it three or four years. I can't understand anyone playing a joke on a nice old man like that."

"It happened before you know. Just before the other murder."

"I know, but what can I do?"

"Why not tell Adeane he needn't play *Vladimir?* You could use a dummy tonight."

"A dummy always looks like a dummy." Milhau pouted like a spoiled child. "A rich man like Ingelow is always making enemies, but nobody has it in for Adeane. He's a harmless little guy who writes bum plays. Just because he's playing *Vladimir* doesn't mean his life's in danger. Besides—"

"Besides what?"

"It's too late now."

Basil's glance followed Milhau's through the gap in the wall. The curtain was rising.

By this time Basil knew that wretched play of Sardou's by heart. Even the fact that he was seeing it from a bird's-eye view failed to give it any novelty. He marveled at the ability of the actors to put so much freshness and vitality into those never-to-be-forgotten lines.

Four! Six! Is the master away?

"Too fast, too fast!" muttered Milhau in real distress.

Basil, his eyes on the stage, heard Pauline's voice: "They're nervous. All of them."

He turned his head to smile at Pauline and caught the glitter of triumph in Margot's eyes. After all, this was why she was doing it—to rasp all their nerves until the guilty one broke down.

It was impossible to see the actors' faces. Even their figures were rudely foreshortened. But their voices came through clearly, each one taut and humming as wire stretched to breaking point. Their words tumbled out of their mouths faster and faster, as if they were frightened amateurs. The gestures that were so carefully formed the first night and even at the rehearsal were sketchy and blurred now—rather like a shorthand version of something that had been written in precise script.

"I'm glad the audience is here from morbid curiosity," whispered Milhau. "Nothing else would hold them in their seats with a performance like this!"

"I don't like the effect of that white dress of Wanda's," said Pauline suddenly. "It is too stark and bleached for such a somber background."

The count's room—quickly!

The people clustered around the peephole could

feel the breathless hush in the unseen audience below as Leonard threw back the double doors. From this angle they could just see the hump under the coverlet made by Adeane's body and the arm that dangled, but his head was hidden from view.

"Well, anyway he didn't move this time," said Milhau.

Just then Adeane's arm shifted slightly. It was hardly more than a shiver, but the audience must have seen it. There was a single shrill titter. Then a ripple of giggling—cheerless and hysterical. Milhau swore under his breath. Margot was vastly amused. Pauline was worried.

From that moment on the actors on stage completely lost their heads. Wanda forgot her next line, and the prompter's voice could be heard plainly. A moment later the same thing happened to the veteran Hutchins. They could not recover the sympathy of the audience. Giggles greeted the most serious lines in the play. At first Basil thought it was purely the hysteria of a morbid audience. Then he realized that the hysteria was in the actors, not in the audience. Their acting was so bad tonight that they were making the play a burlesque of itself. It was vividly brought home to Basil that the acting of Wanda's company rather than Sardou's lines and situations had made the performance two nights ago seem interesting and lifelike. This play was anything but "actor-proof."

Everything that was false or faded in Sardou's ideas of love or politics or play construction was mercilessly emphasized by the ragged performance. Every flaw in each individual actor's technique and personality was exposed. Wanda seemed a gushing *poseuse;* Hutchins a pompous, declamatory windbag. When Hutchins said: *He cannot escape now, every hand is against him* a male voice laughed outright. Yet Hutchins didn't say it so very differently from the way he had said it the other evening. The ambassadorial dignity was only a shade more flamboyant. Even Leonard lost his magic touch and gabbled the part of *Grech.* Rod was phlegmatic as usual when he first came on as *Dr. Lorek,* but the giggling of the audience soon got him so on edge he could hardly remember a single line. An almost clinical demonstration of partial amnesia from shock, Basil decided.

"Oh, God!" muttered Milhau.

"What now?"

"He skipped ten whole lines. They can't go back and pick them up. That this should happen to me! My best company—Wanda and Leonard and Rod—laughed at when they're in a serious play! It'll ruin them and me too! What will the critics say?"

Margot looked as if she could bear it.

"I saw something like this in London once," said Pauline. "The Gate Theatre players did a version of *Little Lord Fauntleroy.* They didn't alter a single line of the original play but by acting absurdly and putting the wrong emphasis on every line they made it perfectly hilarious—much more subtle than an ordinary burlesque."

"Sure, and look what happened to the Broadway version of *Vient de Paraitre,*" added Milhau. "That was the play about the little nobody who became a best selling author overnight through a fluke. When the curtain rises on the second act he's sitting at an enormous desk with an enormous portrait of himself on the wall behind him. It was supposed to be serious, but the minute the curtain rose on that scene the first night the audience laughed its head off. So after that they played the whole thing as low comedy."

"Couldn't you pretend that you had intended this as a travesty of *Fedora* all along?" suggested Basil.

"Too late for that now," moaned Milhau. "All the write-ups have been serious. Wanda's a serious actress!"

The climax of the first act had come. *Dr. Lorek* came down stage from the alcove. *This is the end.*

Vladimir! Wanda, now a vision in white velvet and ermine instead of gold tissue and sable, sped upstage to Adeane. *Speak!* She lifted slender arms like a white swan spreading its wings, and suddenly, like the legendary death cry of the swan, a raucous shriek came from her lips. She dropped like a bird winged in flight and rolled down the three shallow steps that led from the alcove to the rest of the stage. The audience laughed and laughed and laughed. It was so funny the way everyone on stage was overacting this evening—even Wanda Morley!

Milhau was at the telephone. "Ring down that curtain! Tell 'em Wanda is sick. We can't go on like this, or we'll be ruined! Give 'em their dough back, and tell 'em to get the hell out of here—politely, of course. . . . What? WHAT?"

Milhau put the receiver back as if it were too heavy for him to hold. His plump cheeks sagged. Pauline looked at him, her blue eyes bright with fear of the unknown. Margot was still cool and composed, even smiling a little. Would anything short of a kick from a mule ever stir that woman wondered Basil. It was Margot who spoke: "Something wrong? Wanda?" she asked in her small, crisp voice. Basil realized that she hoped something was wrong with Wanda. Perhaps that was her inmost reason for reviving *Fedora*.

"No." Milhau answered her, but he was looking at Basil, dully, uncomprehendingly. "No, not Wanda. I could understand that. I mean . . ."

"What is it?" cried Pauline in a voice that cracked.

Milhau answered in the same lost voice. "Adeane. Just like the first time. Only there was more blood and —Wanda saw it. That was when she shrieked."

II

The medical examiner had gone. Men from the Department of Public Welfare had come to take the body. In the glare of a baby spotlight focused on the alcove, Basil stood taking his last look at Adeane. *My life is so dull . . . nothing ever happens to me . . .*

Basil left the alcove and walked down to the footlights where Inspector Foyle was standing with a knife in his hand—a surgeon's scalpel with a grooved handle of tarnished silver and a newly sharpened blade.

"Same sort of knife—same wound—stabbed any time within the last hour, and the first act lasts almost an hour. Again, a dozen witnesses saw the victim enter the empty alcove alone and shut the door. Again, only three actors entered the alcove during the performance, and it was the same three—Wanda Morley, Rodney Tait, and Leonard Martin."

Basil touched the knife handle with his fingertips. It was sticky. "Better send it to Lambert."

Foyle laid the knife on the domino table, beside a new

book still in its dust jacket. "This book was in his pocket—Victor Heiser's autobiography. Deals mostly with medical experiences in the tropics. What would Adeane want with that?"

"Material for a play no doubt." Basil turned the pages slowly. "He said something about reading Heiser at the medical library."

Foyle looked more puzzled than ever. "Why Adeane?"

Basil smiled. "He had no tact. No, I'm not joking. He really had so little sympathy—so much egoism that he could not put himself in the position of others—including the murderer. Violence fascinated Adeane but he had no personal experience of it until tonight. He got his sadism from the German psychologists and the hard-boiled novelists. Murder was never quite real to him. He didn't understand how real it is to a murderer. How terribly in earnest a murderer can be when he thinks his own life or liberty is at stake. Adeane discovered something. Perhaps that's why he was in such an odd state of elation this afternoon—intoxicated with a new sense of power. It must be quite an experience to bait a murderer—like teasing a tiger. But I think that's what he did. . . .

"Instead of coming to you or me with his discovery, he tried to blackmail the murderer. I don't mean that Adeane sneaked up to the murderer in a dark corner and hissed: *Ten thousand dollars by midnight or I will tell all!* I don't believe it was even blackmail for money. I think he wanted to enlist the murderer's help in getting his precious play produced. That was an obsession with him. And just as he hinted to Margot Ingelow that she owed him something for his giving her an alibi, I suppose he let the murderer know indirectly by some hint or innuendo the nature of the thing he had discovered assuming mistakenly that the murderer would buy his silence by helping with the play."

The Inspector was dubious. "Would a man connive at murder just for the sake of getting a play produced?"

"Ask any unproduced playwright! No, seriously, Adeane was a completely callous egoist, consumed with his own ambition. These men with vast ambitions and slender talents who prey on the arts since the arts became profitable in the last hundred years or so are not quite human. If you have no talent you have to rely on tricks in order to get on, and such a career hardly develops the ethical sense. If you had cornered Adeane he would have said that the thing he discovered didn't prove murder absolutely, so he wasn't really sure of it; but it did cast suspicion in a certain direction, and so . . . what's the harm in making use of that? Such things are done in business every day old man, so why not in play producing, etc., with a wink and nudge, one man of the world to another.

"He played with murder as innocently as a child plays with a loaded gun, and—the gun went off. What we must ask ourselves now is simply this: What did Adeane know that no one else knew?"

"You say Adeane was the witness who gave Margot Ingelow her alibi?" said Foyle. "Could that have anything to do with it?"

"Hardly likely since Margot Ingelow was with Pauline, Milhau, and me tonight when the second murder was committed. She seems to be cleared."

"How did Adeane happen to take the part of *Vladimir?*" asked Foyle.

There was a sudden glint of amusement in Basil's eyes.

"That question can be answered easily, if you send for the boy who was to have played the singing peasant boy in the last act."

A few moments later a patrolman escorted the peasant boy onto the stage. He really looked like a peasant now in the gay green and red costume Pauline had designed for him—a handsome, virile peasant with gold earrings in the lobes of pointed, faun ears under the wavy black hair.

"Tell the Inspector what you did at rehearsal this afternoon," said Basil.

The moist black eyes rolled uneasily. "Aw, gee it was only a gag. I spoke the last line, and they all got mad at me. It's supposed to be bad luck. The guy who was gonna play *Vladimir* says he won't play, and then Adeane says he'll do it, he's not superstitious. What the heck, it wasn't my fault. How could I tell that—that—" The boy's eyes rolled toward the alcove. There was nothing there now but the crumpled coverlet on the couch. He swallowed and dropped his eyes. His hands were twitching.

Basil's voice came into the silence quietly. "How much did you get for that?"

"Ten bucks." The boy kept his eyes on the ground.

"From whom?" cried Foyle eagerly.

"Don't you know?" The boy looked up in surprise. "From Adeane himself. He *wanted* to play *Vladimir*."

The Inspector was disappointed.

"All right, you can go," said Basil.

The boy scuttled through the wings to the stage door.

"Why on earth did Adeane want to play *Vladimir?*" demanded Foyle. "In order to test some theory about

240

the murder by seeing the play from *Vladimir's* point of view?"

"Nothing so impersonal and disinterested," returned Basil. "He did it to attract Milhau's attention to himself and his plays, and he succeeded. He actually got Milhau to say he'd read the stuff."

"And then—just as he got his first real chance—he was murdered." Foyle brooded. "If only he'd given us a hint of what he knew—"

"He wasn't interested in helping us. Adeane was never interested in anything but Adeane."

Foyle turned back to the knife on the table as if he greatly preferred a tangible clue to all these tenuous suppositions. A new idea came to him. "Did Rodney Tait carry that surgical bag on stage tonight?"

"Yes, but the bag was empty. This afternoon all the remaining knives were left in Milhau's office safe."

"Were they counted first?"

"No. Rod just dumped them on Milhau's desk in a heap. Anyone in the theater could have helped himself to a knife before they were put in the safe."

"They should have been counted. I'll have to ask Tait a thing or two about that." Foyle rose grimly. "I'm going to question the whole bunch now in Milhau's office. Want to come?"

"No, I think I'll look around here a bit."

The plywood door at left quivered after Foyle's departure. Alone, Basil prowled restlessly around the stage. He had little faith in the sort of inquisition going on now in Milhau's office. Official questions put people on guard. They only let slip the important things in their unguarded moments when everything was casual and spontaneous. Foyle had left Adeane's copy of Dr.

Heiser's autobiography on the table. Apparently he thought it of no importance. Again Basil turned the pages. Why had Adeane bought the book when it was available at the medical library? A passage on native medical diagnosis in India caught Basil's eyes. He read it with growing interest. . . .

A light footstep distracted him. He turned and saw Margot through the gap in the wings at left. She paused. "It's all right, Dr. Willing. The Inspector questioned me first and said I could go."

He waited as if he expected something more of her. She came through the wings onto the stage. She was carrying the white hat; the smooth brown hair was slightly disordered, the black and white linen dress crumpled. She looked tired. As they were on the stage, he gave her a cigarette and lighted it.

She sank into *Fedora's* armchair before the fire. "You hold me responsible for this latest development don't you?"

"I haven't said so."

"But you've looked it."

"I'm more responsible than you," he replied soberly. "I felt it was all wrong this morning at rehearsal, but I didn't put a stop to it because it was only a feeling— nothing positive."

"I don't think either of us is responsible," she answered. "People make their own lives and their own deaths. Adeane made his. He was the sort of fool who would think it smart to bait a murderer."

Basil held out his hand. "Will you give me the staples you took from his manuscript?"

She looked at him astonished and indignant. "I don't know what you mean!"

"Will you let me see your bag?"

She hesitated. Gently he took it from her—the same patent leather bag she had carried yesterday. He opened it. There were all the usual things—coin purse, handkerchief, lipstick. He opened the zipper compartment. There were a pair of brass staples, and other things— a diamond ring, a bright new paper clip, a tin bottle top, a small pair of gold nail scissors, a shining new copper penny, a glass clip from some Woolworth store, and a scrap of tin foil.

"How did you know?" she asked him.

"You were called Magpie—behind your back. They are extraordinary birds, famous for other things besides their black and white plumage. They are crafty; they imitate human speech like parrots and—they have a trick of stealing and secreting anything that glitters, regardless of its value. Anything from a diamond ring to a scrap of tinfoil. They are almost the only animals who can be considered kleptomaniacs. When I saw your flushed face and shining eyes the day Adeane's staples disappeared I was sure of it. Some nicknames are friendly. Others are derisive. Magpie is that sort."

She took it calmly as if it were an old story to her. "Would you base such a serious charge on a pair of staples and a nickname?"

"I'm not making any charges. But there are one or two points that must be cleared up between you and me. No one else need know anything about it. Was this the cause of your quarrels with your husband? The thing that drove him to Wanda Morley?"

Margot's detachment was almost inhuman as she answered calmly. "Yes. He didn't mind my—taking things, but he said I was . . . cold and unfeeling. . . . You—

a psychiatrist—don't have to be told that people like me usually have a sort of emotional numbness."

Basil nodded. He had had many such cases among patients of less wealth and influence than Margot. He had had disputes with many magistrates who refused to believe that a poor man or woman could steal for any motive other than want. Sometimes they were boys— more often girls for girls were apt to be brought up more strictly than boys. Always the kleptomania had been associated with extreme prudery or frigidity. The pathological thief always prided herself on her moral "purity" and insisted in self-defense that stealing was a far less serious offense than "sin." Yet the pleasurable excitement she derived from uneconomic stealing was obviously erotic. Like the pyromaniac she simply transferred the orgiastic emotions from sex to something else that was also immoral but not in her opinion so "obscene" and "wicked." It was another curious example of the way civilized society's condemnation of nature tends to encourage perversion in myriad forms.

"It started at school, when I was about fourteen," said Margot with the same inhuman calmness. "Things disappeared. There was a secret investigation, and I was caught. They didn't expel me publicly. They just asked my parents not to send me back at the end of the term. I was taken to doctors and so forth, but it didn't do any good."

"Ingelow knew nothing about this when he married you?"

"No. We didn't have the same circle of friends. We met at a horse show. I think it was my calmness and detachment that attracted him to me at first. My parents were delighted. They were old-fashioned, and they believed that marriage would cure any little aberrations of mine. Of course it didn't. I just don't have the sort of feelings about love and marriage and children that most women have. I can't help it. I'm made that way. And yet, the funny part of it was that I did really love John as much as I could love anyone, only I just couldn't show my feelings. Wanda didn't love him at all. But she has strong sensual feelings for all men, and no false shame about exhibiting them. So—he thought she loved him. She's the sort of woman who sees the unhappy marriage of another woman as her opportunity. The moment I took her home and introduced her to John she saw how things were with us and went after him.

"I've learned a lot in the last few months. I've learned that appearances are far more important than actuality. I've learned that to most people—certainly to most men —love is primarily a sensation and only secondarily a sentiment. But all this knowledge has come too late to me to do any good. I know these things intellectually, but emotionally I don't know them at all.

III

When Margot had gone, Basil went down the aisle to Milhau's office. The little room was crowded. Foyle sat at Milhau's desk. Wanda, Rod, and Pauline were looking surprised and angry. Leonard seemed tired; Hutchins, worried; and Milhau himself embarrassed.

"I didn't mean any harm," Milhau was saying as Basil came in. "Glamour is part of a star's stock in trade. She's got to have some guy with her wherever she goes. She can't pop into a restaurant by herself as if she were a nobody. And she's got to have some fellow falling for her all the time. I didn't know about Ingelow and

Wanda because they were keeping it dark until he got his divorce. When he was off in Panama, Wanda started going around by herself. That was awful—bad publicity for her and for the show. I told her to get herself an escort if she had to hire one, but she just laughed at me. Something had to be done so I talked it over with my publicity boys and one of them cooked up this scheme. He got it out of Shakespeare."

"What?" interrupted the Inspector incredulously.

"Sure. Why not? There's a play of Shakespeare's about a couple named Beatrice and Benedick. They don't care a hoot about each other, but their pals play a joke on them by telling Beatrice that Benedick's nuts about her and *vice versa*. So I told Wanda that Rod was nuts about her, and I hinted to, Rod that Wanda was falling for him. They were both flattered. She began asking him to go places with her, and he didn't dare refuse. I had a camera man trail them whenever they were together, and the publicity boys saw the shots were published with captions and—"

"Why, you—"

"So that was—"

"You nasty little beast!"

The three exclamations came from Wanda, Pauline, and Rodney. All three were converging on Milhau. He backed toward the desk as close to the Inspector as he could get. "Now—now—don't get excited!" begged Milhau. "You know it's an old Hollywood custom—these publicity romances. People aren't going to fall for a glamour girl on stage or screen if she's a dud off stage and—"

"Dud!" shrilled Wanda.

"In Hollywood the victim of the 'romance' is in on the secret!" cried Pauline.

Rod doubled his fist and advanced on Milhau without saying anything.

"Listen to reason will you?" Milhau scuttled around the desk, putting the Inspector between himself and Rod. "It was for your own good. I was building you up as a male lead by making every newspaper reader think Wanda was nuts about you—"

"Am I interrupting?"

Everyone turned. Lazarus was standing in the doorway. In one hand he held the bird cage under its burlap cover. His eyes sought Basil. "You said I could leave Dickie in some other place tonight where he would be safer."

This concern for the safety of a pet canary when a human being had just been murdered should have been funny. But no one laughed or even smiled. Milhau's little publicity stunt was forgotten immediately. In a loaded silence, Foyle rose and took the bird cage. He pulled off the cover and set the cage on Milhau's desk. Dickie was asleep, head tucked under one wing. As light smote him suddenly, the head came out and the eyes blinked, but he remained on his perch, a little ball of yellow feathers, as if the presence of so many strangers frightened him.

"This is the canary I told you about," said Foyle. "You'll agree it's a rather curious coincidence, and it has occurred twice. Before each of these murders this canary has been let out of its cage. On both occasions the knife used was sharpened recently—presumably in Mr. Lazarus' workshop across the alley. That explains why the murderer broke into the workshop, but it doesn't explain why he released the canary. Can anyone suggest an explanation? Miss Morley, perhaps you can tell us."

"No. I can't." Wanda was staring at the bird. Her face was twisted out of its usual shape by some fierce emotion. Basil thought it was fear.

"You're sure this wasn't another publicity stunt of some sort, Mr. Milhau?" went on Foyle.

"No." Milhau seemed honestly puzzled. "I tell you what, Jake," he said to Lazarus. "You can leave the bird here in my office if you like. I'll lock the door."

Foyle shut his notebook with a snap and rose.

"Can we go now?" queried Hutchins wearily.

"Yes, that'll do for tonight. But you must all hold yourselves ready for questioning tomorrow."

"Where shall I put Dickie?" Lazarus asked Milhau.

"He'll be O.K. right on the desk." Milhau helped to readjust the burlap cover.

As the others moved toward the door, Hutchins laid a hand on Basil's arm. "Funny about Sam adapting Shakespeare to a modern publicity stunt, isn't it?"

"Yes." Basil looked at Hutchins questioningly.

"Shakespeare is applicable to so many modern situations," went on Hutchins gravely. "All evening I've been trying to recall a line from *Othello*. It goes something like this: *Were it my cue to murder I should have known it without a prompter. . . .*"

Foyle was standing at the door of the outer office, a bunch of keys in his hand. He pressed an electric switch in the wall. Light flooded the lobby beyond. The silence was shattered by a woman's scream.

It was Pauline. Rod hurried to where she was standing—just inside the lobby beyond the door.

"Anything wrong?" said Foyle sharply.

"No. It's nothing. I'm—I'm sorry." She shrank away from all of them. Her face was almost as distorted as Wanda's had been a moment ago and by the same emotion—fear. She tried to smile, but her mouth only quivered. "My nerves must be on edge."

Basil's glance surveyed the lobby. It was empty except for one uniformed policeman standing against a red velvet curtain weighted with gilt fringe.

"You didn't see anything or anybody?" persisted Foyle.

"No. I—I just stumbled." Her eyelids dropped. "I'd like to go home now. Right away."

"All right." Foyle switched off the light in Milhau's office and locked the door on the outside with a key from the bunch he held. "Going my way, doc?" he said to Basil.

"No. If you don't mind I'm going to stay here a little longer."

The little group of people in the lobby halted. Pauline turned. "You're going to stay here alone?"

"If I may?" Basil looked at Foyle.

"Sure. Why not?"

"Do you think it's quite safe?" asked Leonard.

"He won't be entirely alone," Foyle answered for Basil. "We always leave a patrolman on guard at the scene of a murder for a day or so."

"Only one?" cried Pauline. "In a huge place like this?"

"It's largely a matter of form," answered Foyle.

"We've finished the investigation here. Anything that could shed light on the crime—even a section of scenery that was splashed with blood—has been removed to the police laboratories."

"Still . . ." Pauline looked at the sheer walls of the auditorium and the vaulted ceiling half lost in shadows. "One man . . ."

"Let me stay with you," said Rod to Basil.

"No, I'll be all right." Basil smiled as if he didn't think Rod would be much help in any circumstances.

"I don't like the idea Dr. Willing," said Hutchins seriously.

"Neither do I," put in Wanda. "But Dr. Willing is very obstinate."

Basil turned to Milhau. "May I borrow your keys?"

"The Inspector's got them now. He's running everything around here."

Foyle handed the bunch of keys to Basil. "You can leave them with the patrolman when you go." As the others drifted away, he went on in a low voice. "What's the big idea?"

"The theater is the setting of both murders. I want to study its topography and absorb its atmosphere."

"Sure you don't want me to stay?"

"No, thanks. I can do better alone."

Foyle looked down through the glass doors to the outside lobby. The others were leaving by the box office door. "What do you think of that bunch? Do they know anything?"

"At least four of them did—and one of the four is dead now."

"Who are the other three?"

"Pauline, Hutchins, and Wanda."

"What about putting tails on all of them?"

"I wouldn't. I'd give them a little more rope. . . ."

III

After Foyle's departure, Basil went down the aisle and crossed the stage. Beyond the wings he re-discovered the enclosed stairway that led to Milhau's apartment. The door was locked, but he found the key on Milhau's ring and unlocked it. When he switched on the light he saw everything just as they had left it—soiled plates and glasses in disarray on the supper table, chairs gathered before the panel in the wall, the panel itself pulled back to reveal the stage below. Even the stage was unchanged. Again he was looking down on *Vladimir's parlor in the antique Muscovite style with Parisian decorations.* Footlights and spotlights had been turned out, but a single work light was burning.

He spent some time examining the apartment without discovering anything of interest. Then he sat down wearily in one of the armchairs. He smiled a little as he remembered Mark Twain's advice to an apprentice author who had got into difficulties with his own plot: *Have you tried thinking?* The same advice held good in solving a complex crime. He reviewed the case from beginning to end—from the moment in the Washington plane when he had read the item about the canary in a newspaper to the moment when Pauline had screamed in the lobby just now. Slowly the churning sediment of his disturbed thoughts began to settle to the bottom of his mind leaving the clear essence of the case on top. That was the real reason he had wanted to stay in the theater after the others were gone—so he could be utterly alone in an empty place where he could hear himself think. From the first he had suspected the murderer. Now he was morally certain of the murderer's guilt. How was he going to prove it in court? He would have to rely on Lambert's evidence once the knife handles had been subjected to a spectroscope. That was rather a pity because most juries didn't like chemical evidence . . . too technical . . .

Motion drew his eye to the gap in the wall. Far below something was moving across the shadows of the dimly lighted stage. Startled, he leaned forward. Whatever had moved was gone.

He waited. Again there was movement. Now he saw it clearly, in the path of the work light—a small yellow bird—a canary—flying across the stage.

CHAPTER THIRTEEN

Alarums and Excursions

BASIL WENT to the switch and turned out the apartment lights. Then he closed the door and went down the enclosed staircase. His footfalls sounded loud in the stillness. He had no idea if they could be heard beyond the walls that enclosed the stairs. At the foot he paused to listen. There was no sound. He opened the door and stepped across the wings to the stage.

A few hours ago it had been all lights and bustle. Now the work light—a single bald bulb dangling from a wire in the roof—made a patch of sickly white light in the shadowy stillness. A sudden flutter startled him. Again the canary flew across the patch of light and perched on a rope attached to a pulley overhead. Eyes like black pinheads shone in the faint light.

The murmur of traffic from the world outside only seemed to underscore the silence here. There was something disturbing about that silence—a sense of something beyond it, listening and waiting and watching. No wonder the haunted house is always the empty house he thought, as he left the patch of light and stepped into the deep shadow of the wings.

The double doors leading to the bedroom alcove stood

open, as they had stood to-night when the curtain fell, but now the curtain was raised. A faint glow from stars and lighted buildings seeped through a small window in the lobby back of the topmost balcony. In that diluted darkness, Basil faced row upon row of empty seats rising in tiers toward the domed ceiling like something vast and dim in a nightmare. He stood listening to the stillness. There was something else. The sound of a footfall on the other side of the backdrop. He was not alone.

He crossed the stage to the wings at left. He saw only darkness, but he heard footsteps receding. He snapped on his flashlight. The small beam painted monstrous shadows on the dusty tangle of wires and ropes flanking the stage. One of the looped wires was swinging gently to and fro as if someone had brushed it in passing. Underneath it something like a bundle of clothes lay on the floor. He hurried forward and found Pauline.

Forgetting his own danger, he knelt beside her. Dark in the faint light, a thin stream of blood trickled across her wrist. Basil laid his flashlight on the floor and searched for the source of the hemorrhage. To his relief he found it was only a flesh wound in the upper part of the right arm. With a penknife he cut away the sleeve and improvised a dressing with a clean handkerchief of his own. As he worked, he was conscious of a faint odor, familiar yet elusive. He noticed something white on the floor. It was a large white handkerchief, damp and sticky to the touch. When he picked it up the faint odor grew a little stronger. It came from the handkerchief—evanescent and rather sweet like a breath of wind from an orchard. He thrust it in his pocket.

Pauline stirred and opened her eyes. "W-what?"

"You're all right," Basil reassured her. "Just a flesh wound that nicked a vein. How did it happen?"

"Someone jumped at me in the darkness. I couldn't see who it was. I lifted my arm to shield my head. There was a sharp pain in my arm. I don't remember anything after that."

"Why did you come back here?"

"To warn you. It was the red curtain—the one with the gold fringe—I mean when I screamed. I couldn't explain before him, but I saw—"

"Yes. I know. It's all right."

"I should have thought of it sooner. After all it's my job to know about colors."

"How did you get in?"

"I was going to pound on the door until you heard me. But then I saw the fire door at the top of the fire escape was open."

"I'm going to find him." Basil handed her his flashlight. "Keep this on, and if you see anyone, yell."

Basil crossed the stage to the door at left and passed through to the region backstage. Out here on bare boards his footfalls were hollow and echoing through the auditorium. Would there be an echo in a theater building designed with special attention to acoustics? He stopped walking. The echo went on. It was not an echo at all. Someone else was walking toward the fire escape on the other side of the stage set—someone who must have been crouching in the wings listening to his talk with Pauline. Basil might be able to reach the fire escape ahead of this other person if he turned back and crossed the stage.

Moving as quietly as possible, he returned and

through the door at left crossed the stage to the right wing. On the stage itself there was still the vague light from the window behind the top balcony. Beyond the wings there was still that one patch of light cast by a single electric bulb. But in the maze of wings just beyond the wall of *Vladimir's* parlor the shadows deepened into darkness. And he had left his flashlight with Pauline.

As he stepped into that margin of darkness, a slight sound startled him. He turned his head. He had a fleeting impression of a shadow moving among the other shadows that were still. The image had hardly registered on his retina when something heavy collided with his shoulder. He struck out at it, and his knuckles grazed rough cloth. It pulled away from him with such a violent wrench that he was thrown against a flimsy wall of lath and canvas. Again he was conscious of that vague, sweetish odor. Someone was breathing hard quite near him in the darkness. Then footfalls clattered on the boards, receding again. Someone was running away.

He tried to follow the sound, but he came up flat against a wall of lath and canvas. He groped his way through the wings toward the iron stairs that led to the fire escape. There was a thin margin of pale light at the edge of the fire door.

Lightly and quickly he ran up the stairs and pushed the door open. There was no one there—on the landing or below on the stairs or in the alley. The wind cooled his face and stirred his hair.

The stars seemed to watch him remotely. The whole city was spread before him—a theatrically exaggerated backdrop of mountainous buildings lighted up like Christmas trees. He clung to the iron railing, leaning against the wind. At this height it was solid as a wall.

Again the hot, red glare from the Tilbury sign pulsated like the flickering of a great fire: *Time For Tilbury's Tea!* He looked at the clock. It was just half past nine. As he watched, the minute hand jerked forward convulsively. It didn't move the space allotted to a single minute. In one jerk, it traversed the space representing two minutes. He stood still, staring at it. Then he heard a whistle blowing shrilly, in the street beyond the alley. That was the only warning. Suddenly, silently the red face of the clock disappeared. The fatuous message of the Tilbury advertisement—*Time For Tilbury's Tea!*—faded and did not flash again. The lights in the cocktail bar went out. Building after building grew dark and indistinct against the stars. Now there was no light anywhere but the street lamp at the corner and a cluster of small lights that looked like fireflies at the far end of the street. The globe of the street light turned orange, faded and died. The fireflies vanished. There was no sound of traffic now. Faintly lit by the stars the street was empty and silent, the city nothing but a mass of shadows against the sky ghostly as the ruins of Nineveh or Tyre. Basil frowned. He had forgotten that this was the night of the black-out. He turned back into the theater. A woman was standing at the foot of the iron staircase. A long sable cloak was thrown over her shoulders as if she had snatched it up because it was the first wrap at hand. She turned her head at the sound of Basil's footfalls.

He recognized Wanda Morley.

The wind had blown her dark hair into a cloud around her vivid, mobile face. Her tilted eyes shone golden in the dim light and the yellow jewel on her finger flashed as she laid one hand on the railing.

"Dr. Willing!" Her voice shook. "How grim you look."

She stepped back and the cloak fell open revealing the white dress she had worn that evening.

"How did you get in?"

"By the stage door, naturally. I got a key from Sam Milhau."

"When did you come?"

"I don't know why I should answer these questions." Her eyes measured him.

"Would you prefer to answer the police?"

"I came just this minute," she answered breathlessly. "Why should the police question me about it?"

"Did you meet anyone in the alley? Or see anyone on the fire escape?"

"No." She drew the fur cloak about her shoulders as if she felt a sudden chill. "Is anything wrong? Has anything happened?"

Again he ignored her question. "Why did you come here alone in the black-out?"

"Why shouldn't I be alone?"

"You're usually surrounded by maids and press agents."

Wanda lifted her black lashes pathetically. "If you knew how I hated all that sort of thing. How I long for a sane, serene, uncomplicated life . . ."

"In the suburbs doing all your own housework. Yes, I know all that. But I also know that there are some things one doesn't care to confide in a press agent or even a maid."

Wanda moved a little nearer and her voice dropped. "I came to see you. I have to tell you something, but— I didn't want anyone else to know. I'm afraid."

There was a whir of wings. Wanda started convulsively and clenched her hands. The canary flew overhead and alighted on the railing of the staircase. "What on earth is that bird doing here?" she demanded.

"That bird is a valuable witness," answered Basil.

"I—don't understand."

"I think you do," returned Basil. "I think that is what you came to tell me. I saw how frightened you were this evening when Inspector Foyle asked you about the canary, and you were frightened that day at your house when I showed an oblique interest in canaries in general. You suspected the truth the moment you saw that item in the newspaper about the canary several days ago. The possibility of murder was drawn to your attention before the murder took place, when the police asked your press agent if the canary business was a publicity stunt of yours. The murderer saw that you suspected him. Actress as you are you could not hide your fear of him. And when you realized his suspicion of your suspicion you believed your own life was no longer safe. You want him put under lock and key as soon as possible for your own safety and you've come here to tell me about him. Haven't you?"

"Do you really think he would . . . kill me?"

"How else could he protect himself?"

In the dim light Wanda's rouged lips were dark against her ghastly white face. She swayed and clutched the railing of the stairway to steady herself.

"There's one thing I'd like to know," went on Basil. "Does the Tilbury clock keep time accurately?"

A shaky smile quivered on Wanda's lips. "So you noticed? So few people do!"

"You mean it's not accurate?"

Wanda's smile steadied. "Outdoor clocks on tall buildings are never reliable to the split second unless they're covered with glass."

"Why not?"

"Because the hands are blown by the wind. It's not strong enough to affect the hour hand, but at that height on a blustery day the wind does alter the position of the minute hand by several minutes if it's blowing in the right direction. Most people never notice it, because they only glance at such a clock now and then. But I have good reason to remember it. When I had my first small part on Broadway I used to live in that hotel on 45th Street where most actors live in their salad days. I had a room in the back with windows looking toward 44th and Broadway like the room Seymour Hutchins has now. I set my watch by the Tilbury clock and was ten minutes late for an appointment with a producer who had promised me a good supporting role. He happened to be a crank about punctuality, and I did not get the job. I made inquiries then and learned that on really windy days the Tilbury clock may be fast or slow by as much as ten minutes. They ought to put a glass over it, but I suppose that would spoil the looks of the building."

"The police will want to know that and other things," said Basil. "Are you going to tell?"

"I . . ." Wanda's mouth opened and closed. "I . . ."

Something flashed between them with the blue glitter of steel. There was a singing vibration. In the wall behind Wanda a silver knife handle quivered half a foot from her head. The steel blade was embedded in the wall.

Wanda screamed like an animal. "No, I won't tell!

Never!" Her knees could not support her. She sank to the floor in a pool of fur. Her mouth was shapeless with terror. Her eyes stared into the darkness. "Put out the light!" she whispered to Basil. "Please! He saw me coming here this evening. He knew you were alone in the theater—as I did—and he understood that I was coming to see you and why. I think he plans to kill us both. Oh, do put out the light!"

A dark figure moved out of the shadows and set foot on the iron stairway. "Don't follow me. I have other knives—the whole surgical kit—and they're all sharp now." Light feet ran up the stairs. A man's head and shoulders were silhouetted against a glittering slice of stars. Someone was passing through the fire door.

Basil took the stairs two at a time. The door was open. He took a step onto the top landing of the fire escape. A dark figure was waiting for him. Only the face and the knife were pale in the starlight.

CHAPTER FOURTEEN

Scène-à-Faire

LEONARD MARTIN SPOKE his lines on cue: "Reckless, aren't you, Dr. Willing? A little too reckless! You'll be found in the alley tomorrow morning with a knife through your heart, and every bone in your body broken by your fall. But they'll never catch me. Wanda's too frightened to talk even though she's the one who'll be suspected, because she's the one who asked Milhau for a stage-door key tonight. I learned to pick any kind of lock years ago when I played *Raffles*—a concession to Milhau's realism. I slipped in by the stage door when the patrolman was on the other side of the building, and I can slip away now in the black-out unobserved. There won't be anything to connect me with any of these crimes. I stabbed Ingelow and Adeane without leaving one single clue for the police to work on." There was perverted pride in Leonard's voice and something else—doubt.

Basil played up to both. "You were clever—but not quite clever enough. Inspector Foyle has evidence that you are guilty."

"You're lying! I don't believe it!"

Basil knew that if he lived he would never forget

these perilous moments watching that murderous face in the starlight high above the blacked-out city. But if he could only play upon the actors' instinct for dramatizing every situation and keep Leonard talking long enough. . . .

"You overlooked three main clues," said Basil calmly. "A clock, a fly, and a canary."

"What on earth are you talking about?"

"When we found that Ingelow had been murdered, your watch agreed with mine while Rodney Tait's was ten minutes slower. This afternoon in Foyle's office I found that my watch was ten minutes fast when I compared it with the correct time given by the Naval Observatory on the radio. So Rodney's watch must have been right two nights ago. Why was mine fast? Because I set it by the Tilbury clock just before the murder, and the Tilbury clock gains several minutes on windy days. Why was yours fast on the same occasion? Because you had just set your watch by the Tilbury clock, too. The Tilbury clock can't be seen from any point in the theater except the top of this fire escape. So you were the dark figure on the fire escape the night Ingelow was murdered. It was you who dropped Wanda's script when I passed underneath, and it was you who underscored the line that Hutchins spoke: *He cannot escape now, every hand is against him.* . . . From the first, Hutchins said he had not underscored it in Wanda's script, and there was no reason to doubt him as he was not under suspicion. So the line must have been underscored by someone who did not speak it in the play. Why? When does anyone mark a line in a play that he doesn't speak himself? When it's a cue for some bit of stage business. The line you underscored in Wanda's script was not only a clue, but also a cue for a bit of business; and that 'business' was murder. You had to have a cue for stabbing Ingelow on the stage in order to fit his murder smoothly into the chronological pattern of the play, so there would be no danger of another actor interrupting you at that moment. That pattern was changed at the last moment when the actor playing *Desiré* fell ill, and his few lines were cut. You first learned this when I did—at the art gallery a few hours before the opening. When you got to the theater you snatched up Wanda's script—the only script where the deletions were marked—in order to see if they affected your cue for murder. The cut had to be a line spoken by another actor when you were alone with *Vladimir,* and the omission of *Desiré* might have altered one of those conditions. Or it may be that one of *Desiré's* lines was your original cue, and you had to find another one at short notice when his lines were cut. Anyway, in your haste you marked your cue for murder automatically as you would any other cue. You went out on the fire escape so you could set your watch by the Tilbury clock and time the cue as exactly as possible. As Milhau told me, you had never lived at Hutchins' little hotel overlooking the Tilbury clock, so you had never had occasion to notice that the clock was inaccurate. The script fell out of your hands when you were startled by my appearance in the alley. My appearance was startling to you because you mistook me for Ingelow, the man you were planning to murder, just as Wanda did when I knocked on her door a few moments later. We were the same height, and we were dressed alike that evening as I noticed when I first saw him. You dared not recover the script from me in the alley for fear of exciting my suspicion of you when Ingelow was stabbed on cue. There wasn't time then for you to select another cue.

"The next morning Rodney Tait provided me with a time table of the first act. During rehearsal this morning I found that time table was correct, and I added to it the exact time the cue for murder was spoken by Hutchins. Then I saw you were the only actor on stage near enough *Vladimir* to stab him at the moment Hutchins spoke that line. Hutchins himself was the first to suspect that his own voice had been the signal for two murders. He wasn't sure, so he tried to convey the information to me indirectly by a Shakespearean quotation. Even Pauline suspected you tonight when Inspector Foyle turned on the light in the lobby, and she saw that a curtain which looked black in a very faint light was really red. Of all colors, red is the first to lose its characteristic hue when light fails. Just as blood and lipstick look black in a dim light or a photograph, your red dressing gown looked black on the fire escape in the darkness beyond the faint red radiance from the Tilbury clock."

"That is an ingenious reconstruction," said Leonard. "But it's largely surmise. You haven't proved me guilty."

"I haven't, but the fly and the canary have."

"What about the canary?"

"It was clever of you to steal Rodney's surgical knives and break into Lazarus' shop to sharpen them. That way you thought there would be no record that you had ever sharpened a knife or had one in your possession. But there was a record. First, the night before Ingelow's murder you had a cut on your forefinger and Lazarus tells me such cuts are characteristic of knife-grinders whether professional or amateur. Secondly, each time you were in Lazarus' shop you set the canary free. You even did so a third time this evening, when you broke into Milhau's office to get another knife from his safe and saw that the canary's cage was there. What sort of man would feel an irrational, irresistible impulse to set a caged bird free every time he saw one, regardless of consequences to himself or the bird? Only a man who knew how agonizing the sense of forced confinement can be—an ex-convict who had served a prison term that he considered unjust. You were the only ex-convict among the suspects. As Wanda knew about your prison sentence she began to suspect you when she first heard that a burglar who sharpened a knife had also freed a canary. She must have wondered then if you knew Ingelow. But she couldn't be sure, and she was too frightened to talk. None of the others suspected you even after the murder because they didn't know about your prison sentence or your motive. Of course, you never dreamed we would associate the freeing of the bird with your prison sentence, because you had never associated the two yourself. An irresistible, irrational impulse is neurotic, and a neurosis is by definition a failure to associate consciously an act with its emotional cause."

Leonard Martin laughed. "Cobwebs and moonshine! Psychology is a joke to the layman, and juries are made up of laymen. The only things they believe are eye witnesses and material evidence—bloodstains and finger-prints. You haven't got anything like that!"

"Murder is rarely performed before an eye witness. But we have material evidence far more conclusive than most fingerprints and bloodstains. That's where the fly comes in."

"The fly?"

"Do you know how the Hindus diagnose diabetes mellitus? There is an account of their procedure in Dr. Heiser's autobiography. They set the patient's urine outdoors in the sun. If it attracts flies they know it contains sugar and is therefore diabetic urine. The same sugar is present in the perspiration of a diabetic. When I first met you at the art gallery I saw you were a sick man. As I happen to be a doctor of medicine, I soon noticed the principal external symptoms of diabetes in you, just as I noticed that Pauline was anemic. You had the bronze skin of the diabetic in place of the prison pallor one expects to see in a man just out of prison. You had the extreme emaciation of the diabetic and his avoidance of sweet food. You refused French pastry at the art gallery, and you didn't even take sugar in your coffee at Wanda's this morning. Finally, there was the peculiar sweet, fruity odor of your breath which indicates butyric acid in the lungs.

"You wore no gloves when you clasped the handle of the knife you used to stab Ingelow, because Milhau had directed you to remove your gloves during the action of the play, and you couldn't ignore his direction without rousing suspicion. In your character as a Russian detective, you had to wear heavy leather gloves—too heavy for such a delicate operation as stabbing Ingelow in a certain anatomical spot. But there was no danger of fingerprints, because you chose a knife handle that was elaborately grooved. Excitement and perhaps a recent dose of insulin made your palms perspire freely. The grooved surface of the knife handle rejected fingerprints, but it retained more perspiration than a smooth handle would have done. When a fly was attracted to the handle and ignored the bloodstained blade, I began to suspect the truth. The city toxicologist has already reported that he had found chemical traces of human perspiration and sugar on the knife handle. As soon as he subjects it to a spectroscope he will find some indication of butyric acid. This was the one fact Adeane knew that was not known to anyone else. He was the only witness present with the Inspector and myself when the fly alighted on the knife handle. He noticed it as we did and that cost him his life. This morning before rehearsal he told me in your presence that he had been reading about diseases of the pancreas at the medical library when he spoke of the suggestive effect on the body of such reading. He also mentioned Dr. Heiser's book which he was carrying under one arm, and dropped a broad hint about the Fly who witnessed the murder of Cock Robin. Apparently he thought you could be bullied into helping his career. He wanted you to put two and two together—and you did. You knew from experience that diabetes was a disease of the pancreas, and you glanced through Adeane's copy of Heiser's book and saw that the only reference to flies concerned the Hindu method of diagnosing diabetes. You concluded as Adeane wanted you to, that he had read enough medical literature to recognize the symptoms of diabetes in you and that in some way the action of a fly had indicated to him that the murderer was a diabetic. But instead of allowing Adeane to blackmail you, you killed him; and he had so little realization of his danger that he gave you an opportunity to do so by playing *Vladimir* in order to bring himself and his plays to Milhau's attention."

"Anyone who had just touched çandy might have left

sugar and perspiration on that knife handle!" protested Leonard.

"But not butyric acid as well. The knife handle had the same fruity odor as your breath. So did the handkerchief you dropped beside Pauline when you stabbed her tonight. There is enough acid on the handkerchief for it to be identified by chemical analysis. You must have wiped brow and neck and hands with it and—that will convict you of murder."

"Without a motive?"

"You loved Wanda, didn't you? That was why you introduced her to Milhau when she was unknown and gave her a chance on the stage. In the art gallery you said that Wanda's allure was like an X-ray burn—a delayed reaction. You weren't thinking of Rodney then —you were thinking of yourself. You had thought you could get over it, and you were finding that you couldn't. Perhaps she wouldn't let you. She didn't like her victims to be cured. She was flirting with you as well as Rodney when Pauline and I watched her in the art gallery that afternoon. When you came back to New York after serving your prison term in Illinois you found she no longer cared for you or even pretended to do so. You were too shrewd to be taken in by the publicity romance Milhau staged between Wanda and Rodney. You spied on her as a jealous man will—as you did the morning you discovered her with me on the balcony—and so you unearthed something unknown to her other friends: her secret engagement to John Ingelow; and his pending divorce from Margot, which had come to a head while you were in prison. Yet you so masked your feelings that Wanda had no idea you even knew Ingelow by sight. He was younger, richer and more eligible than you, so you had no hope of supplanting him. Your old place as Wanda's leading man was gone. Rodney was the rising star because he was young and attractive; yet you were the better actor. That was a bitter pill. You hated Rodney for that. You hated Wanda whom you had once loved for her fickleness and ingratitude. You were jealous of Ingelow. Since you couldn't have Wanda yourself, you determined that Ingelow should never have her either; and you murdered him in such a way that Wanda and Rodney became the principal suspects. You arranged that cleverly by prompting Hutchins to tell Wanda the old story of Edward VII playing *Vladimir* to Bernhardt's *Fedora,* knowing that Wanda would want her lover to do the same thing because she was always imitating great actresses of the past. Perhaps you even suggested to her that she revive *Fedora.*

"Do you know one reason I suspected you from the very beginning? Because you were the only real actor among the suspects. Margaret Ingelow wasn't an actress at all; Wanda and Rodney just played themselves on the stage. But you played roles entirely different from your real self. Wanda could simulate various emotions, but she couldn't act any personality other than her own. You alone of the suspects were artist enough to simulate a personality entirely alien to your own. You were the only one who could have been a murderer at heart and still have put on a convincing performance as an innocent man."

"You've got most of it right—but not the motive." Leonard's voice was very quiet now. "That prison sentence was unjust because I was not a drunken driver."

"You mean you hadn't been drinking?"

"I'd been drinking all right but—I wasn't driving."

"Wanda?"

"Yes. She ran over the child. She drove on, and I changed places with her. Like a sap I took the wheel before the traffic cop caught up with us; and I took the rap for her afterward. The sudden change to a sedentary life and starchy diet in prison gave me diabetes. You know how it is—an officer transferred suddenly from the field to staff work gets diabetes the same way sometimes. I came out of prison to find my career ruined as well as my health and Wanda all set to marry this Ingelow. The diabetes had produced hardening of the arteries, and the doctors gave me only a few months to live. I had nothing to lose by murder—I was going to die anyway. What did I want in the last few weeks before I died? Just one thing—Wanda. Sometimes a man condemned to death asks for special food or other privileges. All I asked for was Wanda, and the only way to get her was by killing Ingelow."

"No wonder Wanda suspected you," said Basil. "She was the only one who knew all this."

"But she needn't have been afraid of me. I never would have killed her. It was for her I did it."

"And the knife you threw at her a few moments ago?"

"That was for you. You knew too much and—"

A voice spoke from below. "Do you people realize that this is supposed to be a total black-out and there is a light shining through that fire door that's standing open? If you don't close it immediately, I'll call the police!"

Leonard smiled.

"This is my cue for an exit."

Quick as a monkey he turned and clambered upon

the iron railing. Basil sprang forward to seize him. But Leonard had jumped already.

Just then the street lamp at the corner blazed into light. Basil's eyes were so used to the darkness that it looked like a star shell radiating sparks in all directions. As he ran down the fire escape the Tilbury clock flashed red again. The air-raid warden's gray overcoat turned faintly pink in the reflected light as he bent over the dark figure sprawled prone in the alley.

"This man is badly hurt!" he cried aghast.

"He's dead," answered Basil after a quick look. "Better go ahead and call the police."

"There's one little point I'd like to clear up," said Foyle some time later. "Since Rod and Wanda were not guilty, why did they contradict each other in fixing the moment when Ingelow died that first night?"

"Perhaps because they were just guessing," suggested Basil. "And guessing is a form of wishful thinking. When there are no facts for the mind to follow it follows its own fancy. Wanda said Ingelow seemed dead the first time she kissed him—thereby throwing suspicion on Leonard, the only person who approached Ingelow on stage before Wanda's first kiss. She did that, consciously or unconsciously, because she hated Leonard as only such a woman can hate a discarded lover, and she was beginning to fear him. In the same way Rod 'guessed' Ingelow was alive the last time Rod touched him, thereby throwing suspicion on Wanda, the only person to approach Ingelow after that. Rod disliked Wanda because she had pursued him and made Pauline jealous. Actually both Rod and Wanda were wrong in this testimony. Compare Rod's time table of the first act with the timing of the cue for murder, and you'll see that Ingelow was alive when Wanda first kissed him and dead when Rod last touched him. Of course, Leonard, as the murderer, did his best to throw suspicion on both Rod and Wanda by saying Ingelow was alive before either had approached him on stage and dead after both had done so."

One morning a few weeks later, Pauline and Rodney came once again to breakfast with Basil. But this time they seemed like any other pair of young lovers—carefree and rather charmingly absurd. Rodney shook hands with Basil three times and Pauline kissed him.

"I had nothing to do with it!" he protested. "You owe everything to a canary and a house fly."

The End

>>> If you've enjoyed this book and would like to discover more great vintage crime and thriller titles, as well as the most exciting crime and thriller authors writing today, visit: >>>

The Murder Room
Where Criminal Minds Meet

themurderroom.com